TAYLENOR

TAYLENOR

ANNE MARIE LUTZ

Hydra
Publications

ISBN: 978-1-948374-17-0

Hydra Publications

Goshen, Kentucky 40026

www.hydrapublications.com

Thank you to my wonderful family. This book wouldn't exist without your support.

CHAPTER ONE

J aena knew as soon as she set foot in the village that a gifted child lived there.

She opened up her senses and cast wide. *Taylen* lay over the place like a layer of mist floating over fields on a damp morning.

Her first thought was to run away. She could return to Iryor for help, turn Ears around and vanish on the road leading through the ripening grain, leaving the village of Bless-us-goddess none the wiser that she'd been there. Mother Thara could return with Jaena and take over the burden of convincing the parents to let the *taylenor* child go.

Jaena shivered. This was her duty, the thing she'd been trained for above and beyond the years she'd studied to be a priest. Now, with *taylen* so thick in the air it prickled her skin, she wasn't sure she could complete her task.

Small figures appeared between two houses and shrieked a greeting. Two of the children of Bless-us-goddess raced towards Jaena, braided hair bouncing. Her chance to avoid this task was gone.

In only a few moments more children surrounded her, focused on the donkey pulling Jaena's utilitarian cart. These children were all too young to be the *taylenor*.

"Her name is Ears," Jaena told them. The children laughed and clustered close to the donkey's flanks to pet her.

The headwoman awaited them by the market circle. She was lean and sun-browned, with striking silver hair. She invited Jaena into her house to drink tea.

"It's been two years since we've seen a priest -- old Priest Mag it was last time," the headwoman said as she sat and poured the tea. "You're very welcome here. We've had two babies born since the last visit."

"Any deaths?" Jaena asked.

The headwoman had brought out her best mugs, blue-glazed treasures from the artisans in Duscapi. No doubt they'd been purchased at great cost to this tiny village and were brought out only to honor guests. Guilt pricked Jaena. The headwoman might not be so welcoming if she knew Jaena would be taking a child away from Bless-us-goddess.

"Thank the goddess, no deaths. But we have a newly wedded couple, Sella and Gray, who will need their marriage bed blessed." The headwoman smirked. "If we can get them out of it long enough for you to bless it."

"All the better," Jaena said. "Imn-ashu smiles on eager couples."

The headwoman snorted with laughter. "Indeed, we're glad to see you, Priest! You may stay here, in my daughter's room. We'll put up your donkey and your cart. No need to camp outside when you're with us."

Jaena thanked the headwoman. It would be pleasant to sleep in a warm room and have someone else take care of Ears for a change.

The evening was long, filled with tea and then grilled meat, wheat-cakes and beer. Jaena delivered news from the capital and gave the headwoman Master Harling's predictions about weather and crop yields.

In the morning Jaena went to the market circle, and the babies were brought for her to sing over. One child wasn't really a baby anymore – she walked around on chubby legs and clung to her mother.

The other baby grinned up at Jaena, gurgling as she cradled the child and sang the goddess's blessing.

None of the parents complained about Jaena's off-key singing. Nobody asked how a woman with such a flat ear could serve the Goddess.

The heavy sense of *taylen* had receded this morning. Jaena began to wonder if they had hidden the gifted one; but it was unlikely the people in this little village would know anything about the *taylen*. Certainly not enough to want to hide their sons and daughters away.

By Jaena's third morning in Bless-us-goddess, she had come no closer to discovering the source of the talent. She prepared to take her leave, wondering what she should do. As she guided Ears out of town, she noticed a small house at the edge of the village. It stood a little apart from the other houses, in the fields to the north, framed by golden grain.

The sense of *taylen* intensified as she neared the house. Jaena's head swam with its strength. She stopped the cart, wrapped the driving rein around a post, and knocked on the door.

The heavy-set woman who opened the door sighed when she saw the green priest's badge on Jaena's cloak. "I suppose you must come in," she said. "I'm Cedon. Make yourself comfortable in the kitchen, Priest, and I'll get you some tea." She called out to a child of about six who peered from behind a door. "Kio, get your father please!"

Jaena sat at the scarred wooden table and sipped tea. Cedon's silence was like a wall. The woman didn't like priests, or maybe she had a hint of what Jaena was about to tell them.

Then a boy walked into the room, and Jaena knew he was the one she'd been seeking. He still looked healthy and strong, his brown skin gleaming with perspiration from work in the fields. It would be hard to convince Cedon and her husband to let him go.

"Sorry," the boy said. "I was looking for Da."

"Kio went to get him," Cedon said.

Cedon's husband came back from his work. He rinsed his hands in a bucket just outside the door and came into the kitchen still tracking mud from the fields. Kio tagged behind him like a puppy.

"I'm Maloc," he said. "Kio said there was a priest in the house?"

"I'm Jaena, priest of Imn-ashu," she said. "Thank you for your welcome. I wonder if we could talk for a few minutes."

Cedon sighed. "Kio, go outside for a while. Wiel, you go too. Don't go too far, now!"

Jaena waited until the noise of the boys' voices thinned with distance. She took a deep breath. "I have hard news for you, Cedon and Maloc. News I am sad to have to bring."

Maloc looked puzzled. Cedon met Jaena's eyes. Jaena thought the woman must be expecting the news, or why had she stayed away from the rest of the village during Jaena's visit?

"Your older son," Jaena said. "Wiel, is it?"

"Yes."

"I could tell as soon as I approached your village that someone gifted in *taylen* lived here, and I've spent these days trying to find the child. Wiel has a very strong natural ability. I'm sorry to have to tell you this, but I have no choice."

She expected them to look puzzled, ask what *taylen* was. So few knew about it these days.

"I think you have a choice." Cedon sat very straight in her chair. "We know a little about this *taylen*. No one else in this village knows anything about it, but we do. Wiel's uncle – " she nodded toward Maloc – "Maloc's brother, was taken by a Seeker years ago, when they were both young in another town. We never saw him again."

Maloc was in his middle years. His brother must have been taken away as long as a quarter-century ago. They had no idea that the uncle was buried in the *taylenor* section of the cemetery in Iryor, and had been for probably twenty years.

"You suspected then --- about Wiel?"

"The boy looks just like my brother." Maloc's voice was strained. "Every time I look at him I see my brother staring back at me, strong and lean as if he was still fifteen. Of course I wondered if Wiel was like my brother in more than just looks. Of course I did. – He's Imn-ashu's gift to us, my brother's soul come back again."

"You can't have him," Cedon said. The older woman's hands shook.

Jaena sighed. "You don't understand."

Maloc stood, knocking over his chair. He strode to the door. "I can hear you boys under the window. Go! Wiel – get out into the woods! Stay away until I send Kio for you. Go!"

There was a scrabble of sound under the window. It seemed the boys had been eavesdropping on the adults' conversation. Now Wiel had run away, fleeing from the house at his father's command. It would be even harder to explain to him why he must accompany Jaena back to the city.

Maloc returned from the door. He stood with his hands on his hips, feet spread, glowering at Jaena. Cedon sat at the table but her body was like stone.

Jaena closed her eyes for a brief moment. She summoned the memories of what Mother Thara had told her to do. She opened her eyes and faced both of them. "If you love Wiel, you won't put any obstacles to him leaving with me."

"That's what they told my ma. We never saw my brother again. We asked every priest, even every messenger that happened our way if there was news. They just looked down their noses at us, man and woman alike."

"Maloc went to the city once, before we were married," Cedon said. "He said no one would help him."

"I looked everywhere. I had to go back and tell my ma I couldn't find him," Maloc said.

"By Imn-ashu, I swear I mean your son no harm."

Maloc swore. "No harm, you say. And you, a priest of the goddess, really a Seeker. They say a priest can't lie, but you are full of lies, you and all your kind."

That was fear speaking, and pain. Jaena forced her anger down. "Let me tell you what happens to the *taylenor*, and you'll see why Wiel must come with me." She hummed a few notes of Imn-ashu's prayer, under her breath, for strength more than anything else.

Maloc slammed a hand down on the table. The loud crack echoed around the humble little kitchen. "No more praying. Just speak, will you? Don't you owe us that?"

Jaena told them the story her mentor had told her after she'd been rescued from the harsh winter alone in her parents' homestead and brought to the mothers in the hospital. She'd heard it again when she was chosen as a priest and then a Seeker. She'd been taught several different ways to tell it, depending on the emotional state of her listeners. She threw out all those techniques and decided to be only blunt and honest. Nothing else would do.

"*Taylen* is the gift that allows people to learn magery. In the old days there was always great hope when a *taylenor* was discovered. Mages taught the children to use their gift – in fact Mage Herrein still does, just in case such a child manages to escape his fate and live to become a mage."

Maloc cleared his throat. His posture slackened, became less belligerent. "What do you mean, Seeker – if they live?"

Jaena sighed. This was the hard part. "Somewhere in the body of a *taylenor* when he is born, is the potential for magery. It lies dormant until they reach the age when they can be married – then it blooms. But tied to that potential is a Dark Twin. When the *taylen* blooms, so does the Dark Twin. It's a sickness that follows the emergence of the *taylen* like a toddler follows its mother, hanging on to her skirts. It kills the *taylenor* slowly, over a period of months or years. No one has found the cure for the disease, though Mage Herrein and the mothers at the hospital don't give up hope."

"So. My brother has been dead for many years," Maloc said.

Cedon stood and took her husband's hand.

Jaena nodded. "I'm sorry. Yes. Seekers were commissioned to find the *taylenor*. We take them back to the city for two reasons. First – someday we might save one. Mage Herrein was such a child, you know, and it's said that any *taylenor* who lives beyond his growing years may become a Mage."

The sunlight had slipped across the room since Jaena arrived.

"And second?" Cedon asked.

Jaena forced herself to go on. It was hard to speak like this to middle-aged people who were about to lose their son. She felt young and uncertain. "We make them comfortable, Cedon. The mothers care for them. They have medicines for pain. They have therapies to help them stay on their feet longer, so they won't waste away in bed. They spend every moment making things comfortable for the *taylenor*. It extends their lives, and it gives them ease. You can't do that here."

"This is his *home*." Maloc paced across the floor, ending up in the square of sunlight. "We'll take care of him. He is Imn-ashu's gift to us, and there is nowhere he will be better off than right here."

Cedon's hand rose to cover her mouth. Tears shone in the older woman's eyes.

There was a lump in Jaena's throat. She wished Mother Thara were here to handle this. "I'm trying to speak with you honestly about what must be. I can't force you, or Wiel. Please think about everything I've told you. I swear to you on the goddess I serve – it's best for Wiel."

"Priest or not, you're young." Cedon wiped tears from her cheek. "Not long past twenty, I think. How can you know what it is to lose a child? How can you know what's best for him?"

"I've known other *taylenor*. My dearest friend was one. And the mothers have taught me about what they do. But of course I can't know what it's like to lose a child. I'm truly sorry."

Maloc reached out and grasped Cedon's hand. His knuckles whitened; it wasn't a gentle handclasp. His other hand covered his eyes.

Jaena pushed back her chair. "I'll stay another day. I won't impose on the headwoman again so unexpectedly – I'll stay in my cart, just outside the village. I'll come back tomorrow."

"I'd think twice before coming back here uninvited, Seeker." Cedon's eyes flashed.

As if his wife's words had energized him, Maloc shoved to his feet, his chair skittering backwards. He came around the table and grabbed Jaena's forearm.

Her heart skipped as the man hauled her towards the front door. She stumbled and recovered.

"Out," he gritted. "Stay out. Set foot here again and you'll be sorry. We aren't defenseless here, you know."

"Maloc! She's a priest!"

"I don't care if she's the Mage Defender. She can't have our son!" He thrust Jaena onto the front stoop and slammed the front door in her face.

Jaena gasped at Maloc's sudden rage. Staring at the planks a few inches in front of her nose, she tried to catch her breath. She didn't blame Maloc and Cedon. But she must figure out a way to help Wiel before the Dark Twin began to claim him, even if the headwoman set the whole village in her way.

She unwrapped Ears' tether from the post. She climbed into the cart and slapped the rein against the donkey's flank, and headed for the green tree line beyond the standing grain.

CHAPTER TWO

J aena sat on the single step of her cart. She was camped in a clearing, but there was ripe grain all around, too close and dry to risk a fire. The dusk had brought an unexpected chill with it, and she was shivering.

As soon as she finished her dinner of bread and cheese, she stepped up into the cart and came back wrapped in a cloak, with her flute in her hand.

She was far better at the flute than she was at singing. The flute was her favorite means to pray to the goddess – there was little danger she would wander off-key and mar the purity of her prayer. She grinned as she remembered the faces of the village newlyweds as she sang the goddess' blessing on their marriage bed. They had expected a better voice from a priest, that was for sure. Their old priest, Mag, had a clear and youthful baritone in spite of his age.

Their faces had cleared when she brought out the flute. And when the goddess' blessing had descended on them, pure as a drift of snow.

She tilted the flute before her lips and let a trill of notes fall into the sweet-smelling dusk. She would pray to Imn-ashu for Wiel and his family. And maybe also for some warmth while she was at it. The goddess took care of her priests, and might calm the breeze a bit for her.

A rustling in the grass nearby stopped her.

"Who's there?" she asked. She glanced over at Ears, who grazed nearby, but the donkey showed no sign of alarm.

A tall shape emerged from the grain. "Priest Jaena? I'm Wiel, Maloc's son. I need to talk to you."

"I'm glad to see you." Jaena put the flute aside. She'd hoped he would come. She'd thought maybe a boy almost grown would be unwilling to accept the decree of his parents without looking for answers of his own. Her shoulders tensed with nerves. She hoped the ingrained village respect for priests still held true.

"I heard you want to take me away from my family."

"You were listening outside the window, weren't you? Then you only heard part of the story. Please sit down, Wiel."

Wiel backed a step or two away.

"Don't worry. I won't take you against your will, and you're a young man of what, fifteen or so? And much stronger than I am. Sit, please."

"I might be stronger, but you have the power of the goddess," Wiel said. He sat down on the ground cross-legged, keeping a good distance between them.

"This isn't the goddess' concern. This is the business of mages. Do you know what a Seeker is?"

He nodded. "Da told me, just now. Why haven't I ever heard of them before?"

"Seekers are rare. Right now, I'm the only one Mage Herrein employs." She remembered the day Herrein asked her to be a Seeker. Until that day she'd never heard of them either.

"Why were you looking for me?"

"You've inherited a gift called *taylen*. It first shows up in those who have it around the time they're old enough for marriage."

"I think I know what you're talking about." Wiel pushed his hair off his forehead. "Things look different to me sometimes. Like they're deeper than they used to be? And sometimes it feels like if I just reach out and grab, something might happen."

"That's *taylen*. The first thing most *taylenor* notice is a feeling they can pull things with their minds. You have a strong gift; I felt it as soon as I got here. Unfortunately, it comes with a high price. Along with the *taylen* comes an illness that will make you very sick, and probably even cause your death."

"Is that what happened to my uncle?" Wiel looked down, a lock of his dark hair falling over his forehead.

"Yes." Jaena sighed. "This is hard news for you to believe, I'm sure. You're young and I don't see any signs of the illness in you yet. You seem strong and healthy. But before long you'll begin to feel weak, and it'll progress from there. At the Mothers' Hospital they can care for you, make you comfortable, and maybe prolong your life."

"The Mothers of Arifell?"

"Yes."

"They're supposed to heal the sick. Why can't they just cure me?"

"I wish they could. I lost a friend to the Dark Twin, years ago." She paused, watching him. Maybe Wiel had heard all this already, from his overwrought parents; if so, it was surprising he seemed so calm. It was almost dark now, and she could barely see the boy's expression.

But then he glanced up. Fear glittered in his wide eyes. He crossed his arms across his chest, shoulders tense.

Jaena stepped up into her cart. She found her tinderbox and lit her shielded oil lamp, then hung it from the hook set into the frame of the cart, where it cast a yellow glow around them. She found a rug and handed it to Wiel to sit on. "Here. It's getting colder."

He settled himself on the rug. The little interruption allowed them to look away from each other and take a few calming breaths.

"The better news is that Mage Herrein has been working for a long time on how to save the lives of the *taylenor*. He'll work with you there, at the hospital. There's always a chance – a slight one, Weil, I won't lie to you – a slight chance that you'll survive the illness and become a mage. That's how Herrein became a mage – he survived the illness, many many years ago. It's not impossible that the same could happen to you."

"Why can't I just stay here? I don't want to leave my family."

"I can hardly blame you. I can tell they love you. But they can't take care of you here. You'll require a lot of care, Wiel. Your parents will wear themselves out with worry. They'll spend their money on *cernen* who won't be able to do anything for you. Can they afford that pain, that stress? – And how will it be for Kio, watching you die?"

It had been terrible, watching Marki die. She must convince this boy to come with her. Maybe Herrein and the mothers could save this one. There was always a chance. *Imn-ashu, help me make him understand.*

Wiel stood. He began to pace up and down in the narrow area before the cart where Jaena sat. The lamplight illuminated his skin and gleamed off his shiny dark hair. He moved with the liquid ease of a healthy young animal. It was hard to believe that in a few months he would be like Tia, the only *taylenor* child at the hospital right now, who grew weaker every time Jaena saw her.

"Why should I believe you?" Wiel snapped. "You're a stranger."

"A priest," Jaena said calmly. "We don't lie."

"My Da says you can lie as well as anyone else if it suits you." He glared at her. "So I'll wither away and die, useless in my bed here or in the city. What's the chance I'll live to become a mage?"

She shrugged. "Not much. I've seen three *taylenor* children at the hospital since I came to Iryor to live. Two have died, long since. One's still alive, but very ill. It's hard to hear, Wiel, but you'll most likely die here or in Iryor. But Mage Herrein was a *taylenor* child like you, and he survived the illness. He's an old man now, Herrein the Strong."

"The Mage Defender of Cassahn." Wiel stopped pacing, and his eyes glittered in the lamplight.

"Yes. He's shielded us from the ancient demons for more than two hundred years."

"I don't know anyone in the city," Wiel said.

"Your family can visit you."

He made a short angry gesture. "They can't. Da doesn't have any help but me. He can't leave his crops and go off to Iryor for weeks. Ma can't leave Kio. And I'd hate for her to bring him along."

"Then you should sleep on it. I've been as honest with you and your family as I know how. I won't force you. It's truly to your benefit – to your family's benefit, even – that you come with me." Jaena's head was beginning to hurt. There was too much emotion in the air. Wiel's shock and anger troubled the goddess' peace like a gale introduced into a calm summer day.

The boy shoved his hands into his pockets. His shoulders slumped. "I'll come with you."

Jaena caught her breath. She hadn't expected the quick decision. "Thank you."

He shook his head, turning the thanks away. "There's no choice. You must report to someone. Won't they just send someone else out to take me?"

"If you decide to stay here, they'll never know about you." Failing to report that she'd found a *taylenor* would mean breaking faith with Herrein, but there had been too much emotion in Maloc and Cedon's little kitchen. She wouldn't betray Wiel.

"I'll tell my family I'm going. I don't want to be a burden to them. Will you come back in the morning and answer any questions they have?"

"Yes, I'll do that. If they wish to see me."

"I'll tell the headwoman that I've decided. But you should beware. She was angry when I left."

"I'll take care. I don't *think* they'll harm a priest."

"What should I bring to Iryor?" Wiel looked very young all of a sudden.

She smiled. "Bring anything you can't replace, books if you like to read or an instrument if you play. A change of clothes, whatever you need for the journey, but not too much. We'll be walking a lot. Once you're in the city, everything will be provided. You'll be well cared for."

Someone small and fast barreled out of the grasses and flung himself around Wiel's legs.

"You can't go!" Kio wailed.

Wiel cast Jaena a helpless look. He began unwrapping the younger boy's arms from around him. "Come on home, Kio. I'll tell you all about it there."

"You're not a priest, you're a witch!" yelled Kio, whirling on Jaena. "You can't have him!"

"You have an amazing family," Jaena told Wiel. "Kio, Wiel will explain it all to you. I'll come to your house in the morning."

Wiel's reasonable tones and Kio's objections faded away. Finally all was silence except for the hushing of the breeze though the grain. Jaena took the oil lamp into the cart and doused it, and the goddess' peace descended upon her, in the blackness around the donkey cart in the empty field.

* * *

Wiel's parents bowed to his wishes. There were tearful farewells, and stony silence turned in Jaena's direction. She wasn't offended; she knew what it was like to lose a loved one. They would never see their son again.

Their departure was cold and lonely. The children that had clustered around Jaena's cart when she arrived were kept away. The headwoman stayed in her house with the doors and windows shut. Jaena knew that only reverence for Imn-ashu kept the villagers from using force against her. She was certain that some villager would be sent off to Tasa Wimar at the Temple by the end of the day, carrying the headwoman's complaints and demanding Wiel's return.

The weather had turned colder. The sky was an uncomforting iron-gray. The scent of woodsmoke drifted in the air. Travel was slow, since Jaena and Wiel took turns riding in the cart and walking alongside, sparing Ears the extra weight. The donkey had been with her since she started doing the circuit, two years ago. They were used to each other; she wanted to travel with the jennet for a long time.

A day of travel fell behind them, with a stop at a lone homestead along the way to ask if the householder needed anything from a priest. Wiel was mostly silent, looking around at the scenery. He had never been this far from Bless-us-goddess, and everything must look foreign to him.

Near dusk they entered new terrain. Young trees clustered here and there as if frightened of the Arahn Forest that loomed in a gray-green wall just behind them. Scrub brush grew taller than Ears' withers here, but there were clearings, and a creek that emerged from the darkness of the Forest and wound towards the road.

Wiel leaped down from the cart with the alacrity of a teenager with energy to spare. "Why are we stopping here? It doesn't seem safe."

"It isn't, perfectly. But we should be fine. We aren't in the Arahn Forest proper, you know, just on the edges."

"Thoras said the trees are alive in there, and if you go in they'll fold you up in their roots and grow around you while you're still alive."

"Thoras?"

"He's the cloth-merchant, with the summer fair. He tells stories."

Jaena smiled. "Scary stories."

"Kio had nightmares last time, and Ma said he couldn't go listen anymore until he's older." Wiel's face grew somber as he remembered what he'd left behind.

"I passed here on the way to your village," Jaena said. "Nothing bothered me."

"But why didn't we stop beside the plains road?"

"There are dangers there, too, just different ones. Camping exposed on the plain next to the road would make us an obvious target for any bandits that patrol the road at night. But they don't come here."

"They would steal from a priest?"

Jaena smiled at his shock. "Not everyone's deterred by the priests' insignia on the cart."

"But why don't you travel in pairs? Or with a guard?" Wiel stared at her. "I don't understand how you can put yourself in such danger."

"There are a few things I can do to protect myself," she said. "And the goddess takes care of her priests. I've never been injured on the road, but it's best to be sensible anyway. Let's finish making camp. Aren't you hungry?"

Jaena tethered Ears in a clearing close to the cart, watering the animal from buckets she hauled from the creek. Wiel began looking for deadwood for a small fire, keeping to the scrub and away from the

Forest itself. She hoped the fire would keep away any large animals. In spite of what she had told Wiel, this area held its own dangers.

Dinner was bread, hard cheese and apples. The fire burned low, but the half-moon that rose over the Forest provided some light. Jaena was just preparing to go up into the cart when the donkey spooked. Her long ears went up, and she let go with a frightened bray.

"There's a predator somewhere nearby," Jaena said. "Build up the fire a little, and I'll bring Ears closer to the cart."

When that was done she said, "Stay here and keep watch. Shout if you see anything dangerous. There's something I need to get out of the cart."

Wiel gave her a spooked look of his own, the whites around his eyes showing.

"Most wild animals won't attack so close to a fire. Unless something's wrong, or they're hungry in the depths of winter. You'll be safe until I'm back."

Jaena emerged from the cart with her bow and quiver. No sooner had she set arrow to bowstring than Ears squealed. She saw a dark rush of teeth and hair break from the darkness and lunge for the donkey. The white splash on Ears' forehead winked in the firelight as the jennet spun and kicked.

"Wiel, get in the cart!" she ordered, raising the bow. This was some animal she'd never seen before, that dared attack a camp with people and a fire, outside the Forest.

Wiel ignored her order. He kicked at the fire to light the area better for defense. The flames leaped up, casting weird shadows. The trees on the very edge of the Forest seemed to lean closer.

Jaena released her first arrow. It was hard to see in the firelit darkness, but she thought she had hit her target. But the creature galloped onward. She strung another arrow, noticing an odd bitter stink that seemed to surround the creature as it drew closer.

"Go!" she snapped at Wiel.

The boy shoved his arms out at the creature, fingers splayed, then clenched.

The predator's hindquarters swung around towards them as if

yanked. It scrabbled at the dirt, then flipped backwards as if it had been thrown. It hit the ground hard. A yammering wail split the night. The animal squirmed as it rolled over, then ran back into the woods, limping.

Ears brayed, pulling at the tether. Jaena went to the jennet and calmed her. Wiel sat down in the dirt and held his head.

"Are you all right?"

"I feel – a little dizzy. Kind of sick. I think it's going away."

"Where in the world did you learn that?"

"I told you." Wiel got to his feet. He half-leaned on Ears and stroked the jennet's neck. Ears settled, still grumbling. The predator must be far away already.

"I told you back home," Wiel repeated. "Sometimes I think if I just reach out and *pull* – I can do something. I never really did anything before, though. What does it mean?"

"They say the first thing most *taylenor* can do is pull like that. It's – very effective. I had no idea. But thank the goddess you were able to do it! I've never heard of an animal attack on a camp before around here. I still don't – what *was* that animal, anyway?"

"Don't know. Couldn't see," Wiel mumbled.

"It wasn't a wolf." She didn't want to frighten the boy any more, but there had been reports of strange creatures in the East. Why one would emerge from the woodlands, though, and attack them for no reason, left her apprehensive.

Wiel stumbled as he walked back to the fireside.

Jaena made him sit down, then went into the cart and found her flask of spirits.

"Here. Just one sip, Wiel. It'll help." She pressed it on the boy until he took a cautious sip.

He gasped and choked a little, then looked up at her. "Why do you carry that stuff around? It's like fire down the throat."

She laughed. "I have a friend who calls it warm and mellow. It's all in the viewpoint, I think. It was a gift, and good for cases of shock. Go in the cart. You may have the bedroll tonight, and I'll stay out here for a while."

"You're not safe." Wiel sounded exhausted.

"I'll be fine. The goddess will shield me. Go now."

"The goddess never saved anyone that I ever heard," Wiel grumbled, but he was clearly too tired to stay awake. He stepped up into the cart and after a while the small sounds of his moving around stilled. Insects buzzed and chirped in the trees. There was no sign of any wolves or other less-natural predators. Jaena wondered what animal – if it were an animal -- had charged their camp as if bent on their death. She must tell Tasa Wimar about it as soon as she arrived back in the city.

An ember of hope glowed inside her, far down, where she could almost ignore it. Perhaps if Wiel was already using the *taylen*, he might be one of those who could defeat the Dark Twin.

After a while she leaned back on the step, wrapped her cloak around her and dozed.

CHAPTER THREE

"Jaena's back!" The girl in the narrow bed raised her arms. Jaena hugged her with care. She forced herself not to react as she noticed how fragile the girl's shoulders were in her embrace, and how dry Tia's skin felt.

"How have you been, Tia?" she asked.

"Missing you," Tia said. "Look, Mother, Jaena's back!"

"A little early, I understand," Mother Rhody replied. She carried a wooden tray with a mug of milk and a slice of sugared bread. She smiled at Jaena and set the tray on Tia's side table.

Tia made a face. "I can't eat that," she said. "It'll curdle my stomach."

"You must try, dear." Rhody helped to prop the girl up in the bed, supporting her with down-stuffed pillows. Then she sat at the foot of the bed, her beige robe pooling on the floor. "You may have the chair, Jaena. I'm sure you're tired from your travels."

"What have you been doing while I've been away?" Jaena asked Tia.

The girl looked at the simple food as if consuming it were an impossible task. "I saw Mage Herrein yesterday. This time he didn't show me anything new. He said I needed to keep my strength. I watched him do a scrying, though."

"Tia is feeling a little worse today," Rhody said.

"Try to eat, please, dear," Jaena said. "And I'll bring the goddess' blessing to you before I go. Maybe it'll help you feel a little stronger."

"I understand you brought someone back with you," Rhody said.

"Yes, a boy from a village called Bless-us-goddess. His name is Wiel. He seems to have a strong gift."

"I saw him!" Tia said. She ignored her food. The glow that had come from Jaena's arrival had faded, leaving her gray under her dark skin. "I saw him walk down the hall. He's very handsome, isn't he?"

Jaena laughed. "I suppose so."

"There'll be two of us here now. Do you think Mage Herrein will see him soon?"

"I think he will," Rhody said. "He is very quick to visit any new *taylenor*. Remember, Tia, he talked to you on your first day here."

"I was frightened of him," Tia said. "I'd never seen anyone so old."

"But you enjoy visiting with him now," Rhody said.

"Yes," Tia said. She looked down at her sugared bread.

Jaena rose from the chair. "I must go see Wiel. Mother Thara must be done with him by now. I'm the only one he knows here. I should see if he's settled in."

"Go to him," Rhody said.

"Yes, go." Tia drooped back on to her pillows. "I'm too tired to talk any more."

Jaena gave the girl a quick hug. She let her hand drift up to cup the back of Tia's head as she sang the opening notes of the goddess' blessing. Tia closed her eyes.

In the hallway, Jaena allowed her smile to drop away. Only weeks ago, when Jaena had left Iryor, Tia had still been up and walking around, visiting the babies in the newborn room, watching Rhody chop vegetables in the kitchen. Now she was too frail to walk and had lost weight she could not afford to lose. The Dark Twin took its course. It was good that Mage Herrein still tried to work with Tia, giving her something to do to take her mind off her condition.

Marki had been just the same. He'd stopped eating, and then slipped into a limp, unnatural sleep from which he never awakened.

Jaena had been a child then, an orphan newly taken in by the mothers. Marki had been closer than a brother, more precious to her because of the loss of her own family. She had been just as annoying as a younger sister to him, and secretly idolized him. She had not realized that Marki had been fated to die young.

She still remembered the medicinal smell of Marki's sickroom, the drawn window shades, the mothers hovering around the bed.

She shook off the memories and walked down the hall. There was no need to search for Wiel's room. He was still active and strong; he would not be sitting idly in a room like Tia, who was waiting to die.

Jaena heard the boy's voice as soon as she entered the front hall. He was talking with two other young people, novices who might be mothers someday. They sparkled and flirted at Wiel as he made some amusing comment, and he grinned back.

Seeing such a lively scene after visiting Tia was too much of a contrast. Jaena decided to turn around and leave the boy to enjoy the company of his friends in peace.

"Priest Jaena! Stop a minute?" He turned away from the girls, who fluttered off toward whatever their duties were at this hour.

"I thought I'd see how you were settling in. It looks like you're doing fine." She smiled.

Wiel flushed. "But I wanted to see you. They've put me in this huge room, big as Ma and Da's. I'm all by myself in there."

"You'll grow accustomed. Have you seen Mother Thara yet? She's in charge here."

"Yes. She said I'm to see Mage Herrein tomorrow. He's out of the city."

"They will have sent a messenger."

A shriek echoed from the ceiling. Two children raced into the front hall, red-faced and laughing. The smaller one grabbed at the older one's arm, just missing the girl as she dodged away behind Jaena.

"What, Erry, are you afraid of little ones now?" Jaena asked, grinning. She could feel Erry crouched down behind her, almost under her cloak.

"It's just tag, Priest. Don't you know tag?" Erry twisted away as the boy reached for her. "Stop it now! Can't you see Priest Jaena is here?"

The smaller boy paid no attention, diving to knee level to reach for Erry's legs.

"Stop now," Jaena said more seriously. "You know Tia's just down that hall, feeling very sick."

"Children!" A summons rang out. A young mother whom Jaena had not met stood with hands on her hips, glaring. "You know you can't run wild here. You'll disturb the *taylenor*. Back to the common room, now!"

The children obeyed at once. They trailed back across the front hall, elbowing each other but offering no other complaint.

Wiel laughed. "Those two don't look like they belong in a hospital."

"The mothers take care of a few orphans too, until a place is found for them learning a trade or at a religious school." She drew her cloak about her, ready to go to her own room at the Temple. "Is there anything you need, anything that hasn't been explained?"

"There's nothing I could need. There's so much here. It's like a palace." Wiel looked down. "But Jaena, I mean, Priest, there are still some things I don't understand."

"Mage Herrein will tell you everything tomorrow. If there's anything he hasn't explained to your satisfaction, ask me when I return. Or Mother Thara – you can always ask her."

"She's kind of hard to talk to."

Jaena pictured the tall, skeletally-thin mother with her beautiful, severe face. Yes, Thara was hard to speak to at first. "She's dedicated her life to the *taylenor*, Wiel. That's you. She'll answer anything you need to know, get you anything you stand in need of. You can depend on her. I have to go now and report to Tasa Wimar. If you need me, you can reach me at the Temple whenever I'm in the city."

"That's not often, though, is it?"

"Not often," she said gently. The boy looked a little lost now. "But I'll check in on you when I'm here. After tomorrow, you'll be busy with Mage Herrein."

"Thank you. For everything."

Jaena said goodbye. Wiel's thanks shamed her. She deserved no thanks for taking him from a loving family and leaving him here, where he would eventually sicken and die. She knew Herrein worked to find out how to save the *taylenor*, but who knew if the cure would come in time for Wiel?

She drew her cloak about her and went out into the cobbled street. She had already told Mother Thara about the strange predator that had attacked them in the woodlands. Now, she must find Tasa Wimar in Imn-ashu's Temple and report to him. It still bothered her, something about the way the creature had moved, something about the flash of teeth in the firelight, or maybe the stink of it. Mother Thara would inform the mage. If it was something unnatural, it was Herrein's to deal with.

The afternoon bustle of the city was music to her ears after the solitude of her circuit. Hooves clopped on the stones of the street. A driver shouted to make way as some nobleman's carriage swept by. In the little square near the hospital, people were selling vegetables and baked goods. Baskets overflowed with apples, pears and squashes. Jaena turned into the square, fingering the few coins in her pocket. Maybe she could buy a meat-pie from the vendor near the corner.

"Jaena!" someone shouted.

She turned to see a young man with curly black hair slide from his horse's saddle. He shoved his reins into the hands of the hospital's porter and opened his arms to welcome her. She walked into his embrace, smiling at the trace of fragrance on the man's clothing.

"What's this, my lord Metten?" she asked. "You're wearing a floral scent?"

"The dandies are wearing it." A corner of his mouth quirked up. "It's an experiment -- supposed to be subtle. Halpen says no one should be able to tell unless they're close enough to kiss."

She blushed and laughed. "I suppose I'm close enough. Though it doesn't seem your style at all, frankly."

"My friend Halpen is trying to civilize me. A fool's errand, right? Come with me to dinner tonight, Jaena, say you will! I want to talk to you some more, and I can't stay now. Will you come?"

"I was just going back to the Temple."

"You have hours yet! I'm meeting Halpen there, so we won't be alone, but I've missed the sight of you." His eyes were warm and full of humor. She felt at home again, now that she'd seen him. She agreed and watched him take back his reins from the porter. He gave her a quick bow, remounted and was off into the crowded streets before she could forget the warmth of his embrace.

* * *

Dinner turned out to be at the best inn in the city, a restrained brick building surrounded by well-cared-for greenery, and hung with candles in shielded glass.

The babble of conversation hit Jaena's ears as soon as they walked through the door. A servant in spotless black livery inclined his head to Metten and avoided looking at Jaena at all as he bowed them into the dining room.

Tall ceilings bordered in gilt crowned the dining room. The room smelled of thyme – likely they had tossed herbs into the iron basket above the fireplace. People chatted and ate and drank at the tables, which were dressed almost as well as the people seated at them. Inquisitive eyes turned her way, and a bejeweled lady bent to whisper in her companion's ear.

Jaena felt like turning around and leaving. This was not a place for a village-born commoner, even a priest. This was a place of the upper classes.

Metten seemed to notice nothing out of place. He led her across the room to where a young man and woman sat at a table set for four. The woman was lovely. Her dress was crusted with green semiprecious stones around the low neckline, and her hair was an improbable yet striking rose color.

Metten waved at the man, whose sandy hair flopped about his ears. "Lord Halpen de Morn, known him since Verasa College. Hal, this is my friend Jaena. She's a priest, just returned from her latest rounds."

"How unusual!" Halpen sat back, looking at Jaena with a polite social smile on his face. She recognized it: it was the smile the upper classes reserved for the lower. "This is Meleji de Osar, daughter of the Chartess of the southern islands. I'm escorting her to Duscapi to meet family."

Duscapi was an ancient city, full of every race and religion known to humanity. It was known for its crumbling architecture, its school of music, and its decadence. Even its legendary name seemed full of the music of bells and *dirath*, foreign music not heard here in the capital.

"I hear Duscapi is a beautiful city," she said. "I hope you enjoy it."

"Oh, she'll enjoy it," Halpen said, grinning at Meleji. "I'll be with her, so she'll be bound to."

Metten said, "I'll take you to Duscapi someday, Jaena. I'm free of obligations now since I left my master's studies and my parents have basically cast me off. Find some free time, and you and I can go explore the place."

Jaena felt a little thrill. "Oh, I would love to. But Metten -- "

"No 'But Mettens'," he said. "You can do it. You've been on rounds for two years now with no time off. Talk to the Tasa, or the mothers, or whoever. The world lies before us!" He gestured at her, grinning.

This was why she liked him so much -- his willingness to slip the bonds of social barriers and do what he wanted. Metten was in no way careless with what he perceived to be his duty; he simply defined things a little differently than did his peers.

But it was impossible. She lay her head against Metten's shoulder for a moment, then straightened. "We'll talk about it later."

She had no funds for a trip across the country, and Metten, for all his social status, had been put on a minimum allowance by his angry father. He was living in a room above a shop and supplementing his allowance with lucky gambling winnings. The trip to Duscapi did not appear likely to happen.

"Where in the world did you two meet?" Halpen said. "You seem quite familiar with each other."

Metten grinned as the butler poured wine into their glasses. "Met her on her rounds, where else? She came to Verasa with another priest. I guess the masters wanted a note of gravity to help distinguish us older students from the teenagers. They asked the goddess to bless our studies. I think the goddess was busy elsewhere, in my case at least."

Jaena remembered Metten leaving his friends and pulling out a chair to talk to her at dinner that evening. He'd ignored the frowns of the Masters, and Priest Mag's puzzled glances. She'd been enchanted with his charm.

Halpen smirked. "Since you left Verasa few weeks later and have been a wastrel ever since. It's a wonder this priest will even tolerate your presence, since you scorned to follow through on the goddess' wishes."

"The goddess doesn't require people to follow a path they aren't suited for," Jaena said.

"Tell my noble parents that," Halpen said. "It'll be news to them." He lifted his glass. "Cheers!"

The first course was set before them, delicate curls of citrus adorning some sort of custard, sprinkled with rose petals and herbs like a treat for dolls. Jaena watched Meleji's white hands across the table as she chose a fork, and copied her.

"Where are you back from?" Metten asked, the air of excitement still clinging to him. "I didn't expect to see you for weeks!"

"I wasn't too far away, a few days from the city. Have you heard of Homeborn? Or Bless-us-goddess?"

Halpen laughed. "Really?"

"It's a pretty village, very small," Jaena said.

"I think they were trying to cover their bets, with a name like that." Halpen's eyes began to wander. He had clearly lost interest in her.

The food was delicious, and the drink plentiful. Metten, Jaena and Meleji all became talkative and happy, and Jaena was sure her cheeks glowed as theirs did. Halpen had been drinking steadily since they arrived. His face flushed red. He began to make spiteful remarks and slur his words. Meleji pulled farther away from him as the evening progressed.

"Are you staying here?" Jaena asked Meleji, wondering if she should be left alone with the drunken lord.

"Yes. My maid and groom accompanied me, though, so I'm well attended." Meleji returned a friendly smile.

"Jaena came in from rounds with a *taylenor* boy," Metten announced. "This will be the second *taylenor* at the Mothers' Hospital at one time. I've never known there to be more than one before -- and usually not even that, right Jaena?"

"The *taylenor* are very few," she agreed.

Halpen's drunkenness seemed to drop away as his gaze narrowed on her. "You brought in a *taylenor*? Why are you doing that?"

"Jaena is a Seeker." Metten smiled at her.

Halpen goggled at her. "I thought you were a priest!"

"I am. There's no reason I can't be a Seeker while in Imn-ashu's service."

Halpen stared at her.

Meleji said, "What is this Seeker?"

Metten began giving a cheerful, if somewhat garbled description of what it meant to be a Seeker. Halpen sat back speechless and stared some more.

Jaena began to be annoyed at his regard.

"We have no such thing in the Islands," Meleji said. "This is a very good thing you do, Jaena. It is too bad you can't save the young people, but at least they are well cared for."

"Someday we'll save one," Jaena said. "Mother Thara works with Mage Herrein on the problem with every new *taylenor* we find. They'll get to the root of the illness."

Halpen shoved back his chair and stood. "Uh, drank a little too much. Must leave, my apolo-ologies."

She frowned. The young lord was certainly drunk, but his hands seemed to be shaking as well. Meleji began to rise, but Halpen waved her away. "No. Stay. Enjoy. Met, you'll take care of her? I must go now."

"Yes, go on," Metten said. His brows drew together. "Is something else wrong?"

"I'm fine," Halpen said. He began to walk away from the table.

Jaena gasped and sat back in her chair as if she had been slapped.

It had taken the young lord's drunken condition and his sudden fear to bring it to her attention. Now that she was focused on him, Jaena could sense the thing she was used to Seeking, in villages all across the countryside.

Halpen was a *taylenor*.

The nobleman's gift seemed stunted. It was barely discernible under Halpen's loud personality. Unlike Wiel's *taylen*, it didn't call out to her. There was no surreal mist of *taylen* in the dining room. It was the strangest gift she had sensed.

But it was there.

And the young lord was surely in his early twenties, but he showed no sign of any illness. He had apparently never been found by any Seeker. But he knew he had *taylen*, Jaena had no doubt. He was afraid of her. Afraid of being discovered.

She watched as Halpen negotiated the crowded tables and climbed the stairs to the guests' rooms on the upper level. Both Meleji and Metten stared after him.

"That was odd," Metten said. "I wonder if I should go check on him?"

"I think he's fine," Jaena said.

"He only has to go to the first floor suite. Also, he has a manservant," Meleji said. "He'll be attended."

"Halpen's a rich man. He probably has several servants with him. His parents even bought him a private room at college." Metten swirled the remaining wine around the bottom of the glass. The red wine against the green-tinged glass made a color darker than blood.

"Who is he, exactly?" Jaena said.

"Hal's a good friend. Don't be put off by his abruptness," Metten said.

Jaena knew Metten viewed things through his own golden filter, assuming all people were basically good and eager to help each other. Then again, maybe she had been too quick to judge Halpen. "I mean, who are his family?"

"The de Morn family. You haven't heard of them?"

Now Jaena placed them. She paid little attention to politics, but even she knew the de Morns were hereditary members of Cassahn's

Council. The de Morns were among the most powerful in the land. And their son – their only son? --- had *taylen* that was crushed down into a little ball in his psyche, and he had never grown ill from the Dark Twin.

* * *

The next morning, Jaena arose from a sleepless night and pulled her traveling cloak over her shoulders. She slid out the side door of the Temple, avoiding the resident priests on their way to sunrise meditation. It had rained in the night, and the streets were wet, the few early street vendors silent as they set up their wares. She walked until she arrived at the inn.

By the bleak light of a gray morning, things looked very different. There was no glow of firelight and wine; no sparkle of jewelry and laughter. The precious wineglasses she had admired last night had been locked away. The public rooms were abandoned.

She climbed the steps to the suite Meleji had referred to the previous evening. There was no one else in the hall when she tapped on the door. As she waited, she thought she heard a scuffling sound from inside the chamber.

A man Jaena had never seen before opened the door. "Yes? Are the horses ready?"

"I would like to see Lord Halpen," she said.

Apparently the man inside recognized her voice. There was a rush of footsteps and Halpen's bulky form replaced that of the servant. "I don't want to talk to you," he said. "You shouldn't even be here."

"I have a question," she said.

"I'm not interested in your questions. What right do you have to question me? Metten has gone too far this time, inviting you along where you don't belong."

"But -- "

"Goodbye." The door thudded closed.

Jaena waited a few moments, then went down to the parlor to order tea. The attendant there sneered at her, but did not refuse her custom. Jaena drank tea, nibbled on a scone and waited. After a while she heard booted feet in the entryway, and the sounds of something heavy scraping along the floorboards. Luggage, she assumed.

In a few moments she was sure of it; she had actually frightened Lord Halpen de Morn away from his hotel room, and he was leaving – hungover, weary and against his real wishes – at a time when he would usually be fast asleep, just to avoid Jaena's questions about the *taylen*.

After the sounds of Halpen's departure died away, Jaena put her coin on the table for payment, and left the place. She had no idea what was going on, but she knew whom she would ask next.

CHAPTER FOUR

Halpen de Morn shoved at the door into the parlor, ignoring the protests of the novice outside the room. A few of the mothers sat at a wooden table, the remains of a simple meal before them. Mother Thara, at the head of the table, stood and glared at Halpen.

"What's the meaning of this?" she asked. "You have no business here, de Morn."

"Get out!" he ordered the other women in the room. "I must speak to Mother Thara on a matter of urgency. Go, now!"

The other women fluttered from the room, casting nervous glances at Mother Thara in case she wished them to stop or assist her in any way. Thara waved them out, her clear gray eyes on Halpen's face. She waited until the women had scattered and sat down again.

"What do you want?" she asked. "You know footmen will be here in short order, wondering if you've murdered me."

"What? No!" Halpen said, running his hands through his hair. He knew he was being rude, but he couldn't help it. His nerves were tight as guitar strings. He paced back and forth, hearing his boot heels sharp on the wooden floor. After a moment he yanked open the door to verify that no one stood outside, listening.

Thara's eyes were still as sharp as the rest of her bones, Halpen thought.

"Can't you see I'm damned upset?" he demanded. "My secret has been discovered, by one of your people at that!"

"What do you mean?"

"That chit of a priest who, it turns out, is also a Seeker. She has discerned my *taylen*. It was supposed to be hidden beyond discovery. What am I going to do?"

Thara rose. She drew him toward a chair, poured some tea from a teapot in the center of the table. Halpen could feel his breath coming fast with fear. He shoved the tea aside, sloshing it onto the table.

"What good is tea?" he shouted. "What am I to do, Thara?"

"Tell me what happened," she said.

Halpen pushed his hair off his perspiring forehead. He went through the little story: how that fool Metten had become involved with someone below his station, how he had invited her to dinner, and how he had mentioned – too late for Halpen! – that the woman was a Seeker.

"Her eyes were otherworldly," he said. "You should have seen them. She knows, Thara. She was even shameless enough to show up at my door this morning, a single woman alone, and stand at my door to question me."

"What did you tell her?"

"I told her she had no right to question me!"

"I'm sure that allayed all her suspicions," Thara said.

Halpen's temper flared. "Don't talk to me that way! What am I to do, Thara?"

Thara stood by the long window, the light of the gray morning reflecting on her face. "She'll come to me, you know. I'm her mentor. We have another chance to turn her curiosity aside. Think, de Morn! The Seeker has encountered an unusual kind of *taylen*, one she has never heard of. What is there in this to frighten you? We simply explain the situation."

"Easily said!" Halpen said. He looked around the room. "Have you nothing here stronger than tea?"

"Relax, de Morn. You behave like a child found out in a minor transgression."

Halpen felt the laugh bubbling up inside him. "Tell my noble parents that. Tell them there is nothing to worry about here, that it is a – minor transgression."

Thara held up a bony hand. "Yes, I know, we don't wish Lord and Lady de Morn to be troubled by this. They need not be; don't worry."

Halpen sighed. Thara shared the de Morn interests, and she was brilliant at manipulating the opinions of those around her. "I ... would appreciate your help."

Someone banged on the door, then slid into the room. It was a sweating footman, followed by an armed city guard. "Mother Thara! I've brought help!"

"I don't need help, though I thank you for your alertness." She gave a coin to the guard and another to the footman, and gestured them out of the room. "Fools," she told Halpen. "You could have murdered me several times by now, if you really meant me harm."

"What can we do?" Halpen said. "I thought there might be some way to silence her, but ..."

"No need. We simply tell her the truth."

Halpen felt as if the world shifted from under his feet. He stared at her.

The corner of Thara's mouth quirked upward. "You are a sport, Halpen. A rare example of one whose *taylen*, inherited from some distant ancestor we don't even know of, has come down to you a faint shadow of its usual self. Along with that, you've been spared the Dark Twin, but you have no mage ability to speak of, and no facility at learning anything Mage Herrein has to teach."

"It's that simple, then," Halpen said. "Tell her the truth."

"You make things too complicated." Thara walked to the door. Her robe, loosely belted at the waist, seemed barely to contain a physical form as it draped to the floor.

Halpen sighed. "I panicked," he admitted.

"Go now. I'm sure Jaena will be here soon, asking me all kinds of questions about how it's possible to suppress natural *taylen*. You don't wish her to see you here."

"Never see her again, I'll be thrilled." Halpen rose and bowed to her. "My thanks, Mother Thara."

"It's nothing. Go, now."

Halpen went. He felt several pounds lighter as he walked through the hallway to the front door. It was a relief, to know Mother Thara was handling this disaster. He moved quickly, not wanting to see the *taylenor* who currently resided here in the hospital. One was new, but one lay near to death. That child was cursed by her *taylen*, doomed to die at an age when by rights she should be leaving home, perhaps going to some trade or getting married. Halpen thanked the goddess he wasn't cursed to an early death and left the hospital as unobtrusively as he could.

CHAPTER FIVE

Tia died just as the Temple's morning bell reverberated through the walled streets.

It was a bright autumn day in the city, the sunlight turning the stone streets gold. All that light vanished as the front door to the hospital closed behind Jaena. Someone had covered all the windows with dark cloth. There were no children running in the halls or being scolded by the mothers. No novices lingered in the entryway to gossip. Silence ruled the wing that was devoted to the *taylenor*.

Jaena made her way to the closed door of Tia's room. Voices murmured inside, the deep music of a priest's prayer. Wiel leaned against the wall across from the door, alone as if he sat a vigil. He looked up at Jaena's approach. His eyes were solemn.

"I saw her yesterday." Jaena's voice cracked. "It was not unexpected. Poor Tia!"

"How long was she -- " Wiel stopped.

"Tia was fourteen years old. Mage Herrein found her about two years ago."

"So," Wiel said. "I have two years, then."

"Not necessarily. I knew a *taylenor* boy named Marki. He lived for more than three years after his *taylen* manifested. I've been told a gifted girl once lived a decade, back when there were more like you in these halls. I don't know what makes the difference. Mother Thara didn't know."

Wiel pushed himself away from the wall. "I feel fine," he said.

"I can tell. I'll pray to Imn-ashu that you're the exception."

He nodded, fast and jerky as if his emotions were under rigid control. Then he walked away and through the side access door to the courtyard. Brilliant sunlight stabbed into the hall for a moment, along with a burst of birdsong. Then the door closed and all was dim again.

Jaena waited until Tia's door opened. Mother Thara and Priest Mag emerged. Thara gave her a nod, and Jaena went in to pay her last respects to Tia before they came to take her away.

Jaena stood beside the narrow bed, blinking back tears. She reached out to gently touch the girl's face. Priest Mag had sung Tia's soul to Imn-ashu, and there was nothing left of Tia's sweet self in the body that lay on the bed.

Jaena tried to add her own prayer, but the notes stuck in her throat, stopped by unshed tears. She gave Tia's cold hand a last squeeze and left the room.

The funeral was held later that day, a small rite held for the comfort of those who had known Tia. The girl's family was far away, in the south of Cassahn near the closed border with Ull-fasten, and would not attend. A priest would be sent to them with a message, but the family had probably been mourning Tia as dead since the Dark Twin had been explained to them.

Instead, a few mothers who'd cared for Tia filed into the parlor to hear the songs. Four of the older orphans from the other wing of the building attended, wide-eyed and scared in the presence of death. At the last minute Mage Herrein himself slipped through the door into the chamber, robed in unrelieved black, accompanied by one servant. Jaena was glad to see that the old mage cared.

Priest Mag sang the ageless prayers, his rich voice filling every corner. Jaena closed her eyes and listened. It comforted her to hear Tia's last songs rendered in such a voice.

After Tia's body was removed to be interred in the hospital cemetery, Jaena went to the breakfast room and waited for Mother Thara.

She had to wait a while. Mother Thara needed to confer with Mage Herrein. Jaena waited and ate some of the fruit in the carved bowl on the table. By the time Thara was free, the day was well advanced.

Thara took a seat in the chair at the head of the table. "I'm sorry."

"Yes, so am I." Jaena blinked away fresh tears. "I wish you and Mage Herrein could find some way to stop the deaths."

"It's our first concern. You know that."

"I know." Jaena sighed, put poor Tia out of her mind, and told Thara her concerns about Lord Halpen's *taylen*. "It's strange," she finished. "It was as if his *taylen* was ... half there, or buried somehow."

"I'm aware of Lord Halpen's condition. It's extremely rare, but he inherited a weakened form of the *taylen* from some long-ago ancestor. Even his family, which pays close attention to their noble lineage, doesn't know where it came from. He escaped the Dark Twin, has never shown any sign of illness – but then again, he has no ability for magery, either."

"Has he ever tried?"

"He sat with Mage Herrein for hours when he was younger, until Herrein threatened to strangle him – only half in jest, I fear. The man's as ungifted as you or I. It's just a strange vestige from long ago."

"How odd!" Jaena said.

"It's very rare. Not surprising Mage Herrein wouldn't have told you about it."

"Yes, but – he was frightened. I swear he was afraid of me as soon as he heard I was a Seeker. It's what made me focus closer on him. What does he have to be afraid of?"

Thara's already thin lips tightened more. "He's a fool. Maybe his parents have taught him it's something to be ashamed of. The de Morns are very conscious of status, you know."

"I've heard of them." Jaena thought of the regal lady de Morn and her husband, as she had seen them at some public ceremony. Then she thought of Halpen, sandy-browed and chunky. Still, he was attractive enough, if it weren't for the condescension in his eyes.

Thara pushed back her chair and rose. "I must see Wiel soon. I believe he is very upset."

"Yes." Jaena sighed. "Thank you for seeing me, Mother Thara. I'm out on rounds again to the eastern villages tomorrow."

"Good," Thara murmured. "Maybe your luck will hold, and you'll find another *taylenor*. I advise you not to go alone this time, though."

Jaena flushed. "Lord Metten is at loose ends. I've received permission for him to join me, if he promises to place the goddess' work first and above his own."

"An interesting man, your Lord Metten," Thara said, and smiled. The smile transformed her thin, severe face. If Jaena ever wondered if this reserved woman really cared for her, all she need do was remember that smile.

"Well, he's had some training in arms, and I think Tasa Wimar is just as happy not to have to send someone else out with me. Apparently there have been more sightings?"

Thara nodded. "Yes, some people in the east have claimed to see demons. Take care, child. It's good that the young lord is going with you."

"That thing I saw near the Arahn Forest. Have you told the Mage Defender about it?"

Thara nodded. "It might have been a demon. There's no way to know – you didn't see it clearly, and it left no sign. Arahn is known for dark visions, after all. But there are reports of strange creatures as far in as Uthen's lands – Arahn is further west, but there's no telling. If the stories are true, we have dark times ahead. That ancient evil has been entombed for centuries, and Mage Herrein isn't as strong as he used to be."

Jaena thought back to the days when she had sat with Herrein, learning about *taylen*. She'd been intimidated by the old Mage Defender, and he'd done nothing to allay that. Strict and quiet, he'd explained the duties of a Seeker to her without ever venturing into the territory of a personal connection with Jaena. She got the idea his task of defending the land lay heavy on him. She remembered his hands shook after their lessons, and sometimes he needed to support himself by leaning on a table as he walked across the room.

"Mage Herrein is very old. Is he still able to defend us?"

"I hope so." Thara's eyes glanced away and did not meet Jaena's.

CHAPTER SIX

The line of travelers waiting to board the Uthen ferry stretched along the dirt road at the river's edge. A painted wagon that proclaimed a troupe of traveling actors had drawn a cluster of the curious. One of the actors was singing. It was a glorious autumn day that almost chased thoughts of Tia from Jaena's mind.

But not quite. Part of Jaena was relieved that Tia was at peace at last. Part of her still mourned. Tia had been so delicate, so eager to see Jaena, almost like a little sister might have been. Jaena had loved her like a sister. She could barely remember loving her own sister, who'd died in the frozen winter of the plague so long ago.

Ears waited patiently in the harness, ears swiveled to catch the music and laughter from the direction of the painted wagon. Every now and then she stretched forward to lip at tufts of hay from the farmer's wagon in front of them.

The song broke off as the aging ferry drew up to the dock. It took a while for the foot travelers and the single crest-emblazoned carriage to rumble down the walkway and disembark. Metten, who stood near her with his mount's reins looped around his forearm, leaned closer.

When the last traveler leaped from the walkway and slung his pack onto his back, the ferryman reached out to ring the bell. "Come on aboard! Five coppers a wagon."

Metten removed his other arm from Jaena's waist. Jaena pushed him gently away, flushed and smiling from the quick kiss he'd given her. He put a foot into the stirrup and swung back into his horse's saddle, ready to ride onto the ferry.

Two women and the hay wagon in front of them boarded. The ferryman turned the brim of his hat around against the glare of the sun and waved at Jaena. It seemed there was room for the donkey cart.

She clucked at Ears. "Come on, donkey."

Ears must have disapproved of the ferry. First she put her ears back, listening; after two steps forward she planted her feet and refused to go any further. Jaena looked behind them at the line waiting to cross the river.

"Awww, come on!" came a shout from a traveler behind them. "I've someplace to be!"

"Ears wants a better class of transportation, I think," Metten said, lounging in the saddle. He looked undisturbed by the possibility of being stuck with a stubborn donkey and angry travelers stacked up behind them.

Jaena made a face at him. "Maybe you can convince her to board."

Metten leaped down and handed her his reins. His thoroughbred mare shook her head nervously. Jaena hoped the mare didn't follow Ears's example.

"Well, donkey," Metten said conversationally. "You aren't a horse, but I suppose the same rules apply. Come on, now." He grasped the donkey's halter and pulled.

Ears dug her feet in.

"Uh-oh, that's bad," Jaena said. "She's not going anywhere for you, my lord."

The ferryman strode towards them, frowning. "Here, what's with your donkey? I've got people waiting, and a schedule to keep."

"Get out of the way!" yelled someone two wagons back. "Let someone else go!"

"Hurry it up!" called the horseman behind them.

Jaena gave the reins to Metten and went to the donkey's head. "Come on, Ears, come on," she coaxed, pulling on the bridle. "Just a few steps now."

Ears tried to back up.

"Look," the ferryman said, exasperated. "If you can't go forward, you're going to have to go back. You, on the bay – give them some room to turn around!"

"I'll do better." It was the farmer with the hay-wagon, who'd boarded ahead of them. He grabbed an armload of hay from his load. He threw a few handfuls of hay down in front of Ears on the ramp to the ferry, and threw the rest down on the deck. He looked at Ears. "Smart animal," he said. "Gotta give her a reason to go."

Ears perked up. Jaena loosed her hold on the bridle so the donkey could lip the wisps of hay. The donkey took several steps and was aboard the ferry, where Jaena managed to get her out of the way of the fuming traveler behind them before Ears settled down to munch the rest of the hay.

"Now there's a man with intelligence!" said Metten, smiling at the red-bearded farmer.

"I've got lots of experience with asses, take my word," the man said. "Not referrin' to you o'course, sir."

"Of course not." Metten grinned as he slid from his saddle.

"Donkeys are wonderful beasts – smarter than Whiskey here – but when they don't want ta go, they don't want ta go." The farmer dipped his head at them. "I'm Goras."

"I'm Jaena. I apologize for Ears. She's usually not this stubborn." She handed their fare to the glowering ferryman, who had not forgiven them.

"Glad to meet a priest of the goddess," Goras said, inclining his head. He'd seen the Temple's insignia on the little cart, green-and-blue wisps of stylized music issuing from Imn-ashu's flute.

Metten introduced himself. "Thank you for your help. May I repay you for your hay?"

"That little bit?" Goras snorted. "Repay me by buying me an ale in

Uthen. You're an unlikely pair. I'm curious – it's always been my worst sin."

"Happy to!"

The ferry pulled away from the line of travellers on the dock. Brown water slapped against the hull. The ferryman, intent on making a good day's wage, had crowded his deck – aside from Jaena's group and Goras' hay wagon, there were four foot-travelers, clustered in a group in the bow, staring towards the clutter of Uthen on the other riverbank.

Jaena stroked the donkey's forehead. "I'll look forward to it. It'll be good to take a break before heading out on my circuit. Thank you again, Goras."

Goras' smile vanished. "You're headin' east?"

"Out of Uthen, yes," Jaena said.

Goras lowered his voice. "Then I have news for ya, Priest. Word is, there've been some weird things seen in the eastern villages. Demons, some say."

"There've been no demons seen for hundreds of years." Jaena kept her voice noncommittal.

"The mage is gettin' pretty old, I think. Maybe he can't keep the demons in the pit the Eastern Mage sent 'em to, back when my great-great-great-gran was a toddler."

"You believe these rumors?" Metten frowned.

Goras patted Ears' forehead. "Maybe a few of 'em? I don't know. There's been an unusual number of tales from the far-eastern villages. Thought you'd like to hear about it, seein' as you're headin' out that way. Hope the Eastern Mage isn't stirrin' as well."

"Thank you for the warning," Jaena said.

"The Eastern Mage has been entombed under Mount Nimn for five hundred years," Metten said. "Assuming that's not all myth and legend."

Goras shrugged. "All I know is I was taught that when the demons appear, the Eastern Mage soon follows. Probably liars' tales, as you say, sir."

"Either way, I'll keep my sword ready."

A river-bird swooped down over the ferry, sunlight flashing on its wings. Jaena's hair whipped in the stiff breeze. The low buildings of Uthen's docks and river district drew closer. A chill swept through her. It felt as if something awaited them in the city.

CHAPTER SEVEN

There was no Temple at Uthen. There was a resident priest, a fiftyish man named Hathar who had been stationed in the town for most of his life. His one-room house was near the inn that supplied all his meals in return for supposed favor from the goddess and a tiny stipend from the Temple.

Jaena stopped as a matter of courtesy to let the man know they were in town. Then Jaena drove Ears to the inn and Metten went inside to reserve their rooms. She pulled the cart into the yard, and stayed with the donkey in the warm, horse-smelling stable until the stableboy brought hay. Then she and Metten set out to explore the city.

Uthen had narrow streets, and a three-story stone house where the local lord, who was responsible for the protection of the town and its environs, lived. Bright banners flew from its roof, and a single guard stood at the front door; the lord was in town.

"It's Lord Uthen, of course," Metten said. "His family predates the town. Never have any trouble remembering their name."

"You know him?"

"I knew his son, at college. And his lovely daughter."

Jaena poked Metten in the ribs. He laughed.

"Tell me," Jaena said. "I've always wondered. Why did you leave college?" Metten had a curious intellect; she thought he would have been in his element at Verasa.

"Verasa College isn't what you think. It's a school for training lords and governors, learning about money, making contacts we'll use to influence others the rest of our lives." He made a sour face. "I wanted to go to the Masters' School in Duscapi, but my father wouldn't hear of me going there. He said it's full of thieves, charlatans, and drummers from the south."

"He's not wrong, from what I hear." Jaena sighed. "I still want to go, just to hear the music."

"You'd love Duscapi. You and your flute would fit right in."

Jaena smiled at him. He loved to listen to her play the flute and didn't even object to her singing. "Did you learn all the noblemen's names at college?"

"Yes, and the banner of each house, and their cousins and *their* cousins and so on. And of course the rules of precedence."

Jaena tried to picture her relaxed lover learning about formality and protocol. "No wonder you escaped."

"There were some redeeming things about it. I hated the rules of trade and treaties, but there was a sciences instructor I loved to listen to. And the history of the gods, that was good."

It wasn't a market day, so the square was empty of all but a couple of food carts. They left the central area and walked past a communal oven and along one of the crooked streets. Painted signs indicated a candy store and a tavern. Further down the street was a dry-goods store with bolts of cloth lined up as if in formation under the shelter of the front awning.

Jaena was considering going into the candy store when a shriek of terror rang out from somewhere nearby.

There was another scream, and many voices crying out. Jaena and Metten rounded the corner and saw people running away, trying to crowd into the nearest doorway. In the middle of the street was something out of nightmare.

The thing was about the size of a wolf. It was black and hairy and had strange humped shoulders. It crouched over the body of a child and snarled at Jaena and Metten, who were by now the only people left in the street. Its fangs dripped an ominous pink, blood mixed with saliva. A jagged wound gaped from the child's chest down to its belly, exposing the red-and-gray of perforated organs. Blood spread like glistening paint on the stones.

"Get back!" Metten snapped. "Here, in this shop." He pushed her towards the door and turned back to the street, loosening his sword in its sheath.

"The Guard will be here," Jaena said, suddenly very afraid. "You don't have to – "

"I don't see any Guard coming."

"Come in here, come in fast!" said a voice from the shop. Hands gripped hard on Jaena's forearm and pulled her in. Inside, a cluster of people craned toward the window to see what was happening in the street. An older woman sobbed in the back corner, hands covering her face.

Jaena twisted away from the hands holding her. A heavyset man in wool crossed his arms and looked down at her, refusing to allow her to pass.

"Don' be a fool, girl," he rumbled.

"What is that thing?" she asked.

"Could be a demon."

"Right in the street, in the middle of the day," Jaena breathed.

Legend had the creatures tied to the darkness of night; it was shocking to see such a creature of hell here, on Uthen's prosaic streets, just after noon. Jaena's thoughts flashed back to the thing that had attacked Wiel and herself in the woodlands on their way to Iryor; that thing, too, had behaved atypically for an animal.

Jaena shoved her way between two men. "I must see. That's my friend out there."

The men let her through. She slipped past rolls of fabric and racks of thread and cord to edge over to the shop window and peer out.

Metten had drawn his sword and approached the creature. He

stepped like a dancer, centered on his feet so he could leap any way he needed to.

The demon crouched above the body, one paw on the child's ripped-open chest. There was no chance at all that the child lived.

Now that Jaena examined the creature more closely, she saw it was different from a wolf. It had spiky hair that stuck out more like quills than fur, especially from its humped shoulders. Its fangs were longer than a wolf's, and its eyes were red. It snarled at Metten, craning its neck and turning its head sideways in a very unwolflike motion that gave Jaena chills up her spine.

Metten came a step closer, and the thing leaped at him, neatly avoiding the swing of the sword.

Metten staggered a step back as the creature slammed into him. The demon was too close for sword-work now. Metten dropped the weapon. Fangs snapped a finger's length from his neck.

Imn-ashu, breathed Jaena, too terrified to make a song of prayer.

Metten clutched the demon's neck with both hands, trying to hold the fangs away from his throat. The monster growled loud enough to vibrate the wooden planks under Jaena's feet, viscous saliva curling from its jaws.

Jaena looked around the shop frantically for a weapon. If no one else here would come to Metten's aid, she would. If only she had her bow! A pair of spring scissors lay on the shopkeeper's counter. She grabbed them, then tried to shoulder past the heavyset man.

The man grabbed her upper arm. She struggled to pull away, but his grip was like iron. "I'm not lettin' you risk yerself out there, Priest."

"It's not up to you," she said desperately. But the big man's hand still held her solidly in place. None of the others huddled here was willing to help.

She spun and looked out the window again.

Metten's right hand moved away from the demon, stretched toward his boot. The demon opened its jaws wide. A bitter stench rolled into the air.

Losing the one-handed battle against the thing, Metten let go fast, ducked under the demon's body as it lunged for where he had just been. He yanked a knife from his boot sheath. He shoved the blade up under the demon's neck, slitting the throat straight across even as the creature's jaws seemed to graze his neck.

Jaena screamed and tried to get to the door.

"Stay here!" ordered the heavy man. "What do you think you can do to help him, you daft child?"

Outside, the demon had not died from the grievous wound that would have killed any other creature. It pawed at its gaping throat in obvious pain. Blood dripped onto the stones. Then the demon shrieked and ran off down the street, disappearing around the closest corner.

Metten dropped the knife, clutching his hand.

The heavyset man stepped away from the door. "I'll go for the Guard," he said.

Jaena pushed past the exiting people, ignoring their frightened noise. She went straight to Metten. He bent over on the cobblestones, his curls hiding his eyes from her as he held onto his right hand with his left.

Before him, wisps of vapor – smoke or steam? – rose from little spots on the cobblestones.

"Metten, are you all right?" She dropped down next to him.

"Stop!" he gasped. "Stay away from those." His eyes were on the little smoking spots. There were spots like that all the way down the street where the demon had run. Curls of smoke rose from them and dissipated a few inches in the air.

"Those spots are from the thing's blood," Metten said. "Goddess that hurts."

"Did it bite you?"

"No, no, I'm fine." Panting a little from strain, Metten accepted her help to get to his feet. He still protected his right wrist, holding it close to his body.

"Let me see," she said.

"Its blood burned me when I cut its throat. Went right down my hand. – Goddess!" He'd bumped his hand into his own belt, jostling it.

The demon's blood pooled in the street and spattered on a nearby wall. All of it smoked and hissed. Metten was lucky the blood hadn't gotten into his eyes.

There was a woman next to Jaena, perhaps the shopkeeper; she made a little sound under her breath and then said, "I'll get a cold cloth. Or some oil. No – cold, cold is what we need." The woman went into the shop.

Large splotches of red, blistered skin marred the back of Metten's hand. One blister extended up onto his wrist. The skin there was almost black, as if burnt with fire.

The shopkeeper came back with a jug of water and some ice wrapped in soft cloth. She poured water over Metten's outstretched hand, washing away the poison. Then she offered Metten a mug of water, which he gulped down as if he hadn't had a drop for days.

"More?"

"Of course. Here, put this ice on your hand until we can get you to a *cernen*. Sit down, here in the shade. – You, Hass, would you please see to that poor child. Get the body covered decent before her Ma gets out here."

Metten's eyes went to the body of the child, still sprawled on the street.

"Sit down," Jaena told him. His pallor frightened her.

He sat on a bench in front of the shop and leaned his head back against the wall. "Is there more water?"

"It's coming. Here," she said taking it from the shopkeeper's hands. Metten once again drained the mug. The shopkeeper followed that with a tiny cup of something alcoholic Jaena could smell from two feet away; Metten tossed it back and looked up at the woman with a faint smile in his eyes.

"That did it," he said. "My thanks. I can walk to the healer now."

"I think not," the heavyset man said. He had returned without any guards. "The *cernen* is coming to you. My thanks for your protection, sir. Is here anything else you need right now?"

"Nothing, thank you," Metten said. "Jaena, are you all right?"

"No one else was hurt," Jaena said. Down the street, two men lifted the covered body of the child onto a pallet to be moved indoors.

Metten's eyes followed hers, and he frowned. "I accomplished nothing, here."

"You got rid of the thing." Jaena was still frightened because he looked so pale. "It didn't hurt anyone else."

"I hope not," Metten said. "But I don't know where it went when it ran away."

"Nor do I, but it's gone," the heavyset man said. "Guard station said there were others, though. They were all out chasing them when I got there. Demon down by the River Gate, one near the manor, and one in the city stables."

Jaena grimaced, imagining what carnage there must be in the stables. Thank the Goddess she had not chosen to stable Ears there, but left him with their innkeeper instead.

Metten said, "Look at all those little holes in the street. That's where the thing's blood dripped."

There were scars in the dirt between the cobbles, all the way down the street. She looked again at Metten's arm. He was fortunate. It was a wonder Metten seemed no more than severely burned. The blood might have eaten through his hand completely.

CHAPTER EIGHT

The *cernen* slathered salve over Metten's burned arm and commended him on the use of ice, then dosed him with something thick and purple he said would ease the pain. Jaena left him at the *cernen's* house and checked on Ears, then went to offer her assistance to Uthen's resident priest.

Hathar was sweaty and pale. "These are demons, demons out of history. I can't believe they're wreaking havoc right here, in Uthen, in the middle of the day!" He twisted his sash between his hands.

"It's frightening," Jaena agreed.

"You need to cancel your rounds," he said. "It's not safe, not safe at all. If we're under attack here, the eastern villages might have been overrun. Go, tell the innkeeper you're leaving!" He opened the front door as if rushing her outside.

Hooves clattered on the street. Jaena glanced outside Hathar's open front door. A group of horsemen rode up. A gray-bearded man wearing mail over a fine red tunic slid off the lead horse and crossed the priest's threshold. He glared at Hathar.

"Priest, why aren't you out in the streets?"

Hathar bowed. "Lord Uthen. We're just about to go. This is Priest Jaena. She was on her way to her eastern circuit."

Uthen's eyes scanned her. "You are not to continue your rounds," he ordered.

"They'll be in need, my lord," Jaena said, though she didn't like the idea of heading out alone.

"We're in need here. Make yourself useful. When we get things in order here, I'll send some men to escort you back to Iryor. Hathar! I want you out there. People are milling around in the streets asking for you. I'm sending a message to Herrein immediately, and a followup in a few hours. I want your report, with anything at all you've learned, before me or my second by dusk."

"Yes, my lord." Hathar's voice wavered.

Uthen turned on his heel and went back out. He mounted and pulled his horse's head around. His men rode off toward the town center, sunlight glancing off their mail.

Hathar dithered for a few moments. Then he and Jaena set off for the River Gate area where at least one demon had been spotted.

Hathar proved almost useless among the frightened people on the streets. He himself was too shocked, and Jaena thought he seemed frail and brittle. He knew this town and its people too well to be the calm support he should have been to them in this crisis. She wished the older man could go back to his house and pray to Imn-ashu in peace, but this was his job, and Lord Uthen had commanded him here.

After a few minutes watching his fussing, Jaena decided she could help more elsewhere. Hathar was singing a prayer in the midst of a small group, but he nodded to her as she slipped away. She began the walk up the long stairway to the upper city alone. There were signs that the fight continued in that area: shouts and clamor, and a gout of black smoke that crawled up the sky. She would go where she was needed.

Metten awaited her at the top of the weathered wooden logs that stepped up the flood plain from the riverside. "All well?" he asked.

"I suppose. Should you be here?"

He raised his bandaged arm and shrugged. "I'm well enough. The *cernen's* house is full, and I kept thinking of you. Why are you wandering around all by yourself? They're still searching for demons in the upper town."

"The priest here is no help. I thought I'd see if I could be useful."

"All by yourself, with no guard?" Metten released an exasperated breath. "Good thing I came back."

"I'm glad you came back, too." She smiled.

He frowned. "I'm serious, Jaena. The things are still running around loose."

"You're here now. Do you know your way around this place?"

Metten led them through Uthen's narrow streets. Jaena saw no one else in this section. Houses were closed up tight, shutters drawn. Open merchants' stalls were abandoned to whomever might care to take the goods that were left behind. Down one twisty alley, past some fruit scattered on the ground from an abandoned cart, Jaena saw the telltale pockmarks of demon's blood on the cobblestones.

They turned a corner and were surrounded by guards. The smell of sweat mingled with woodsmoke as a guardsman shoved Jaena back, hard, against the wall. Stone rasped against her skin. The man gripped her arm, fingers digging in.

"Get back! There's demons here."

Jaena stumbled away. The guard shoved her into a fenced enclosure that smelled of horse. Metten was already there, shaking off a guardsman's grip.

"Stay there! My lord's orders."

Hooves echoed in the alley. Lord Uthen rode up, trailed by a guard with his sword drawn and a wild look in his eyes.

"What are you doing here?" Uthen demanded.

"I came to sing the souls of those who need it."

"Well, that was a damned fool idea, Priest. There's a demon still alive here. Stay put!"

"With my good will, my lord," she said. She had no desire to find out what was causing the stink she now detected mixed with the smell of wood smoke.

"You too. Stay with her," Uthen said, his eyes on Metten's wrapped hand. "I'll leave a man to guard you both."

"No need, sir," Metten said.

Uthen pointed at him. "You'll do as you're told. Your father would have my skin if he knew you were here. Bad sword hand and doped up, too, I have no doubt. I don't know why that fool *cernen* let you go."

"My golden tongue, sir," Metten said. "I'll stay back. I have no wish to get in your way. But this hand isn't useless, and there's no need to spare a man to stay with us when you need him in the fight."

"Imn-ashu has always protected me," Jaena said.

Uthen grimaced. "Humor me, Priest. Stay alert then, Metten." He wheeled his gray mare around and called, "Let's go!" to his men.

The men rode back down the narrow street towards the square. Jaena looked around to see a stone wall to one side. She sidestepped a pile of manure. This place had been recently occupied by at least one horse. She hoped the animal was still alive somewhere because there was no sound from the open shed behind them.

"Get back into the shed," Metten said. "I think the thing is just around this corner." He drew his sword.

Black smoke billowed from between the buildings.

Someone yelled, and a horse screamed. Something dark ran across the street; Jaena couldn't see it well, but the way it moved told her it was a demon.

Then the thing rolled over on the cobblestones, a length of spear through its belly. It yowled and scraped the wooden shaft along the cobbles. Something shiny and black dripped from its gut. A guard lunged for the end of the spear, but the demon twisted away. It rolled again, forcing the spear to tear loose. Its blood spurted into the air, into the guardsman's face.

The guardsman screamed. He threw both arms across his eyes.

Two guards and a townsman raced to the first man's aid. The demon scrambled between the legs of one of the frightened horses and disappeared into a dark doorway.

Jaena shivered, thinking of the open shed door behind her. *I hope none of those things are in there.*

The guardsman fell to his knees, wailing. His companions clustered around him. A girl rushed up with a bucket of water and a cloth. She tried to squeeze water from the soaked rag into the wounded man's eyes.

The injured man, lost to reason, thrashed wildly. He knocked the girl away across the street. Jaena winced as the guardsmen forcibly pulled the injured man's arms from his face so he could be treated.

More shouts echoed from the houses around the square. Uthen's men were finding what they had been seeking.

Metten shifted his grip on his sword hilt. "How many demons are there, I wonder?"

"Where is everyone? I haven't seen any people except for Uthen's men." Jaena hoped the townspeople were all in hiding in a cellar somewhere. She hoped they were not going to have to go house to house, collecting bodies. She hoped she would not have to sing so many souls to the goddess tonight. An old memory seized her, unexpectedly: an empty house, and a line of narrow mounds in the snow. She'd thought that memory long buried.

Eventually, Uthen rode back to them. Sweat and ash streaked his face. The fine cloth of his shirt was eaten through, revealing the blistered, red skin beneath. Another wound on his thigh still bled.

"You may come out now," he said. "We're cleaning up. Be prepared – it is not a pleasant sight. You, Priest, you are to stay with Lord Metten and one of my men at all times."

"What did you find?" Metten asked. "Are there many dead?"

"Not as many as I'd feared. There were three demons running free. They're dead now. There's a big pyre in the square – someone threw them onto the fire. It works, apparently – the only thing we've found so far that can actually kill the things."

"Good," Metten said.

"It's not a pleasant sight," Uthen growled at Jaena. "If you weren't a priest, and badly needed, I wouldn't let you in. You either, son of my childhood friend."

"I'm twenty-four, sir, not the boy you remember. I'll guard her. You need not fear."

Uthen barked a bitter laugh. "So you say. After you've seen the things, you'll have the right to tell me that." His expression softened as he took in Metten's wrapped right hand. "On second thought, you've fought one of the things. Come on, then. And no word to your father about this, Metten."

"I don't see him much any more," Metten said. He slipped through the opening in the gate, waving Jaena behind him. They crossed the alley and rounded the corner.

In the central square a fire burned, spewing greasy smoke. The scent of wood smoke was overlaid by a foul odor, apparently the stink of burning demons. Two blackened, shriveled demon corpses disappeared into the hungry flames of the pyre.

Uthen's men were on foot, swords drawn, quartering the square.

"In there," Uthen said. He tilted his head towards a big house fronting on the square. The house had been hung with silk banners, as if they had been anticipating a party that day. Now the banners were flecked with ash and blood. As Jaena watched, a girl began to haul the decorations down. The girl sobbed as she worked.

"Go. Help Lord Uthen," Jaena said to Metten. "I have work to do."

He frowned at her mulishly and took up a position beside the front door, arms crossed, on guard. After a few seconds he uncrossed his arms and began to help the girl take down the party banners.

Terrified people clustered inside the house, their faces pale and shocked. Some of them had burns from the demons' blood. The wooden table in the main room had been pushed out of the way against the wall, and four bodies were lined up next to each other on the floor. Two men, a woman, and a child, shoulder to shoulder, burned and showing the ragged gashes of demon claws. An older man covered them with a colorful woven blanket, probably someone's bedcover.

A woman walked through the door, her hair dusted with ash. The woman's eyes were red from smoke and tears.

"I'm Nitay. My father is one of the dead," she said. "Will you sing their souls for us, Priest?"

"Of course I will." Jaena had sung souls to Imn-ashu before, but this duty would be different. These people had died violently, unexpectedly. She hoped their sundered souls would understand it was their time to go. She stifled her own reluctance; this was her duty, and the only thing of value she could do for these people.

"I'll call the others together."

Jaena pressed her back into the wall, harder and harder as one person after another streamed in. They stood crammed into the front room, only a couple of feet between the living and the dead.

Nitay gave Jaena the names of the dead. "Marha tried to save the boy, but it was too late. She has a baby at home. I don't know what they'll do now."

Jaena tried to ignore the stench of violent death and the fear all around them, so that she could bring the souls of the slain to her mind. The child's soul in particular flapped around like a frightened bird, stunned and unable to comprehend what had happened. The older souls waited for Jaena to release them.

The copper smell of spilled blood filled her nose and stifled her voice for a moment. A red stain crept out from under the woven blanket.

Jaena's first notes were nowhere near the correct key. Nitay looked at her in surprise. Jaena stopped and cleared her throat. Someone stirred in the crowd, maybe displeased with her voice. She was used to that. She closed her eyes, tried to feel Imn-ashu's presence, and started over again.

After a few moments of awkwardness, Jaena's voice smoothed out. The goddess' voice filled hers and overcame the disharmony. Her voice resonated, filling the death-laden air with comfort. The sounds from outside in the square faded until they were alone in this room with the dead, their friends, and Imn-ashu's peace.

Imn-ashu beckoned. The souls of the dead took wing and were gone.

The enclosing peace thinned. Sounds of the fire and the guardsmen penetrated the room again. The people lining the edges of the room shifted and began to murmur to each other. Jaena's throat hurt, and her hands trembled.

Nitay appeared at Jaena's side with a stoneware mug. She frowned. "You're shaking like a leaf."

Jaena could only nod. There was no explaining the power and incandescence of the rite she'd just completed.

"Priest, you need to sit. Let me help you." Nitay helped Jaena out of the house.

In a few minutes, the bodies would be removed and prepared for their families' private goodbyes. Wooden pallets were propped against the outside of the house, waiting to transport the dead. A woman stood near, embroidered covers folded in her arms.

Nitay led Jaena across the square, away from the smoke of the pyre, and helped her to sit on the grass under a tree. The earth was damp and cold. Jaena shivered and looked around for Metten.

"I have heard souls sung before, Priest," Nitay said. "But never like that. You didn't even know my father, but I felt his soul going to Imnashu."

"I think the goddess is with us even more closely than usual today." A fragrance of *hibon*, the goddess' flower, drowned out the scent of demons and death. If Jaena could hold still one more moment, she might feel the goddess' touch.

Something brushed her arm. She startled. A blanket settled over Jaena's shoulders.

"I'm sorry, Priest," Nitay said. "You looked cold."

Jaena looked around, shaken. The scent of *hibon* was gone. No one but Nitay was near her. The fire snapped across the square.

Metten showed up and expressed his condolences to Nitay while Jaena collected herself. The young woman left to attend to her relatives, and Metten sat down next to her. He nudged her with his chased silver flask.

The first sip burned her parched throat like fire. The second was smoother. She handed the flask back to him.

He leaned into her, putting his bandaged arm around her shoulders. "Better?"

"I think so." Jaena relaxed in the warmth of Metten's closeness. He was a good man. She was afraid she was beginning to depend upon his presence.

"Nitay asked me to thank you again when you felt better."

"Imn-ashu is very close. It's as if she sympathizes. But that's not all. I think she wants me to do something, but I have no idea what it could be."

"The Goddess tells you this?" Metten frowned. "Jaena, you can really feel Imn-ashu?"

She shrugged. Some people didn't believe Imn-ashu was real. She hadn't thought Metten was one of them.

Uthen found them as the sun sank towards the rooftops. "I'm sending a second messenger with reports for Herrein. Priest, you're heading back to the capital at first light. Lord Metten will accompany you, and I'll send an escort in case you run into problems on the way."

"I'll report to the captain of the city guard," Metten said.

"The faster the better." Uthen stared around at the aftermath of the fight. "We can't take much more of this. We need Herrein to fight this scourge back with his magery. I pray he's not too old to do it again. Goddess' eyes, the Eastern Mage herself may waken and invade us at any time. Tell your superiors as well, Priest."

"I will."

"You may both come up to the manor and stay with us. My wife will welcome you." Uthen frowned at Metten. "You'll be safe there."

Metten laughed. "He means there's no way I'll be able to get to your room past his disapproving servants."

Jaena was surprised. "Lord Uthen, there's no need to guard my honor. The goddess guards me."

"I think she's busy tonight," Uthen said. "She has more important things to tend to than making sure her priest doesn't succumb to a bit of charm and some curls. I know Metten's father, you know – he was a lot like you when he was young, Metten, though neither of you will admit it."

Metten's grin froze on his face. "Indeed."

Uthen shrugged. "But you'll both do whatever you choose, after all. I must go see that the town is settled."

Jaena looked at Metten. He was indeed charming, and so were the dark curls, and the shoulders, and the whole effect, she thought. She glanced away from him, feeling suddenly shy. Then she felt exasperated with herself. She was twenty-three, and a priest, a strong woman who was used to traveling and serving the goddess alone, and not some chit who blushed when a handsome impoverished lord smiled at her. Even one who had fought a demon for her.

CHAPTER NINE

They left as soon as the sky turned pearly with dawn.

Ears had been skittish at the innkeeper's stable, kicking at the stall and braying. Now she happily plodded along in the traces, no doubt glad to be leaving a place so infested with demons.

The mounted men escorting them were grim-faced and serious. They bristled with swords and spears. One of the men carried a glowing pierced-metal firepot. The lead rider, Captain Eus, carried a bound torch as a means of defense against any possible demon attack; the flame looked weak and strange as the sun rose, its smoke curling back towards Jaena.

Saddles held more lengths of wood and fiber, the long-burning torches of the northern tribes, ready to light if needed. Jaena had one by her feet in the front of the donkey cart, and her bow within reach.

Metten rode near her but did not speak. He held his bandaged right wrist close to his body. He had been using the hand more often than she thought was wise.

The road between Uthen and Iryor was the main artery for trade. A crew paid by Lord Uthen kept weeds and brush cut back from the verge all the way to his border. Uthen also maintained a road patrol to discourage bandits, so the road was usually well traveled. Today it was almost empty; word had spread that the demons were at large.

The party passed a farmhouse and a few homesteads with doors and gates barred, animals and people indoors. In spite of the brilliant sunshine, the day bore an air of foreboding. Jaena tucked up tight on her seat behind Ears, all her muscles tense.

At midmorning a messenger on a fast horse galloped past, Uthen's colors streaming from her shoulders. She would be carrying reports to Mage Herrein in her pouch. The woman raised a hand in greeting as she rode by. Jaena watched her until she was just a vanishing dot on the long stretch of road.

The first demon barreled out of nowhere. It lunged for the neck of Captain Eus's horse before the captain could shove his lit torch into the thing to force it away. The demon slashed the horse's neck. Blood spurted as the horse gave a terrified scream and fell.

Captain Eus leaped clear from the dying animal. The dropped torch rolled in the dirt. Metten slid from the saddle and dove for it, but it was out.

Ears brayed and planted her feet.

The man who carried the firepot had opened it and lit a torch from the banked fire inside. The end of the torch flared. Another guardsman grabbed the torch and shoved it into the demon's face.

The demon cringed away, but another one scuttled in from wherever they were awakening, and Jaena thought she saw another one after that, a black tangle of teeth and hair in the mid-distance.

The captain crawled to his horse. The mare lay in a pool of blood that had pumped out from her jugular. Eus ripped at the ties on the saddle, freeing another bundle of fiber and wood. He thrust it at Metten.

"Here! Light it, fast!"

Metten grabbed for the torch and thrust it into the flame from the other torch. He pushed it at Jaena. Jaena couldn't take it; her hands were full with Ears. The stoic donkey was terrified in a way she had never seen before. Ears scrambled in the traces, trying to run. Jaena rushed to hold her head, to keep her here where she would have at least a little protection from the demons' acid teeth.

Around her, guardsmen were readying spears and lighting torches with disciplined speed. Two men formed a barrier in front of Jaena.

Metten gave the lit torch back to Captain Eus and grabbed another. Just as one of the demons leaped forward, Metten lit the new torch, drew his sword and spun around to join the guardsmen in defense.

Jaena tried to clear her mind, bring a few notes of the goddess' song to her lips. The goddess would help, somehow; she had been close and responsive the last few days. The din of growling, snarling and the guardsmen's shouts and curses jangled her nerves. She could not even begin Imn-ashu's song.

Jaena held onto Ears with all her might. Her two guards straggled out in a futile attempt at attack. She grabbed her knife and cut the traces, and pulled Ears over behind Metten. The donkey made a loud, screeching bray Jaena had never heard before.

A yowling scream filled the air; a guardsman struck out with his lit torch, and the demon's odd spiky coat crackled and crisped as it burnt.

Another black shape was in the undergrowth, then on the verge beside the trade road. Jaena stifled despair. *How many more were there?*

The sunlight darkened. Jaena looked up to see a roil of dark gray clouds, solid-looking as mountains, sweeping across the sky. It came from the southwest, the direction of the capital city. The front, if that's what it was, moved fast. In only seconds they were in a stormy dusk, winds whipping so hard that all the torches snuffed out like nightcandles blown out before bedtime.

Jaena gripped Ears' bridle. Something blew off the cart, which had been left on the road with the cut traces on the ground – Jaena's blanket, the solid thump of her flute case.

The guardsmen and Metten clustered back-to-back, turned outward in a futile defensive effort. Jaena knew they had no hope without the torches. Something gibbered and growled, too close.

She clutched at Ears' rough coat. Maybe it would be better to let her go after all. Ears might outrun the demons. Her hands loosened on the donkey's bridle.

It was night under the whirling dark storm. She couldn't see the guardsmen, or Metten, or any demons. Every nerve jittered as she waited to be attacked. She crouched down low to avoid being knocked down by the wind. Someone grabbed her shoulder, fingers tight, anchoring her.

Jaena closed her eyes and prayed this would all be over soon. Reaching out for the goddess, instead she felt the power behind the storm – *taylen*, thick and alive in every blast of air that rasped against her skin. This was an active *taylen*, magery she'd never experienced, so strong she could almost hear a voice in the wail of the tempest.

Lightning lit up the inside of her eyelids, but she heard no thunder. She ducked her head and saw another flash, so white it was almost blue.

The scream of the gale stopped between one breath and the next. The darkness blew away. Jaena looked up at a clear sky, sun beaming down on an open road.

She turned to look behind them. The line of slate clouds advanced towards Uthen.

She whirled to check the position of the demons. Maybe it was not too late to defend themselves, even without the torches.

"What the hell --?" One of the guardsmen stood up. "Where are they?"

Metten paced a few steps from their frightened defensive cluster. He looked around, sword still at the ready in his bandaged right hand. "I don't see them."

"There they are," the captain said.

All Jaena's muscles seized up in fear again. Then she looked where the man pointed and saw a desolate pile of tangled black a short distance from the road. Another lay across the bushes at the side of the road as if it had been tossed.

Jaena exhaled in convulsive relief. Her legs shook. She held onto Ears' bridle and watched the others pace over to the miserable pile.

They stepped around it cautiously, hands on weapons, waiting for any sign of movement. After a circuit around, Metten reached forward with his span of wood and poked at it.

The demon's body gave with Metten's shove. Jaena cringed and waited; but the thing didn't move.

"Is it dead?" she called.

The captain crouched down and examined the body. Two men were canvassing the area, looking for at least two more dead demons – surely there had been four?

Captain Eus called, "Dead as near as I can tell, Priest."

"But what killed them?" Jaena looked at the now-empty sky. That storm had been sudden and strong. It had nearly knocked her down. Unsecured items from the donkey cart were strewn across the empty road: her cloak, a blanket, the bucket she used to water Ears. Stripped-off branches littered the road. The captain's horse lay still, its blood soaking into the hard-packed surface.

Metten was back next to her. His hair was even more tangled than usual, his cloak in disarray. He pulled it over his shoulder and began unwrapping it from itself. "That wasn't a natural storm, obviously. Do you think Herrein did that?"

"I think so." The storm had been thick with *taylen*. She hoped yesterday's messengers had arrived at Iryor and Herrein had responded, using the magery she had never seen to fight back their invaders.

"Glad he isn't too old to defend us when we really need it," Metten said.

"I hope he got every one of them."

"Or he'll have an even bigger task ahead of him."

Jaena's knees were still shaking. "I don't understand."

Metten put an arm around her. "It's in Phorau's histories. The demons show up when the Eastern Mage begins to wake. They terrify and weaken us, and then the Eastern Mage rises to finish the job."

Those were ancient stories. Jaena had learned them years ago, at the Temple with the other novices. Metten called them "histories", but

Jaena thought they were more the stuff of legend. If they were true, Mage Herrein was about to be tested in a way he had never been before. He was the only true mage remaining in the land, facing a threat that had almost defeated the gods.

CHAPTER TEN

J aena had expected Iryor to be a city on edge, tense with military readiness, preparing for war.

Instead, a guard gave their group an offhand glance and waved them through the city gate without asking any questions. When they came out of the shadow of the gates into the walled area, Jaena was surprised to see everything much as usual. Travelers asked locals for directions to inns, and a musician played his guitar in the corner, hat out for contributions. A rich man's carriage, drawn by four purebreds, maneuvered through the path made for it by a grinning boy clutching his payment of a copper coin.

She twitched the reins and urged Ears onward.

"Don't they know what's coming after them?" Captain Eus muttered.

"Apparently not." Metten looked around in confusion at all the signs of normal daily life going on in the city.

Jaena pulled Ears to a stop when they reached the square closest to the Temple. Wailing pipes and drums echoed off the stone walls. Three men and a woman sang and waved strips of colored cloth in the air. A few barefoot children jumped and spun in time to the music. A matron hurried by, frowning at the dirty children.

"This is really odd," Metten said. "What happened to Lord Uthen's reports? All these people should be behind barred doors."

"I don't see the city guard mobilized, either," the captain said. "Lord Metten, Priest Jaena, I should leave you here."

"By all means go," Metten said. "Get them on their toes."

"My thanks," Jaena told the man. "Goddess' peace."

Eus nodded. He signaled to his men, and they wheeled their horses and set off for the headquarters of the City Guard.

Metten left her at the Temple door. "I'll see Herrein, I suppose."

"Good! Tell him the demons may still be on our heels."

A novice slid past them and stood at Ears' head. "You haven't heard the news, then," he said. "Mage Herrein sent a magical attack. Didn't you see it? The nearest villages have sent word that all the demons are dead."

Metten's mouth set. He looked grim. "They're fooling yourselves if they think that scourge is beaten back. This may be just the beginning. Jaena – I'll go find out what fantasy these people have in their heads."

The novice grinned. "It's all over, my lord. Mage Herrein got the message from Uthen two days ago. He locked himself in his rooms for a day after – scrying, I suppose. The new *taylenor* boy was in there with him. We all prayed – Tasa Wimar declared a day of song, and we all called the goddess' aid. Now we're celebrating."

Jaena handed Ears' reins over to the novice. The boy opened the carved-oak door for her, but Jaena shook her head.

"I think I need to go check on Wiel."

"But Tasa Wimar will be waiting," the novice said.

"I know. But I have to check on Wiel." The thought of Wiel in Herrein's rooms while the ancient mage fought off the attacks from the East set her on edge.

"Don't worry," Metten said. "The mothers will take good care of him."

"I can't help it, I brought him in. Thank you for taking care of Ears – please tell the Tasa I'll be back as soon as possible." She touched Metten's arm. "Go report, and I'll meet you later."

* * *

Jaena looked for Wiel as she entered the *taylenor* wing of the hospital. There was no sign of him in the main hall or in the courtyard. Mother Rhody was in the pantry area, preparing some infusion from herbs when Jaena poked her head in.

"Oh yes, he just came back from working with Mage Herrein again," Rhody said. "He's in his room. Very exhausted, Jaena. This isn't a good time."

Jaena nodded and went to Wiel's room anyway. The door was pulled to, but not completely closed. She tapped on the door and it slid open a little further.

"Wiel?" she said. "It's Jaena."

A gasping sound came from inside the room, then a choked, "Come in, Priest."

The windows were covered. A lamp burned low in the corner of the room. Wiel sat on the edge of his bed, hunched over. His arms were wrapped around his belly, and the odor of sickness hung in the air.

"What's wrong?" Jaena said, alarmed. "Should I call Mother Rhody? She's right down the hall."

"She knows I don't feel well." Wiel straightened. "She's mixing me something. Goddess, I'm glad to see you, Jaena."

Jaena went to the window and pulled one drape aside. The room grew bright enough for her to see Wiel's face. He was pale, and his forehead shone with perspiration.

"Poor boy," Jaena said. "What happened?"

Wiel turned a little away. "Just sick, that's all."

"Was it sudden?"

Wiel laughed, a short barking sound. Then he paled even further, rubbing his stomach. "You could say that."

"May I sit with you a while? Is there anything you need?"

"Please stay," Wiel said.

Jaena found a low stool in the corner and sat on it, pulling her cloak around her. "I'm sorry," she said. "You were healthy when I left. Is this the Dark Twin, come so soon?"

"Oh yes," he said. "This is it."

"It seems to be striking harder than it did with Tia." Jaena frowned. "And so sudden. Are you sure this is not just some stomach complaint?"

Wiel looked up at her then, eyes very dark in his pale face. "Don't pretend you don't know," he said. "I hate all this pretending."

Jaena stared at him. "Know what?"

Wiel hunched his shoulders over. "Oh, don't worry, I don't blame you," he said. "It's not as if there's anything else you all could have done."

Jaena waited a moment, but he said nothing else. "I really don't know what you are referring to," she said carefully. "I'm sorry, Wiel. Have I injured you in some way?"

He gasped and leaned over, vomiting a little liquid into the tub that waited there.

"I'm getting Rhody," Jaena said. "This is taking too long."

"No!" Wiel held up a shaking hand. "It'll pass. Don't go. Besides, after the drink she's making me I'll feel much better."

"Were you ill at Herrein's house?"

He nodded. "Herrein has needed to do some demanding workings, Jaena. With the demons killing people in the eastern towns. It's pulled a lot of strength from him, strength he doesn't have to spare at his age."

"But you're new, and untrained. What is it he relies upon you for?" Her breath caught as a horrible suspicion occurred to her. "When, exactly, did you get sick the first time?"

He gave her a twisted smile that was more like a grimace. "You actually didn't know," he said. "That's even stranger than all the rest."

Jaena's breath came fast as fear rushed through her body. "I – I'm still not sure -- "

Mother Rhody bustled in, carrying a steaming, fragrant pot. "This will help, dear boy. It helped Tia, though she was never quite so violently ill."

Tia had never been so violently ill. Tia had learned from Mage

Herrein — helped Mage Herrein — and grown sicker, and frailer, until she could not survive.

Jaena's vision greyed out as she lunged to her feet. "I have to go out for a minute."

Wiel stretched out a hand to her. "Come back. Don't go yet, Jaena."

"I'll be back before you finish that tea," she promised, and hurried out of the room.

The door to the courtyard was a short way down the hall. Jaena stumbled to it, ignoring the greeting from a novice passing by. She went outside, closed the door behind her, and leaned back against the sun-warmed wall.

The sky spun. Her whole world was not what she thought it had been, and her part in it was far different from what she had thought.

Wiel had no reason to lie to her. He might be too sick at the moment to lie. Less than two weeks ago, she had left with Metten on her rounds, leaving Wiel brown and strong and flirting with novices in the sunny hallway.

Now she returned, the country under magical attack that could only be turned by Mage Herrein's strength and skill. And Wiel was ill. There was no doubt about it. He was very ill. Jaena had never seen Tia so sick, so suddenly after a visit to Mage Herrein. Circumstances were clearly different now.

She put her head back against the wall and closed her eyes. *Goddess, I hope I'm understanding this right. Help me know what I should do.*

A few minutes later the world stopped spinning. She took a deep breath and went back in.

Wiel had drunk some of the tea Mother Rhody had left. He sat back against the wall at the head of the bed, no longer clutching his stomach. There was a little more color in his face.

Rhody had opened the window a crack and taken the tub away. The room smelled better. Jaena stepped in and sat down on the low stool again.

"I still don't understand," she finally said.

He shrugged. "I don't either. But I've learned a little more. —

Though what I don't understand, Jaena, is how you could not have known all this."

"If I'm not mistaken, very few know. It's the Dark Twin, remember? All the *taylenor* have it, even Mage Herrein survived it, the stories say. What else should anyone suspect?"

"Well, Herrein is needing more strength right now than he has for a long time. I think it's pretty apparent now what kills the *taylenor*."

"Oh goddess, did Tia know?"

He shrugged. "I can't say. I understand it took a long time with her – years. She might have known just a gradual decline. Herrein wasn't defending the land against demons when Tia was alive."

"This is the wing for *taylenor* children. Not many people come here regularly – they wouldn't suspect. The mothers must know, Wiel. Even Mother Thara."

"They have to. I don't know why you didn't know."

She shook her head. "I came to the city when I was a child of six. My family died in the Winter Plague. They found me, the only one left alive in my family's house, and brought me here to be cared for. I lived here, in the regular wings, until I went to learn the priesthood.

"There was only one *taylenor* then, a boy named Marki. I met him in the courtyard one day. I remember my teachers were angry that I had intruded into this wing – we weren't supposed to be here. But I liked Marki, so I kept sneaking back in to see him. We would play games, tell stories, pull pranks on the mothers. They ended up tolerating me. I watched him grow sick from the Dark Twin, I thought, and then die – it took years, Wiel, years. I was grateful to the mothers for their care, especially when I learned that if he hadn't been here he would've died miserable and in poverty."

She paused, but Wiel said nothing.

"I went to be a priest, but I wanted to do anything I could to help find children like Marki. The thought of what would have happened if he'd never been discovered as a *taylenor* bothered me. I knew there could be others out there, and I wanted them to have the same love I thought Marki had here. Mother Thara asked me if I would become a

Seeker, and I agreed. Before that, I didn't know what a Seeker was – I had never heard of one."

"You did it all in memory of that boy," Wiel said.

"Yes. Ironic, isn't it?"

He shook his head.

"I'm so sorry I cannot express it," Jaena said. She heard her voice shake. *Poor Marki. Poor little Tia.* And poor Wiel, whom she had delivered to his fate.

Wiel shrugged. "There's no need. I can see you didn't know." He sighed and slid off the bed. He stood and stretched. "I'm feeling better now."

Jaena was pleased to see him looking stronger. But there was a greenish tinge about his face, and a wheezing sound when he breathed. Wiel was not going to get better from this, especially if he kept visiting Mage Herrein. Especially if Herrein must find the strength -- from somewhere -- to fight off demons and a stirring Eastern Mage.

She forced back the guilt at what she had done. "Wiel, I'd like to make what amends I can."

"Like what?"

"I'll take you back home."

He looked at her in disbelief. "You think Herrein will let me leave? I'm the only one now, and he's got a crisis on his hands. He needs me."

"I can get you out. Perhaps you shouldn't go back home, though – they'll look for you there. I can help you cross the border into Ullfasten. There's a border guard, a permanent camp just across the river. Herrein can't follow you there." At least, she hoped he couldn't.

He sighed. "I want to go."

"Good! I want to get you out of here." Jaena began to think of options. How would she get Wiel past the mothers? How would she avoid the guards they would call? Could Wiel even stand long enough to get to a carriage?

"But ... Tia was a hero. Mother Thara said so."

You're going to listen to Thara, after how she's betrayed you? Jaena stopped the thought before she voiced it. "Why was Tia a hero?"

"Even when she was dying, she went to spend time with the Mage Defender and help him."

"He was slowly killing her, Wiel."

"I know. It's awful. But Mother Thara says he's our last defense. He's the one who keeps us safe against magical attack. The demons, the Eastern Mage, defending us against the mages of Ull-fasten. Tia was the one who helped him keep us safe."

Wiel shook his head. Jaena thought that just now he seemed more mature than she was. She knew what he was going to say before he said it.

"If I go, Herrein won't be able to fight back against the demons. They'll overrun us. I don't want to be responsible for all those people dying. There's no way I can go."

"The city guard said all the demons were dead."

"What if they're not?" Wiel asked. "What about the Eastern Mage?"

"The Eastern Mage may not even exist. No one knows her name, and she hasn't been seen for half a millennium. Besides, it's not your responsibility," Jaena added, not believing it herself.

"It is. How many people do you think will die if those demons get here, to Iryor? What if the Eastern Mage wakens? How can I just stroll off and save myself?"

"All right. We must think of some other way, then."

Wiel sat back down on the bed. "Not now. I'm feeling kind of sick again. Please come back and see me later today, will you? You're the only one I can trust now."

Jaena's throat grew tight as she forced back tears. "I'll be here after your evening meal," she said. "I don't know what I can do, but I'm responsible for you being here. I'll think of something."

CHAPTER ELEVEN

S he said the same thing to Metten, an hour later, as they sat in the little square just outside the boarding house where Metten had a room.

"Maybe the goddess will help," she added.

He had given her his full attention as she talked about what was happening to Wiel. Now he frowned. "You're a priest, you know better than I do. But I don't think I've heard of the goddess intervening in the affairs of humans since the days of legend. And who knows if those stories are even true?"

Jaena remembered how she had felt the goddess' presence in the blanket of stillness that had wrapped her while she sang the souls of the departed in Uthen. That had felt very real to her. It was still a long way from Imn-ashu providing comfort to active intervention.

Another thought occurred to her, and she pulled away from Metten. "There's something I have to ask you. Did you know about all of this?"

"What? That Herrein was sucking the energy out of *taylenor* children? Of course not!"

"You're a nobleman's son. You went to college and learned how things work. You might know."

"Well, I don't!" Metten stood up and glared at her. His black curls fell into his eyes; he pushed them back impatiently. "You think they teach this as a class at Verasa? How would I know?"

She shook her head. He seemed sincere.

Metten looked down at her for a moment. He sighed and sat back down, pulling her close again. This time she allowed her head to fall onto his shoulder. He gave her a squeeze, part loving, part exasperated. She grinned into his shoulder because it was so like him.

"Jaena. I have never heard of this. It is not common knowledge. I swear it."

"All right."

"If I were Herrein, and doing such a thing, I wouldn't allow the information out to anyone I couldn't watch."

"The mothers must know," Jaena said. "The ones who work in the *taylenor* wing." She thought of Mother Thara, whom she had always respected, and felt even more betrayed. Thara had been her guide, arranging for her teachers, for her novitiate at the Temple. *How could she have used me like this?*

"I wonder if the Council knows? How old is Herrein, anyway, Jaena, more than two hundred? He had all this set up long before any of us were born. Gods, the bastard did all this to save his own life!"

"It would be easy to resolve, if that were all," Jaena said.

"Yes, we'd slay him and be done with it!" Metten leaned back into the back of the bench. He sighed. "It's not so easy, now."

"I always wondered why there are so few *taylenor*. In the histories, there were many. They say there are mages in Ull-fasten. But here, we have the "Dark Twin". Is that all Herrein? Could it be?"

"I wish I knew."

"I offered to get Wiel out of the city. I thought I should, since I brought him to this."

Metten was silent a moment. "What did he say?"

"What do you think he said? What would you say?" Jaena knew she was snapping at Metten, and that he didn't deserve it. But she was close to tears again, because of the fate that awaited Wiel, and the part she had played in that.

Metten drew her closer. "Calm now, sweet," he whispered. "No one blames you. You didn't know."

"The mothers knew. They groomed me, and sent me out to look for more sacrificial lambs. Why me, I wonder?" She shook her head, dismissing that thought. Now was not the time to nurse her own betrayal. Now was the time to decide how she could help Wiel.

* * *

Jaena left Metten after promising she would not take any action until she consulted with him. Then she went to fulfill her obligation to her superiors at the Temple. Betrayal churned through her mind, erasing her ability to think reasonably. She didn't know what to do, but she had to do something. She couldn't live with herself otherwise.

The deep notes of Mag singing prayers echoed through the greenery-filled halls as Jaena entered the Temple. Mag was known for his voice. He was an old man now, and had given up traveling his circuit, but his voice never changed. Jaena remembered hearing it when she'd first arrived here, an awed and intimidated girl of thirteen. She remembered wondering how she, with her imperfect singing voice, would ever be a priest when priests apparently sounded like *that*.

She still didn't quite know. Imn-ashu was music -- the music of song, the music of water, the music the stars made as they danced in the night sky. Even the music that hung suspended in silence. Every other priest here praised the goddess with magnificent voices. Jaena was the exception. But Imn-ashu had never rejected her efforts, or the more serene prayer Jaena managed on her flute.

Jaena was just grateful, that was all.

The Tasa waited for her in his garden. Water from the roof cistern dripped down the garden-wall, feeding the bright plants that grew there. This place belonged to Imn-ashu and held her peace. It was a refuge from everything outside.

Tasa Wimar spent much time meditating here. Jaena didn't understand yet what purpose that served. She was too young, Mag had told her, to understand the value of such a task. Wait until she saw more of the world, its joys and sorrows, he'd said. Then she'd understand why Tasa Wimar's task helped hold the world together.

"Welcome back," the Tasa said. His rich voice blended with the sounds of the running water and the songbird that flitted behind the stones. He wore the green-and-blue emblem of the Temple on a tunic no finer than the one Jaena wore.

Jaena looked at the Tasa's expression and her own peace fled. Had this man known about Mage Herrein and what he'd been doing to the *taylenor*?

The Tasa's eyes narrowed. "You're full of heavy news, Priest Jaena."

The words rushed out. "Demons attacked Uthen while we were there. Lord Uthen forbade me to continue on my rounds, so we returned. We fought them off again on the return trip until Mage Herrein destroyed them with -- "

His raised hand stopped her. "I know all this already. This isn't what you really want to tell me."

Jaena bit her lip. The words caught in her throat. *I'm afraid to.*

"I see." The Tasa sat down on a low stone wall. "It's a matter of trust, then."

She hesitated, embarrassed. This man was closer to the goddess than any other human in the world. Anything she could tell Imn-ashu, she could surely tell him.

But Herrein's betrayal, Mother Thara's betrayal were too recent. She was still shocked inside, wary.

"You're like a small animal starving in the winter, a wild thing that sees food offered from an open hand." The Tasa nodded. It was a short, decisive move. "You have Imn-ashu's trust, Priest, as well as mine. Go, then, and do what you have to. Think well. Pray. I'll be here at sunset, and also at dawn, awaiting you. Then we'll see if the words can pass your lips."

"I'm – I'm sorry."

"If I'm not mistaken, there's no need for you to be sorry." He nodded. "Go. As of yet, there's no reason for you to fear."

This was an unexpected reassurance. The Tasa trusted her. That was odd, since she barely knew him. She hummed a prayer of thanks under her breath to Imn-ashu, who surely was responsible for this reprieve, and bowed to the Tasa. "I'll try," she promised.

He turned away towards the sunbeam that streamed through the window, lighting the falling water to brilliance. For just a second, Jaena thought she heard some deep and solemn music, a prayer that lay beneath the ambient sounds of the little garden. A voice she couldn't hear struck a shiver from her. This was new, this was frightening at the same time as it was wonderful. She pulled her cloak closer against the chill, and fled.

* * *

Jaena did as she'd been told, singing prayers to the goddess in her tiny room, asking for help as she decided what to do. Then she headed back to the hospital, determined to learn more before it was too late.

She crossed the cobblestoned street and went to the side door she usually used. No sooner had the door swung closed behind her than a guardsman stopped her.

"Who are you?" he demanded.

As her eyes adjusted to the dim interior, she saw that the guard wore a scarlet hawk on his chest: Herrein's insignia. His large form blocked her view down the hall.

"I'm Jaena, a priest of Imn-ashu. I was here this morning."

The man's eyes narrowed. "I wasn't told about you. Wait here."

He took a few strides down the dim corridor to consult with another armed figure Jaena now saw standing near the front hall. After a few moments, he waved her in. There was no apology for the man having questioned her presence.

Jaena walked down the hallway, her heart beating fast.

There were two more guards at the doors to the *taylenor* wing. Once again she had to identify herself to them, and was not allowed in until Mother Rhody came and vouched for her. Then they waved her through, and Mother Rhody walked with her down the hall towards Wiel's room.

"What's happening?" Jaena whispered.

"They're taking the boy away," Rhody said.

"Where are they taking him?"

"I assume he'll go to Herrein's house. He's to be under guard, and only one of us will be permitted to go and care for him."

Too late, Jaena breathed to herself. She was too late to do anything to help Wiel. There was no way she could run off with him under the eyes of the Mage Defender's guards, and she knew she would not be permitted free access into Herrein's house to visit with him. Wiel would be a prisoner.

"Mother Thara is going?" she asked.

Rhody nodded. "I'll prepare and send over the herbal preparations he'll need. But Mother Thara is the only one permitted to stay with him."

"Did they say why?"

Rhody's plump face turned secretive. She shook her head.

The drapes were open in Wiel's room. Late afternoon sunlight shone from the open door into the hall. Mother Thara waited outside the room with a packed bag on the floor beside her. When she saw Jaena she gestured her in. "You may as well say goodbye to him," Thara said coolly.

Jaena shivered at the double meaning. Thara's skeletal face was expressionless; perhaps she had said that on purpose. For the first time earlier today, Jaena had doubted Mother Thara's benevolence. Now she was seeing actual ill will. There was no doubt that Mother Thara knew what Wiel went to, at Mage Herrein's house.

Wiel stood at the foot of his bed, arguing with the servants who were trying to help him to a stretcher. "I don't need the cursed thing!" he said. His color was high, and his hands were shaking. He knew where he was going and was afraid.

Then he saw Jaena at the door. "Jaena!" he said. "Tell these fools I don't need a chair or a stretcher. I'll get there under my own power."

He looked strong enough, to her untrained eye. She said to the servants, "Let him do it."

"I can't, Priest. I have orders."

Jaena put her head out the door. "Look," she said to Thara and the guard who waited there. "If you want to make things easy, let him walk. He can do it, and you'll get out of here quicker."

The guard nodded, and the stretcher was carried away.

"Thank you!" Wiel said. He shoved a spare shirt and the book he was learning to read into the bag he had brought from his village.

She sighed and held out her arms. He walked into them as if he were a small boy and not head-and-shoulders taller than she was. "I'm so sorry," she said. "I want you to know, I haven't given up on you."

He stepped back. "That's good to know," he said. "I'll remember it, Jaena. But you know I have to go. – Look, here's the Mage Defender's man, all ready for me."

Jaena stepped outside the room and waited near Mother Thara. "Why are they taking him away?"

"He'll be safe there," Thara said. "Things are different now, with the recent demon incursion. Herrein needs to make sure his – resources are protected."

Too angry to respond, Jaena turned her back on Thara and began to walk away.

"Where do you think you're going?" Thara's voice cracked down the hall.

Before Jaena could turn, a hand clamped down on her upper arm. Disbelieving, she stared at the guardsman that towered over her.

The big man had an apologetic look on his face. "Sorry, Priest. I got to take ya to the mage's house."

"I won't go!" Jaena yanked her arm away. "You have no right!" What could she do to help Wiel if she were imprisoned too?

"I said Herrein is making sure his resources are protected." Thara drifted closer. "That includes you."

"I am a priest of Imn-ashu. I belong to the Temple, not Herrein or the mothers."

Thara smiled. "You belong to us, Jaena. Tasa Wimar won't dare object. Didn't you ever wonder why you were the only one who could sense the *taylen*? You are all Herrein's."

The guardsman shuffled his feet. He was very young. "I'm sorry, Priest, but I have orders."

Jaena cast a look around. Most of the guards had departed with Wiel. But there was still a man at the side door, and one at the front entrance. She gave Thara a last, angry look and walked down the hall with the young guardsman at her side.

Her guard opened the outer door into the reddish light of late afternoon. He put a hand on her arm to keep her from running off. An enclosed carriage was pulled up close, its door hanging open. Next to it lay another guardsman, limp on the cobblestones.

By the time Jaena registered what must have happened, her own guard had shoved her into the carriage and reached across his body to draw his short sword.

She stumbled over the lowered step and half-fell onto the carriage floorboard. Her shins struck hard on the door's lower frame. Pain stabbed through her legs.

There was a sound of a heavy blow striking metal. Steel glittered in the sunlight. The guard stepped aside and swung a backstroke at the dark-haired figure that had sprung out from behind the carriage's open door.

Metten blocked the guard's arm on his forearm, so close the sword was useless. Jaena scrambled up into the carriage the rest of the way as Metten crowded into the guard. The young guard grunted and swept a booted foot at Metten's legs.

Metten danced back. "Damned fool, do you want to force me to hurt you?"

The guard's face was red with determination and effort. "Hai!" he yelled the alarm. "To me! I'm under attack!" He swept his weapon back for a full strike.

Jaena positioned herself in the carriage doorway and kicked with both legs. Her feet slammed into the back of the guardsman's knees. He crumpled and grabbed for the open door to support himself.

Metten brought the wrapped hilt of his own sword down on the back of the guard's head. There was a dull thud as the man fell onto the cobblestones next to his colleague.

"Hurry!" Metten rasped. He sheathed his sword and began hauling both of the fallen men to relative safety at the side of the road.

Jaena looked around and noticed that the rest of the area was empty; the market-sellers had disappeared behind their stalls, and there were no shoppers or casual passers-by anywhere around. She hurried to the front of the carriage and eased the frightened horses away from the hospital's side doors. The animals shied and snorted, not trained to be steady around violence.

Metten leaped up onto the driver's box. "Are you crazy? Get out of sight. You're wanted, and they'll be searching for you. We have to get out of the city as soon as possible."

She nodded and jumped back into the carriage. She pulled the door closed behind her. Metten urged the horses away with a slap of the reins. The horses were spooked and eager to be away; the carriage lurched as they started forward.

Jaena sat far back on the worn leather seat, sliding as Metten took the street corners a little too briskly. She made sure to position herself where she would not be easily visible to people outside. The sun sank low over the rooftops to the west; the sunlight was giving way to long black shadows, and the early autumn dusk was not far off. The tang of wood smoke tickled her nose and fought against the musty smell of the carriage's worn interior.

After a few minutes, the pace of the carriage slowed. Undoubtedly Metten thought he was far enough away from the immediate pursuit and didn't want to draw further attention by racing through the narrow streets as if a demon were after him.

The sound of the horses' hooves changed: no longer echoing on stone, now they were muffled as if the horses had entered a grassy or unpaved area. Jaena looked out the window to see only the wooden walls of an enclosed stable yard. There were iron rings on scarred posts near the wall, and an old nag tethered to one of the posts.

The carriage stopped, then bounced as Metten must have jumped off the box.

"Lord Metten, what're ya doing here?" cried a man's voice, cracked as if by age or illness.

"Hush," Metten said. "Look, I need a favor, Sim."

"My favor is I won't tell Lord De Rell. Get out, boy, before the others hear ya!"

"I need the old day carriage. Hurry, Sim. I'll leave it at the first changehouse, you can get it back tomorrow."

"What trouble are ya in, Lord Metten?"

"Just hurry, will you, Sim?" Jaena heard footsteps and the nicker of a horse from the stable that must be at the end of this yard. Wheels rumbled over wood, then stopped.

The door to Jaena's carriage opened, and Metten peered in.

"Come on. We're changing carriages. They won't let a guard carriage pass the gates unchecked."

An old man was muttering to himself as he harnessed the horses to the smaller day carriage. He glanced at Jaena, then glared at Metten.

Metten held up a hand. "I don't have time, Sim. You'll have to hold your tongue until next time I see you, then you can berate me to your heart's content."

"Thank you for helping," Jaena said to the old man. She climbed into the day carriage and waited, watching the shadows lengthen into dusk. Maybe the gate guards wouldn't stop them. Maybe they had been warned to look for a guard conveyance, and would pay no undue attention to a wealthy family's old carriage, driven by a young nobleman. She had no idea why Herrein thought she was one of his resources, to be protected like Wiel, but she feared once she was guarded in Herrein's place of strength she and Wiel would never get away.

This was only a temporary setback. She intended to race for help as fast as she could, even if that meant braving the closed border to Ullfasten. She hoped Wiel could hold on that long.

Goddess, help us.

Lamps were being lit in the squares of the city as they eventually approached the West Gate. Torches were set in the big sconces at the guard stations. The merchants who set up inside the gate had packed up and gone home. Foot traffic was light, except for a group of loud young men Jaena assumed might be out for an evening of drinking.

"Halt!"

Jaena caught her breath. She'd foolishly hoped they would just drive through. She sank back on the cushioned seat, hoping her face was lost in shadow. The evening chill came in through the window and touched her face.

"Lord Metten de Rell," Metten said. His voice sounded strange to Jaena, sharp and arrogant. "What do you want?"

A slight pause, then: "My lord. We've been ordered to watch for a fugitive."

"What does that have to do with me?"

"Mage Herrein requires us to make sure she's not leaving the city."

"Well. I wish you good luck with that, then." The slap of reins carried back to Jaena's ears. Harness jingled. The day carriage lurched forward, then stopped again.

"My lord, she is a young woman with -- "

"Do I look like a young woman? I have people waiting for me – I can't be delayed any more." Another slap of the reins. "Good night, Captain."

The carriage moved forward. Jaena lay down on the carriage seat, fast, and pulled her cloak over her face. If the guard should try for a fleeting torchlit glimpse inside as the carriage passed the gate, she might look like nothing more than a pile of blankets.

She remained flat on the seat for a while as Metten drove on, mercifully without being called to a halt by more guardsmen. After a while she sat up and looked outside as the buildings outside the West Gate began to thin and scatter. The first changehouse was not far away; she had passed it often on her travels with Priest Leir when she was mentoring Jaena on the way to her own priesthood. Metten could arrange for the return of the day carriage there and get two fresh horses for the journey.

Leir was restricted to the Temple now, one of the priests who kept the eternal music going in Imn-ashu's shrine. A door seemed to be closing on all Jaena's past life. Mother Thara had proven her enemy, and all the other mothers complicit in her deceit. Herrein, whom Jaena had honored, was a ghoul who stole the energy from others to preserve his own life. Even her travel companion Ears was gone, thank the goddess safe in the Temple stables, but lost to Jaena nonetheless.

Only Metten remained with her, dear to her heart and willing to brazen his way past armed guards to rescue her. Thank the goddess for Metten. He was the only bit of comfort she would have as she set out to find a way to rescue Wiel.

CHAPTER TWELVE

Halpen de Morn had not spared himself, or his horses or servants, since they'd galloped out of Iryor. Now his Elarian gelding stumbled over nothing, head sagging. The gelding's flank was lathered, and the post house was still an hour away. Halpen slapped at the animal's shoulder. "Go on, then, keep moving! When I think what I paid for you – "

Halpen's manservant rode up to his side. Rall's face was sweaty and caked with the dust that had been flung up from Halpen's mount's hooves as they fled.

"Lord Halpen, you must slow down. You're killing the horses."

Halpen turned on the man. "I paid twenty silvers for this nag, and even you are mounted better than a servant has a right to be! The horses will have to hold up until we make the post house."

"My lord." Rall sighed. "They're flesh and blood, no matter how well-bred. What's the hurry, my lord? Is someone after us?"

"None of your business!" Halpen snarled.

Rall stepped back, expressionless. "Please slow down. If you stop and water the horses, then walk a ways, we can make it to a change of horses at Bishett."

There was nothing he could do about it. Better to walk, even with hurry biting at his heels, than be stranded with a dead horse on the southern road. "All right then!" Halpen waved the man away.

It took longer to get to Bishett than Halpen had hoped. The horses, overheated and exhausted, were allowed only a small amount of water at a time. Then they walked, then they watered again. Eventually, the gelding's head came up and he showed some sign of the spirit Halpen had paid twenty silvers for, but anything more than a walk was still out of the question.

Rall took over when they arrived at Bishett. At Halpen's insistence, he paid one of the stable hands to watch for signs of pursuit. He ordered ale and meats for Halpen, as well as an apple tart the innkeeper's wife had made that morning. Halpern visited the pisser, then went in to drink in comfort while he awaited new horses.

In less than an hour, Rall and the innkeeper presented themselves in front of his table. Halpen chewed his meat and glowered at them. He knew what it meant when people looked like that. There was a delay.

"What!" he demanded.

"My lord, there are not enough horses here for all of us," Rall said calmly.

The innkeeper bowed. "My lord, there was a group through this morning needing remounts. I have a fine horse for yourself, and I can borrow one from a friend's farm for your man here. But as for your escort – " He shook his head. "We must wait for your own mounts to be recovered until they can follow you to the next stage."

Halpen stared at them with narrowed eyes. Full of meat and ale now, he was able to handle this latest problem with grace. His parents would be proud. "Send them on at your first opportunity," he ordered. "Rall! You must carry my pack as well as your own."

"Yes, my lord." Rall went to inform the three men who comprised Halpen's personal guard that they would be staying the night here. Halpen watched as the men shed their mail in the front hall, then settled in and called for more ale. They did not look unhappy to be spared their duty. He wished these men served him out of loyalty instead of just the desire for pay. Apparently they didn't care if demons caught up with him and chewed his face off, or if Mage Herrein's men succeeded in catching him before he reached the southern border.

The horse the innkeeper had promised Halpen was beautiful, a strong mare, black as a moonless night. Rall's remount would do the distance, he promised Halpen, but not fast. So Halpen needed to slow down if he was not to arrive at Ull-fasten alone and with no baggage. They proceeded as fast as Rall's farm horse could, but Halpen's temper stayed at a slow boil. If Herrein's men were to crest that rise just behind them, Halpen would never make it out of the country alive. The mage would be searching for *taylen* – strong or weak, it would not matter, as long as the old man could feed off it to fight the demons.

Just as he thought that, there was a glitter on the hill behind them. Sunlight had struck something metal. Perhaps it was a bit of a horses' bridle, or a stirrup, or a weapon. Halpen stood in his stirrups and stared behind them, but the glaring sunlight made it hard to see.

Rall said, "There are two of them, my lord. Mounted. I see metal, perhaps a sword?"

"Not guardsmen, then, if there are only two," Halpen murmured, then started as Rall turned confused eyes to him. "What are you looking at? Find a place for us to wait until they pass, man."

Rall found a shed that was probably some sheep-herder's shelter. It didn't matter that the place looked about to fall down, Halpen told himself. He planned to do little more than wait there while the unknown travelers passed, since Rall's horse could not outdistance them.

Rall took their horses around back. Halpen wandered into the rundown shelter. Rall was probably wondering why his noble master seemed to be on the run from authority, but the man had not said a word to question him. That was as it should be.

Halpen wandered around the little room. There was a pot sitting in the ashes on the hearth, blackened up the side with fire. A small gray table sat in the middle of the room, and there was just enough room between the table and the fireplace for a sheepherder to wrap himself in a cloak and sleep in warmth. Halpen pulled his own fur-lined cloak close about him. It was getting damned cold.

"Hey! Who's there?" came a voice from the road. It seemed the travelers had seen some sign of life at the shed. Halpen raised his eyebrows unbelievingly, then poked his head outside. He knew that voice.

"Metten de Rell, is that you?" he said. Then he saw who rode the second horse, and words died in his throat.

"It's me and Jaena," Metten said, sliding down from his mount. "I can't believe it's you, Hal, without a whole train of servants easing your way. – Oh, I see you have Rall. Hello, Rall."

"Lord Metten." Rall bent his head.

"What in the goddess' name are you doing here?" Metten asked, looking around at the tumbledown shack, the two horses tethered behind it. "Were you hiding from us?"

Halpen flushed. "Of course not. Not from you."

The Seeker had not moved from horseback, nor had she spoken. Her clear gray eyes were altogether too penetrating. Halpen didn't like it.

"I am going to Ull-fasten," Halpen said. "As speedily as I can."

The Seeker looked scornful.

"Huh," Metten said. "Just took it into your head, then?" He smiled at Rall. Halpen had always envied Metten his smile. Then Metten said, "There was quite a group of guardsmen back at the last change house. Yours?"

"I had three," Halpen said. "There weren't enough horses, and I couldn't wait for them."

"You must be in a hurry indeed. That is unlike you," Metten said. "You'd best mount up friend, because there were quite a few more than three guardsmen drinking at that change house. I'm sure many of them will continue on their way as soon as they hit the pisser – the facilities, pardon me Jaena -- and water their horses."

"Gods above, let's move!" Halpen cried to Rall. "I must make it to Ull-fasten without hindrance."

Jaena and Metten spurred their horses on. Halpen and Rall followed, and then they were an unlikely group of four, running from Herrein's guardsmen.

The Seeker had not spoken to him. She did not seem to be a seasoned rider – easy to understand, since she was of low birth. She paid close attention to her mare, and Metten kept a close eye on her as well. But they made some speed. Halpen became aware that his friend and the Seeker were in a hurry as well.

"Who are you running from?" he asked, bringing his horse up beside Metten's.

"Later for that," Metten said. "How far is it to Ull-fasten?"

"Never been there. According to the maps, we have an overnight yet. It's still hours away."

"If I may, my lords," Rall said. "Ull-fasten is about three days from Iryor at its closest point, where the river bends inward toward us. We must find a place to spend another night and not be discovered."

"Good thing your man paid attention while we were at Verasa," Metten told Halpen.

Rall grinned.

"There ought to be a town soon," Halpen said. "Did you not say so, Rall?"

"Yes, my lord. A little town named Goddess-eyes. But won't the men following us ask for us there?"

"I would," Metten said. "How badly do they want you, Halpen? And what in the world for?"

The Seeker had not told Metten, then. He'd thought she would spill his secret as soon as she could.

"Let's continue on to this Goddess-eyes place. Surely there will be a tavern or someplace we can just wait until they pass, then stay overnight there."

"Must we?" The Seeker demanded. "I don't want to spare the time, Metten. You know we must hurry!"

"The horses won't do it, dear. We go as fast as we can." Metten squeezed her hand gently, and the Seeker turned away.

Halpen spurred the black mare. "Let's get moving, then, before they're upon us!"

They made good progress. There was no more wearing out the horses, as much as Halpen wanted to set spurs to his mare's sides and get as far away from Herrein's men as possible. There was safety in staying with Metten and his Seeker chit, he thought. Metten had always had a pretty good mind; perhaps he could figure out how to avoid the border garrison at the Rivasha bridge.

The countryside changed as they proceeded south. There was more tree cover near the road, and green-and-gold foliage on the rising hills. Homesteads sat at the end of occasional dirt tracks, surrounded by browning autumn fields. A caravan snaked down the dusty road from the south, dropping from the hills.

"Hsss!" Halpen waved at Metten. "Are we going to go right past that caravan?"

Metten looked from side to side. A straggly copse stood in the mid-distance, and a farmhouse with the day's laundry fluttering on a line nearby.

"Where would we go?" Jaena asked.

"You know the guardsmen behind us will stop them and ask about us. And the traders will spill everything they know!"

Metten shrugged. "There's nowhere to go, Halpen. I say we just brazen it out and hope for the best."

"You would say that." Halpen fumed as the first wagon of the caravan drew closer.

The Seeker frowned as the caravan grew closer. She looked as if she were thinking hard. Halpen was about to ask if she had some idea, but the first wagon of the caravan drew abreast of them before he could say anything.

They nodded, back and forth as they passed. The wagons creaked and rumbled. Halpen covered his nose with one sleeve at the strong smell of horse and sweat. The drivers, men and women both, wore damp cloths over their noses and mouths to filter out dust, but Halpen had no such protection. He kept his sleeve over his mouth, drawing stifled breaths until the van had vanished to the rear. Then he blinked dust from his eyes and swore.

Rall trotted forward and offered him his flask. "This is water, my lord. It may help."

Halpen upended the flask over his face and let the sun-warmed water drip across his eyes. "Let's go! They'll be on our trail faster than before once they question the caravan."

They had to slow as they climbed the hills. For one thing Metten insisted on pampering their nags, stopping to rest far more often than was necessary. At one point he handed his horse over to Jaena, and he and Rall climbed a slope to look behind them for pursuit.

The Seeker waited until they are alone, then said, "I have not shared your secret."

"Yes, thank you," Halpen said. "It wasn't yours to share."

She grimaced. "You're welcome."

"If you can, spur Metten along a little," Halpen said. "I must get to Ull-fasten, or I may be feeding Mage Herrein's magery by tomorrow."

"I thought your *taylen* was a remnant, too weak to be of any use?"

Halpen gritted his teeth. Apparently he must tell the truth; she already suspected. "My parents paid heavily for Mage Herrein to suppress my *taylen*, so I wouldn't be taken by a Seeker like yourself. They wanted me free to live my life, maybe end up on Council as they are, not choking my life away in that hospital. Herrein was agreeable. He wanted the money, and had no need for more *taylenor* children."

"That's changed now."

"Yes, it has, curse you, and what Herrein put the lid on I am sure he can uncover again. It's still there, as you saw for yourself. I think the Lord Mage is desperate for any *taylenor* right now, and their social status matters not at all."

Above them, Metten and Rall slid down the grassy slope from the hilltop. They vanished into the skirt of autumn-red trees and bushes at the foot of the hill.

"So desperate that they've taken the *taylenor* boy I brought in and put him under armed guard at Herrein's house. He's in great danger."

"See?" Halpen cried. "All bets are off!"

The Seeker cast him a disgusted look.

There was a rustle from the undergrowth, Metten and Rall emerged from the woods, filthy from their climb. Burrs from the autumn bushes dotted their clothing.

"Enough of this," Metten said with no humor in his voice at all.

"Up this next hillside, fast and as quiet as you can, and into those trees. They are close behind us. We have no time to get to Goddess-eyes, especially with tired horses."

Halpen needed no further urging. He slid down from the saddle and led his mare up the hillside and into the cover of a stand of dark old trees. The way up was treacherous, with ridges of knobby roots protruding aboveground. The mare's hooves slid on the slope, but he pulled her on. Behind them, Metten urged his own mount on softly. They were still making noise, too much noise, as the saddles creaked and Rall's nag groaned with the effort.

Green and gold and red closed around them as if they were in an autumn-colored tent.

"Stop there," Metten whispered. "Quiet now."

Halpen stood by his horse's head. Next to him, Rall took the rein. The others stood awkwardly, close to him, stopping where they had been forced to. He was shoulder to shoulder with the cursed Seeker, but dared not move away.

Halpen first heard the jingle of bits, then a voice. He froze. His high-strung mare made a low rumbling noise in her throat; Rall stroked the horse's nose, trying to comfort her into silence.

There was a questioning call from below, "Who's there?" And the sound of horsemen pulling their horses up on the road.

Damn it damn it damn it, Halpen thought. *Stupid horse.*

He knew Mage Herrein was desperate for strength now, strength to defend against the demons sent by the Eastern Mage. If Halpen allowed himself to be taken back to the city, he would be dead within a week, used up by the cursed Mage Defender who should have died more than a century ago. And his parents wouldn't be able to help him, Council members or no.

There was a crooning sound beside him, low, but certainly enough to give them away. Halpen jerked his head around, staring at the Seeker. The woman had chosen this, of all times, to sing? It was a low hum, possibly one of the goddess' songs, and off-key.

He gestured wildly at Metten. Perhaps Metten could get the Seeker to shut up. His friend didn't seem at all perturbed by the inopportune humming, though. Instead, he smiled slightly as he watched what was going on down on the road.

Halpen thought his heart would burst out of his chest. Then he felt a muffled sort of presence, like someone had pulled a curtain around them on the hillside. He waved his arm at it and touched nothing, but he knew it was there. It muffled sound from the road, and even the Seeker's raspy humming was silenced, though he could see that she was still doing it. In a moment Halpen could no longer hear his mare's tired wheezing either. He rubbed at his ears, wondering if he had been struck deaf.

Metten crouched on the ground, looking through the trees and down to the road. It seemed forever, but eventually he raised a hand, and the Seeker's face lost that look of concentration. The weird stuffing fell from Halpen's ears.

"They've gone ahead," Metten said, getting stiffly to his feet. "You saved us there, Jaena."

"What do you mean, saved us?" Halpen sputtered. "She nearly gave us away with that cursed humming. I knew you hated me, woman, but to try to deliver me into the hands of Herrein's men ..."

The Seeker ignored him. She sagged down onto the muddy ground, her head drooping. Her hands shook. What had she done but stand there and endanger them all?

"Thank the goddess, not me," she said.

Rall handed his reins back. Halpen took them, frowning at the man. "What happened here?" he said. "Why are you all so grateful to the chit?"

Metten was in his face, the good-humored smile gone, a glittering look in his dark eyes. "*Not* a chit," he said. "Remember that. And she just saved your ass, whether you deserved it or not."

Halpen stepped back away from the unexpected steel in his easy-going friend's face. "I don't understand."

"Clearly not," Metten said. "Rall, do you have any kind of flask still about you? She needs it."

Rall went into his pack – Halpen's own pack! – and took out the silver-chased flask. In it was some of his father's store of *aum*. He unstopped it and gave it to Metten, who offered it to the Seeker.

"Hey!" Halpen protested, but no one listened.

"The Priest concealed us when she sang, my lord," Rall said. "Didn't you feel the shield she put around us?"

"Is that what it was?" Halpen said. "I've never heard of such a thing! Are you sure it was that damned singing that did it?"

"Many things out of legend have been happening lately," Metten said. "This is one. Jaena's goddess just shielded us from being captured, Hal. Now, let's make her gift useful, and proceed on to Goddess-eyes as fast as we can."

Things began to fall into place in Halpen's mind. "Wait!" he cried. "You think that was *Imn-ashu*? But don't you see -- "

The others were already half down the slope, winding in and among the tree trunks. Halpen stopped talking. He stared after the others and yanked on his gelding's rein to follow. They were deluded, all three of them, maybe the Seeker most of all. Unless she knew – surely she knew, and merely tried to fool Metten because of his family and influence? Either way, he could make use of their blindness before the end of this mess.

CHAPTER THIRTEEN

The town of Goddess-eyes was no help to them. Rall went on a scouting trip and found that Herrein's men were quartered there and had set a sentry. They slipped past the town cross-country and spent the night in the open, huddled under thin blankets while the horses rested and grazed. They did not dare light a fire, in spite of Lord Halpen's demands, so they shivered until there was enough light for them to proceed.

Jaena rode behind Metten, hungry and sore from the previous day's ride. All night she'd thought of Wiel. It was bitter to remember that Wiel was in danger while Lord Halpen whined his way to freedom.

We have to hurry. Surely they'll help us in Ull-fasten.

Rall was proving himself invaluable. He scouted as they rode, coming back with information on where Herrein's men were and how many of them were in the group. It seemed they had gained a little on the guardsmen by leaving their cold bivouac before the sun was up. Because of this, they pushed themselves and their horses in a steady pace that nonetheless wore all of them out.

Then they rode down a long hillside that sloped down to the river and into the border town of Rivasha.

Rall came galloping back to them from a curve in the road. "Off the road!" he shouted. "Guardsmen ahead, many of them."

"And behind," Metten said. "Here, into the town."

They hastened between two outbuildings and through someone's unfenced lumberyard. Stables and cheap inns clustered in this area, on the outskirts of the town. They came out into a dusty side yard, facing toward the street. Jaena kept looking over her shoulder toward the main road, sure that Herrein's men would see them at any moment.

"Here!" A girl stood in the road in front of one of the stable yards. "Feed and water, ten for all four horses!"

"Not now!" snapped Halpen, trying to push past.

"You won't get a better deal!"

"Wait," Metten said. "Everyone, hold up." He pulled his mount around and leaned over the saddle, elbow on thigh, and smiled at the girl. "You know your way around this town pretty well?"

Metten's smile had its usual effect, even on this belligerent little girl. She stopped glaring at Halpen and looked confused. "I live here, don' I?"

"Yes, you do. Want to earn ten pennies for yourself?"

Hands went onto skinny hips. The girl cocked her head. "Wouldn't say no. Gotta tell Mistress if you want me to show you somewheres."

"Tell her, then, and hurry." Metten swung around to stare at Halpen. "Got ten pennies?"

"You don't?" Halpen stared at his friend.

"I'm at the end of the quarter," Metten said.

Halpen snorted. "Yes, I have it. Rall, I do, don't I?"

Jaena's mouth dropped open as the manservant searched in his leather purse for a moment. "Yes, my lord, we are in funds."

"Good to go, then!" Metten said cheerfully, grinning at Jaena as the girl returned. "Now, girl, what's your name?"

"I'm Lotte, and I'm a groom," she said. "Give me your pennies, and we'll go."

"Suspicious, aren't you?" Metten said. "Well then Rall, pay the girl."

After the transaction was completed, Metten said, "We need a way across the river."

Lotte shook her dirty-blonde curls. "A way that stays away from the Mage's men?"

"You've got it," Metten said.

She thought a moment. "Horses can't get across."

Lord Halpen sighed. "I should have known it could get even worse. Soon I'll be reduced to being dragged on a sled in the mud."

They all dismounted. Rall shouldered his pack and Lord Halpen's larger one.

Lotte took the horses into the stable yard and yelled for another groom. "Gray'll take good care of 'em."

"And they will still be here when we return?" Rall asked.

"Yes, if ya *do* return. We keep 'em three weeks, and if you don' claim 'em we sell 'em for charges. Fairer deal ya won't find, I say."

"Then I suppose we say so, too," Rall said. "If you are agreeable, my lords."

"We can send someone back for them," Metten said.

Halpen snorted.

"What? I'm no longer a rich man." Metten turned to Lotte. "We'll send someone back, with a note."

Jaena said, "Shouldn't we be on our way?" If she were captured and returned to Iryor, there would be no way to help Weil escape his fate. She shivered as she remembered how sick Wiel had been, back in the *taylenor* wing of the hospital. They must hurry.

"Yes, yes," Halpen said. "Herrein's men ahead of us and behind."

"Follow me." The girl took off at a trot through the dusty side street.

Rivasha was situated on the lower slopes of the hill they had ridden down, its feet in the river. The town lay below the cliffs that made the eastern half of Cassahn's southern border impassable. There was a garrison maintained here at all times, guarding against incursions from Ull-fasten. Further west began the Wall that had been built by Herrein and his predecessor. If they could not make it across the border here, then Jaena's cause would be lost, and Weil would surely die.

This area was full of stables, storage sheds, and cheap inns that Jaena assumed housed travelers and traders. A smithy belched its burnt-iron smell into the air. Uphill, banners floated from the eaves of more fashionable establishments, and people walked or shopped in the streets. Lotte led them away from areas where people were out and about until they walked into a wooded area cut through with little channels spitting water down at the river.

"My feet hurt," complained Lord Halpen.

"Where are you taking us?" Jaena asked Lotte.

"You said you wanted to cross, away from the Mage's men? They're mustered down by the port, fifty of 'em. I'm taking you to where the cliffs end, where they think nobody can cross. Never seen a guard there."

"Yes, but can we cross?" Metten murmured. There was dirt on his breeches and smeared across one cheek. He looked better than ever. Jaena sighed at herself and directed her attention back to the tiny trail they followed.

"This," Lotte said proudly, "is a deer trail. See? You can hardly see it."

"I noticed," Lord Halpen said.

The path crossed an awkward slope, steep enough so that sometimes Jaena walked with one foot higher than the other, or sidled through shoulder-high brush. Twigs snagged at her cloak. The woods closed in, autumn-dry and silent except for their passing.

"Yes, well, I do see why the guardsmen feel they can't cross this way," Metten said after a few minutes. "But can we? We aren't trailbreakers, Lotte."

"As if I can't see that! You're rich men, and he's yer servant, and she's a priest." Lotte gestured with a dirt-smeared hand at Jaena's badge, green-and-blue on her cloak. "It's why I trusted you. I knew you wouldn't rape me or kidnap me with *her* around."

"Lovely," Halpen said.

Metten sighed and stopped to wipe his forehead, which only left another smear of dirt across it. Lord Halpen leaned against Rall's shoulder, panting. Rall looked unperturbed, but there were three red welts across his cheek where he'd been bitten by something.

Jaena shuddered. She had forgotten about spiders. The sooner they were out of here, the better.

"Look!" Lotte waved downhill. "Gray an' me hauled it up here."

Jaena peered through the underbrush. The woods and streams ended abruptly in front of a steep rock face, the first of the Cliffs of Cassahn. There was a little cut in the earth under the cliff, made by a stream of water that had been diverted by a fallen tree. It had left behind a ditch that would easily double as a trail down to the water. At the foot of the trail lay a little rocky spit where the river curved away. There, pulled to the side in a muddle of tree roots, lay a small low-sided boat, oars resting in the bottom.

"Huh," Jaena said. "What's on the other side?"

"The current will take you down a little ways, but there's another good place to pull the boat in, with a big old tree leanin' over the river. There's no wall on t'other side. You'll see it."

"I hope so, or we're back in the hands of Herrein's men," Metten said.

"There might be a guard on the Ull-fasten side, but he's a friendly sort," Lotte said.

"What do you mean? You've met the man?" Rall asked, using a cloth from their packs to help his lord wipe the mud from his hands.

"We cross here sometimes, Gray and me. Just for fun, ya see? The Ull-fasten guard just laughs and sends us back. He's got a whole army up behind him – I've heard them. But he's never kept us there, not once."

Jaena looked downstream. The current was not as swift as it would be in the spring. The river came down fast from the eastern mountains, but lost some of its energy as it spread over the flatter land near Rivasha. This stretch of river was just out of sight of the docks. On the other side of the clutter of the garrison town rose the beginnings of the gray Wall that Cassahn had built two hundred years ago to keep the two lands apart.

This little section was hidden from the garrison and the guarded path that traced the ridgeline.

"Wonderful," Lord Halpen grumbled. "I feel like a boy again, catching frogs in the mud by the creek."

"Don't tell me you ever did that, or I won't believe you." Metten grinned at his friend.

"Enough," Jaena said. "Can we go? Remember, Wiel is suffering while we make our way out of here."

"Yes. We'll get help from the mages of Ull-fasten, and get Wiel out of there directly," Metten said. "Let's go."

"Good luck," Lotte said.

"Hey!" Halpen said. "Where are you going?"

"Home. I showed you the way, din't I?"

"She did what she said, my lord," Rall said. "We can see the path and the boat."

"Damn it," Halpen said. "Go, then."

Lotte stuck her tongue out at Lord Halpen before vanishing back along the trail.

They half-climbed, half-slid down the cut. When Jaena reached the bottom, Rall was pulling the boat out from the nest of tree roots where it had been cradled.

"Will we all fit in there?" Jaena asked.

"Certainly, Priest," Rall said. "It looks perfectly safe."

Metten and Rall stood on the riverbank for a moment, identifying the big tree that leaned over the river where they would land. Jaena looked further down. The beginnings of the port sat a little downstream. Tumbled rocks from some long-ago inundation lay dumped in the streambed, wet and shining in the sun. There was no sign of any guards.

"Good to go," Metten said. Jaena noticed he was holding his right hand close to his chest. She remembered that it hadn't been many days since he was burned by his fight with the demon, and that his wrist was still wrapped.

"Are you all right?" she asked.

"I'm fine," he said, but his lips were pulled into a thin line of pain. "Just scraped it a little on the climb. I'll have it seen to in Ull-fasten."

They climbed into the boat, Lord Halpen with a good deal of complaint. Jaena wished she could tip him over the edge into the white-water and be spared his contempt and his whining. But even he did not deserve to be taken by Mage Herrein and used up against his will. And besides, he was Metten's friend. Which fact she could not account for.

The bottom of the boat scraped against the rocks as Metten and Rall shoved it into the water. Metten leaped in, making the boat dip alarmingly. Then Rall rolled over the gunwale, wet to the thighs. Lord Halpen drew his cloak closer about him and was, unexpectedly, silent.

Rall braced his paddle against the rocks, shoving the boat away from shore. The little boat slotted into the current. They drifted downstream, Rall and Metten doing their best to guide the craft with the paddles.

It was beautiful here. The trees beside the water cast dark shadow patterns that broke up the frothy, sunlit gold of the water's surface. Jaena dipped a hand into the water. Some creature croaked from the bank, and Halpen gave a little shriek.

"Quiet, Hal," whispered Metten. "We're not too far from the port. Sound carries over water."

They moved out into the center of the water. The river curved to the southwest. A dock leading up to a short gray shed sat at the river's curve; Jaena thought that was the beginning of Rivasha, and hoped they could get across to Ull-fasten before they were seen. The town was the only gap in the mage-built fortifications that sealed off Cassahn's border until the Cliffs began to form their natural barrier. The town had an ancient bridge that was zealously patrolled even under normal conditions. Herrein wanted no contact between Ull-fasten and the country where he held sway.

Jaena had never understood the perpetual stand-off between Cassahn and Ull-fasten. With everything she had learned in the last few days about Herrein, it was beginning to make a kind of muddled sense.

The current swung to the south, almost depositing them below the leaning tree Lotte had pointed out to them. Rall rowed nearer while

Metten grasped an overhanging branch and pulled them in toward the rocks.

Then he and Rall stepped into the water and hauled the boat up, Halpen and Jaena still in it. Metten was still sloshing around with water in his boots, trying to drag the boat ashore, when there was a shout from above.

"Halt! Who are you?" Two men jumped down from the embankment and unsheathed their swords. Another guardsman stood above, arrow nocked to the bow. They wore close-fitting leather helmets and gray-brown coats that allowed them to blend into the rocks and tree trunks. One of the swordsmen had a tattoo on his cheekbone, sweeping black lines like a bird's wings. They all had skin as brown as chestnuts.

Lord Halpen brushed himself off and glared at them. "Put those away," Halpen ordered. "Do we look like we came prepared to attack?"

The guard with the tattoo smirked. "I'm not sure what you look like, other than cold and wet. Who are you?"

"Lord Metten de Rell," Halpen said grandly, pointing to Metten, whose cloak was soaked with river water and sticking to his thighs. "I am Lord Halpen de Morn. Jaena is a priest of the goddess. And my man, Rall."

"Very impressive," said the guardsman, sheathing his sword. "Why don't you come up the bank to us, before you slide down. Uh, Lord Halpen, right? Do you need a hand?"

Halpen accepted the man's arm. They clambered up the hill. Jaena's feet did indeed slide out from under her on two occasions, and only Metten's strong arm saved her from an undignified slip into the river. The last time she grabbed for his arm, he made a stifled sound, and she realized she was holding onto his injured wrist.

"Oh, sorry, sorry!" she said.

"It's all right," Metten said, but his teeth were clenched in pain. He stood and nodded to the guardsmen and the waiting bowman, who still kept his bow ready. "Thank you. We need to see your commander, as soon as possible."

"That you will, and soon."

In another moment they were the center of a group of suspicious armed men who searched them for weapons and took away even their personal knives. The tattooed man seemed to be in charge; he gave directions in a clipped voice and was instantly obeyed.

In the end, five armed men escorted them up the steep cut above the river to level ground. Jaena's feet slipped around in her soggy shoes. Lord Halpen was driest of all of them, but even he looked worn and dirty from their long ride and dusty hike.

As they walked away from the river toward the encampment nearby, Jaena stopped in shock. A wave washed over her, magnified and powerful. There were *taylenor* here – many of them.

Jaena whispered to Metten: "There are many *taylenor* here."

"No talking!" The tattooed guardsman snapped. The escort began marching them across the brown-grass field to a collection of tents large enough, at least to Jaena's eyes, for an invading army.

This must be more than a defensive outpost. Behind the basic wooden structures of what might have been a permanent garrison was what looked like a transient encampment. She saw many people and their mounts, and sensed the immense *taylen* of at least five mages, as well as smaller clusters of *taylen* everywhere. Dusk was near, and cook-fires sprang up in tent-encircled clearings. A savory aroma wafted through the crisp air. Jaena's stomach growled. She turned once and looked behind them and saw the cut in the earth where the river was, and sentries stationed there to watch for incursions from Cassahn.

Their guards stopped before a large tent. A middle-aged man in a leather surcoat over an embroidered tunic appeared at the tent flap. He wore rings and a coat of bronze paint on his fingernails; clearly a courtier or official of some sort, not a servant.

He seemed to know about them. Perhaps the tattooed guardsman had sent a messenger ahead. He said, "Please come in, Priest. You are welcome to Commander Sri's tent. Your companions may come in, for now."

The space inside the tent was large, suited to the status of a commander. An actual carpet covered the dusty earth. A table sat to one side, scattered with maps and papers. A wooden partition screened off the back of the tent, probably to hide a cot or sleeping roll and the commander's personal belongings. Jaena and her companions stood just inside the entrance, guardsmen behind them. Lord Halpen began to speak, but a guard jabbed him in the ribs and he fell silent.

Jaena fidgeted. "Why are we being treated like this? We're here to ask for help for someone who's in great danger."

"You're hostages," said a new voice from the back of the tent. A dark-skinned woman with cropped hair, faded toward gray, came out from behind the screen and sat down, eyeing all of them. She was heavily built – stocky but not fat – and wore mail and a chain of office. "I recognize one of you, do I not, Lord Halpen? You'll make an excellent bargaining chip when dealing with Herrein, and so will your nobleman friend there. The woman though, is a priest of Imn-ashu, so she will be welcome and free to go where she wishes."

"My name is Jaena. Yes, I am a priest of Imn-ashu. I can tell you, Commander Sri, that we mean no harm. We came to ask aid from you in getting a *taylenor* boy safely out of Cassahn. His life is in danger. Lord Metten is a friend who's helped me get here, and Lord Halpen – is *taylenor* himself, and is seeking refuge."

"*Taylenor!*" Sri grimaced. "He's more like a twisted thing. I recognize you, Halpen de Morn. How much did you pay, to have the monster Herrein stifle you like that, and escape your fate?"

"It's a cruel fate," Jaena offered.

"It was my parents," Halpen muttered. "I was just a boy."

The Commander snorted. "It seems you didn't worry about it until you were afraid Herrein wouldn't honor his agreement. Take them away, guards. Except for the priest."

Metten quirked a reassuring smile at her as the men were escorted out of the Commander's tent.

"Where will they take them?" Jaena asked, feeling very alone now.

"You'll see them soon enough. Priest, we honor Imn-ashu. You have the freedom of the camp. You do not have the freedom to leave, however. You may spend time with your companions or not, as you choose."

"Thank you for that," Jaena said. "I need to explain more about why we've come. Well, Lord Metten and myself, anyway. We came to ask your help to get a gifted boy out of Cassahn. Guards took him to Mage Herrein's house three – no, four days ago now, and I'm afraid if we don't rescue him soon he'll die." As she spoke the crushing weight of what she had done settled on her again. *Goddess, be with Weil!*

"You're probably right. With the Eastern mage stirring and sending demons to soften the way, I have no doubt Herrein's running through *taylenor* like sticks on a bonfire. Why in the world did you waste time running here, instead of trying to remove the boy yourselves?"

"We've no way to rescue him. There's no way to get close enough. We were pursued out of Cassahn ourselves. Wiel is heavily guarded. I knew Ull-fasten had mages, and I thought you would be willing... "

The Commander snorted. "Willing we may be. But there are larger concerns now. Mage Herrein sent men by sea to abduct *taylenor* from Ull-fasten, and we ride now to liberate them or avenge them."

Jaena swallowed. If Mage Herrein was so hard-pressed he felt the need to kidnap *taylenor* from foreign lands, then Wiel's chances of surviving were slim indeed. "Please," she said. "If you won't go after Wiel, then I'll have to go back alone."

"Herrein is a monster," the commander said. "For more than a century we in Ull-fasten have tried to save *taylenor* children from him, bringing them back here to learn magery. Did you know that? It's our sworn mission. Our mages work strategies to get into Cassahn and find others with *taylen*. *Taylenor* are becoming rare in Cassahn – that's due, in part, to us. So we'd save your boy as well – but our own must come first."

Jaena's heart lifted. "That's why there are so many *taylenor* in your camp," she said, smiling. "Are they all refugees from Cassahn?"

There was a pause that lasted only a heartbeat, and the air chilled as if winter had come early.

"Tell me, Priest, how you know such a thing." The Commander's hand tightened on her sword hilt; Jaena could see it from where she stood, the knuckles taut on the plain hilt.

"What do you mean?" Jaena asked.

"Surely you cannot be the Seeker. You, a priest of Imn-ashu."

Shame flooded her. "I didn't know. I swear, by my goddess I didn't know until just days ago what would really happen to Wiel. I still wouldn't know, except Mage Herrein was forced to use *taylen* to defend against the demons, and I returned to Iryor to find Wiel very ill."

Sri's dark hand still clutched the sword hilt. "Seekers are an evil beyond compare – much worse than that petty selfishness your Lord Halpen displays. I don't understand how Imn-ashu could stand for such a thing in her own priest. How can we house you in our camp?"

"Since I found out, I've been trying to right the wrong I did. That's why I'm here." Jaena's voice shook. She looked down at the worn carpet. She couldn't stand to look at the scorn in the older woman's face. She waited for the metallic scrape of a weapon being unsheathed, waited for the killing blow.

"Some wrongs can't be righted." The Commander's voice was hard, but she turned away from Jaena. "Whether you knew what you did or not, you delivered a boy up to be sacrificed – his life eaten away by that monster. It's just as well you pay a little guilt. I should slay you, but you belong to Imn-ashu."

Jaena's legs trembled as the pressure of guilt seemed to double.

"Oh, I believe you. I don't think you even know why it's such a terrible sin." Sri's voice took on a weary tone. "Don't you understand Priest, you're *taylenor* too? That's why you could be trained to find it in others. That's what a Seeker is, and why there have been so very few in all of history. I don't know why Herrein didn't just take you and use you up."

Jaena knew. As if the girl stood right next to her, she heard Tia's lilting voice teasing, before the little girl grew too ill to laugh. Herrein hadn't needed Jaena. He'd been able to draw on Marki, then on Tia, and there had been scant need for him to use great power before the demons began to stir. Instead, Herrein had sent Jaena out to betray her own kind, to bring them in to be consumed.

She drew a sobbing breath. Mother Thara's voice said in her memory, *Did you never wonder why you were the only one who could sense the taylen? You are all Herrein's.*

Sri turned back to her. The disgust had left her narrow eyes, but there was no sympathy there. "Can you stand?"

Jaena bent every bit of her willpower to keeping her shaking legs strong under her, to quelling the nausea that roiled her stomach. She was the lowest of the low, who had betrayed her own dearest friends, but she was still a priest of Imn-ashu. She would not fall down before this woman, no matter how mighty Sri might be.

"Well. Consider yourself detained. I will find guards that know how to beware of such as you. I can't look at you more right now."

CHAPTER FOURTEEN

The Ull-fasten had given Jaena a tent to herself. There was a narrow cot made up with blankets – a luxury, she supposed, in a camp where most would sleep on bedrolls on the ground. A chamber pot was tucked away under the cot. She heard the sounds of men laughing and swearing, and the clang of cookpots. A chill crept through the canvas, reminding her that autumn would soon give way to winter.

She lay down on top of the blankets and closed her eyes.

Goddess, forgive me.

She had been so disdainful of Lord Halpen and his deceit. At least Halpen and his noble parents hadn't delivered others into Herrein's imprisonment.

She didn't deserve to be a priest of Imn-ashu, nor to ask for the goddess' forgiveness. She did not deserve Metten's love and loyalty, or the respect these Ull-fasten guardsmen gave her when they saw her insignia.

It seemed no time at all before a voice outside her tent rumbled, "Priest, do you want dinner?"

"Thank you. No." Her voice rasped with unshed tears.

The man went away. Jaena opened her eyes to find that dusk had filled up the corners of the tent. A glow on one side of the canvas came from a campfire in the mid distance. She heard the jingle of metal, perhaps someone cleaning tack or weapons. She drew a deep breath. The air chilled her nostrils.

Jaena forced down her guilt; she was not entitled to sit and wallow. The least she could do now was justify the undeserved favor of her goddess. She breathed a soft prayer for strength. Her shoulders relaxed as comfort eased into her, along with the soft scent of *hibon*. Imn-ashu had not given up on her.

She poked her head outside the tent flap. The two men who sat on the woodpile outside turned and gave her identical looks of wary interrogation.

"Can I go and see the people I'm traveling with?"

The taller man stretched into a standing position. He slanted a look at the other guardsman and shrugged. "No one said not to. I'll take her."

The other tent was guarded, too. She ducked inside to find it barely large enough for the three men. Her companions sat on bedrolls, staring at each other across a shielded lamp that sat on the ground in the center of the tent.

Jaena found a space that was not crammed with bedrolls and packs. "This is cozy," she said. She heard the slight hoarseness in her voice, but no one else seemed to notice.

"It's a hovel!" snapped Halpen. "I can't stay here."

"There's enough room, Hal, and it'll be warm," Metten drawled. Even in the golden lamplight, his face looked greenish and ill. He sat forward on his bedroll, legs crossed, and rested his bandaged right hand on his left.

"How is that?" Jaena nodded at his hand.

"Hurts." Metten shrugged. "A *cernen* was here before. Looked at me, shook her head and went back out to find some herbs or something. Maybe there's a mage-healer instead, with something to put on it. This is a war camp, after all – they're expecting wounded."

Jaena stepped out to speak to the guard about finding another *cernen*. When she returned, Metten was lying down, shivering.

"What did the Commander say?" Rall asked. He handed her a thick slice of bread from a wooden trencher. It was covered with slices of meat. Jaena took a bite, and the warm savory juice flooded her mouth. It seemed like forever since she'd eaten a hot meal.

"Apparently," she said when she could, "Mage Herrein has kidnapped some mages from Ull-fasten. This army rides to get them back – or avenge them, Sri said."

"Taking us along with them like leaves carried in a flood," Halpen said.

She shook her head. "No, Lord Halpen. You're her backup plan. I think she intends to exchange you for one of their own if she must."

"We're bargaining chips," Rall said. "Lord Metten, perhaps she plans to use you as such, as well."

"Not worth much," Metten said. "I've got no *taylen*, you know."

"No, sir. But you're a nobleman."

Metten shook his head. "My father cut me off. Can't see him paying good money for me."

"I'm sure they would ransom you, some way or other," Rall said.

"Not so sure," Metten said, still shivering. "Father told me he'd be happy if he never saw me again. Mutual, too."

Jaena finished her bread and meat and looked around for water. Rall handed her a mug.

"What I don't understand," Metten said, "is what she said about you, Hal."

Lord Halpen said, "It's a thing my parents did when I was young. To save me from Herrein."

"He's *taylenor*," Jaena said. "Since he had money, he paid for the signs of his *taylen* to be suppressed – so no Seeker would ever find him and bring him in. That fate was reserved for those too poor to pay."

"Hey!" Halpen protested.

"It's true," she said. But the disdain she'd felt for Halpen before was gone.

"I had nothing to do with it. It was all my parents. They thought, since they were on Council -- "

"My lord," Rall interrupted. "I remember this, I think. You went off to take some cure. When you returned you were sicker than when you had left. You were fourteen."

"Well, I am a de Morn of Cassahn. Would you have me consumed like fuel?"

The tent flap opened and a tall man stooped to enter. His gray hair brushed the tops of his shoulders, but his face was unlined. He wore a leather surcoat over tunic and breeches and no insignia of rank or status. But Jaena sensed his *taylen*, like a mist of armor that surrounded him.

"I'm Othane," he said. "I'm here to look at someone's wound?"

"You're a mage?" Jaena said.

Othane's face twisted. "Seeker," he said as if it were a curse. "I am a mage-healer."

Jaena flushed and stepped back. "He's over there," she said, pointing to Metten.

Mage Othane bent over Metten in the flickering lamplight and began to unwrap the wrist. After a moment the mage sat back, and Jaena saw that Metten's hand was red and swollen, and the wound was weeping fluid. She gave an involuntary gasp.

Metten grimaced. "It's all right, Jaena."

"It doesn't look all right."

"This is from demon's blood. It doesn't stop burning when the blood is washed away," Othane said. "This hand has not been treated properly."

Lord Halpen wandered over and stared down at his friend's hand. "Ugh. You've been killing demons, then?"

"Trying. Only fire kills them, I believe." Metten's face flushed as Othane smeared some grayish salve over the wound. "Hurts like a damned -- "

"Priest present," warned Rall.

"Don't mind me." She knelt on the floor next to Metten and placed a hand over his good one. The wound was worse. The blisters had spread, and red lines ran up Metten's arm, along the path of his veins.

A chill of fear ran through her. She'd seen red lines like those before, and she knew what they meant. "Will this salve cure him?"

The mage shrugged. "It's the best we have. It looks like the venom has been progressing for days. Lord Metten, how do you feel?"

"Not too bad. But pretty damned cold," he gasped.

It was not at all cold in the confines of the crowded tent.

"Give me the hand again," Othane said. The mage bent over Metten's hand and closed his eyes.

"What's he doing?" Halpen squawked.

Othane opened his eyes and shook his head. "I can't quite see it, I don't have the strength. I can't use my energy on this when we may well see battle tomorrow."

"If I understand how this works, I can help." Jaena pushed back thoughts of poor Wiel being drained unto death.

Othane's head whipped around. "We do not do that. It's an abomination. How dare you bring Herrein's ways here?"

"I'm offering. I can see how bad it is." Jaena looked at Metten's swollen, infected arm and knew it was too late for any salve to cure him.

"What are you talking about?" Metten gasped.

"Getting you healthy again, I hope." Jaena leaned forward and brushed a curly lock back from Metten's sweaty forehead.

Rall looked from Metten's fevered face to Jaena. He stood and bowed to Halpen. "My lord, we should step out."

"Step out where?" Halpen glared. "I for one have no desire to be spitted by the guardsmen because they think we're trying to escape."

"I'll make sure that doesn't happen. We'll simply give the mage-healer more room."

"What about her then?" Halpen said, but Rall nudged him through the tent flap before the nobleman could protest any more.

Jaena helped Metten lie down on a spread-out bedroll. He closed his eyes and turned his head away.

Othane sat back cross-legged on the ground. He frowned. "You don't understand. What you ask me to do is a crime."

"You won't try to heal him yourself."

"It would make me useless until I recover my strength. Healing something that goes throughout the body demands great strength – more than joining a broken bone, for example, or healing a wound. I'm a mage of limited power, Priest, and I owe my strength to our own wounded after the battle."

"So he'll die. You must have seen this before. The wound-sickness will kill him if you don't draw from my strength." Jaena put all her desperation into her voice. She must not allow Metten to die.

Othane sighed. "It's supposed to be a sweet feeling, or so the legends say. Using mage power with no cost. There are many reasons it's forbidden."

"Please."

"It's bitter, that you should have to beg me to heal a dying man." The mage's mouth twisted. "Well, then. You're a Seeker, so I must suppose you understand what you're offering."

"I understand." Jaena sat down on the ground next to Metten's bedroll. She stroked his hair back, but this time he did not respond. "His mind has gone somewhere else. He's getting worse, fast."

"He may have been hiding the symptoms for a while." The mage frowned at her for a moment; then his face relaxed and she saw the trepidation behind his eyes. "I'm not sure I know how to do this."

There was no answer to that. Jaena sat still, watching as Othane kneeled next to Metten and extended both hands over him. After a few moments a soft radiance enveloped Othane's hands like gloves. The mage placed one hand on Metten's wounded wrist, one on his chest, and closed his eyes.

Jaena waited, every nerve drawn tight. What would it feel like? Would it hurt? She remembered Wiel, sick and shaky in the hospital, too weak to stand. She hummed a silent measure of prayer to Imn-ashu, lifted her chin and waited.

The golden light from Othane's hands spread out, enveloping Metten's body. *Taylen* surged in a way Jaena had never felt before. Quick as a snake striking, Othane grabbed Jaena's left shoulder and gripped, hard. The long fingers dug in as if the mage was holding on for his life. Jaena forced herself not to jerk away.

The golden light began to sink into Metten's skin.

Something pulled hard at Jaena's gut. She put a hand to her stomach, trying to ease the strange feeling, but the pulling intensified. She hunched over, instinctively trying to protect her core.

The tent shifted, lurching sideways. She clutched for something to keep her anchored as the world spun. She dropped to the ground, hands pressed to the dirt, feeling as if she was about to be flung away. The mage's hand dropped from her shoulder, then folded up against her forehead.

The pain burst through her skin and exploded.

Golden light illuminated the blood vessels behind her closed eyelids. Through her pain she heard Othane's voice chanting. Her blood thrummed in her veins. Just when she began to think she couldn't do this anymore, the hand released her forehead and the radiance vanished.

Relief from pain manifested as a cocoon of dead silence. Jaena rested in that cocoon until a voice began to permeate the cloud surrounding her.

"Seeker. Are you all right?"

She opened her eyes. Othane leaned over her, his face huge in her uncomprehending vision. She stared up at him.

"Seeker?"

Jaena took a deep breath and was surprised when her lungs expanded and allowed the fresh air in. She pushed herself upright and was about to speak when her stomach rebelled. She waved desperately toward the chamber pot near the tent wall. Othane pushed it over to her just as she threw up.

When she thought it was over, she lifted her head. "Did it work?" she rasped.

She followed Othane's gaze to the bedroll. Metten lay with his face turned away from her. His chest rose and fell in steady, deep breaths. His outstretched arm showed clear skin, the wound pink and healthy. She crawled over and lay a hand on his forehead. It was cool and dry, the fever gone.

"It worked," she breathed.

"I'm glad, but don't ever ask me, or any mage to do that again." Othane's voice shook.

Startled, she turned to look at him. His face was flushed, and his eyes were very bright.

"Are you all right?"

"Dangerously so. This may have even added a month or two to my lifespan." He got to his feet, his hands trembling.

"You mean -- "

"It feels like a drug," he interrupted. "A mage could become addicted to this, Seeker. No doubt Herrein became dependent long ago. It's a dangerous feeling, using power like that with no cost. I repeat, do not ever ask that of me again."

Jaena stood up. The tent swung about her. Othane gripped her arm to keep her from falling.

"I'll be all right. It was just one time. Surely it takes much longer before a person can't recover?" Marki and Tia had lived for years, all the while feeding Herrein their energy.

"I've no knowledge of this. Sit down and stay with him until he awakens. I'll order food and drink brought to you." His leather surcoat swung as he turned and ducked under the tent flap.

CHAPTER FIFTEEN

Footsteps close to her tent awakened Jaena. She opened her eyes to the slate color of early pre-dawn. There was only a dull ache behind her eyes to remind her of last night's ordeal.

Someone stumbled outside, maybe tripping over something in the dim light, and let out a muffled oath.

Alert now, Jaena sat up and listened. The camp seemed to be awake. The movements she heard seemed furtive, without any banter between the guardsmen. Something was happening.

She had gone to bed in her clothes, with her cloak wrapped around her against the cold. All she had to do was shove her feet into her boots. She swallowed water from the mug on the table and stuffed an apple into her pocket.

She threw open the tent flap just as Ael, the rangy man who had been on guard the previous evening, walked up.

"Priest, it's time to go. Quiet as you can. You'll be in the rear, but you have to be ready to cross."

"But what's happening?"

Ael shook his head and did not reply. Jaena grabbed her pack and followed him to a cluster of people in the center of camp. Most of the others there were noncombatants: *cernen*, support people, a guardsman with his arm splinted, sitting glumly on a bench. In the middle of this group, Lord Halpen stood out like a bluejay in a flock of wrens.

Halpen pulled his fur-lined cloak around him. "I demand to know why I've been brought here!"

"Hush," Metten said from beside him.

A guardsman shouldered into their space. "Quiet, please!"

Halpen turned his back on the guard. He lowered his voice, but its petulant quality was grating as ever. "This is ridiculous."

"There's some kind of action going on, my lord," Rall said from his seat on the bench. "Would you like to sit?"

"No." Halpen glowered at the others clustered on the benches: the wounded guardsman, a washerwoman, two Ull-fasten priests Jaena had not met.

"Are you well?" Jaena whispered to Metten.

"Much better." He grinned and waved his hand at her. "It seems Othane was able to do the trick."

As the sky lightened she could see his face was flushed with the cold, not fever. His smile was full of good humor. Tears of relief sprang into her eyes. She looked away to hide her emotion.

The camp had been wrapped up and loaded. Even her tent was already gone. Carts waited in the rear, laden with supplies, horses already harnessed and blowing their breath into the frosty air.

To the north, billows of mist marked the line where the river cut through the ravine between Ull-fasten and the town of Rivasha. The stark outlines of the bridge fortifications rose out of the fog. There were soldiers up there: Jaena saw them clustered, some on foot, some on horseback, but no one seemed to be moving much or advancing at all.

Then the fog turned blue.

The mist seemed to glow from within. It was a luminous blue that brightened and shaded toward yellow as Jaena's eyes followed it from the billowing mist down toward the old bridge.

"It's a shield," Metten said.

Jaena caught her breath. The thought of mages having enough power to create such a thing was amazing. She imagined them standing with their hands extended to draw on their *taylen* and create the shield, which must be protecting the military as they advanced across the bridge in what was apparently a frontal assault on the border guard at Rivasha.

"Come on, now, we're going," Ael said. "Follow the column to the east. Quiet as you can, no talk at all."

"Where are we going?" whispered Halpen. Metten elbowed him in the ribs, and Halpen fell silent, glowering.

Jaena fell into line behind the others. The sky was lighter. There were far more people in their column than she had imagined. Behind her, wheels creaked as the horses threw their weight into pulling the supply carts.

She had no idea where they were going. There had been no chance to talk to the Commander again. She hoped this line of people was headed into Cassahn behind the military, but they seemed to be walking away from the battle at the Rivasha bridge.

She turned and looked over her shoulder at the shield, fading into the lightening sky but still limning the curves of the billowing river mist. Even from here she could hear the shouts and alarms from the Rivasha border guard and the Ull-fasten attackers. The mist hid the actual assault.

It was light enough now to see the brown grass under her feet as they passed the area where just yesterday they had been escorted to the interview with Commander Sri. Now, there was little but trampled grass to remind her of what had been a crowded camp.

She followed the column through a copse of trees and closer to the embankment at river's edge. Just below them was the overhanging tree where they'd pulled Lotte's boat to shore. They passed that and began climbing a path that headed farther up the cliffs that rimmed the river. The sky shaded to a pearly gray, heavy with low clouds. The beginnings of the Cliffs of Cassahn loomed before them.

The path snaked through a fissure edged by boulders taller than two men and vanished into the rocks. Jaena's mouth dropped open as she saw the number of people before them. This was not the small group of servants and noncombatants she had imagined, heading to some safe location to wait out the battle away from danger. There were armed guardsmen here, bristling with weapons, their hardened leather helmets making a distinctive silhouette against the lowering sky. This was the main force.

She glanced at Metten, walking to the side and a little behind her, and found him looking around with his eyebrows raised. She let her gaze linger, relieved to notice the spring of energy in his step even as he negotiated the steeper trail. Then her boot heel caught on a tree root, and she turned her attention back to their path.

Behind them there was a thunderous crash. The glow of the mage shield flickered, then steadied.

"Siege engine?" Metten whispered. He shrugged and fell back behind her.

She wondered if a projectile thrown by a siege engine could disturb the mage shield or destroy the bridge. How long could the Ull-fasten mages hold firm against the force of concerted attack before they succumbed to exhaustion?

The incline leveled out onto a spacious plateau of dimpled rock. In spite of its size, the space was crowded. The vanguard waited grim and ready, some mounted, some with their shoulders up against the rock face. The remainder of the guards straggled into the brush and rocks surrounding the plateau, making a little room for the noncombatants streaming up the trail. The line stalled behind Jaena's group. She imagined the other noncombatants jammed into the trail that was just wide enough for the supply wagons to squeak by. Where in the world were they going? This looked ill-considered at best.

Ael awaited them. "Wait," he said in a low voice. "Don't go anywhere, and keep quiet."

Rall was ahead of them, peering around a jutting escarpment. He turned and waved at them.

They peered around a boulder to see a wonder.

Mist still roiled up from the river, but didn't reach the high plateau where they stood. Jaena looked across the gap into Cassahn to see a twin plateau, almost reaching for them across the gorge. And between the two abutments, a wavering outline, as if drawn by charcoal – two parallel lines, and a path between them that appeared to be made of scribbled net.

Three people stood adjacent to the construction, and one somehow on the other side. As the mist dropped away below them, they drew the charcoal lines like string through their hands. A fluorescing glow about them reminded her of the mage shield she'd seen above the Rivasha bridge.

"No." Halpen's voice was loud. "I won't cross that thing."

A red-bearded guardsman was in Halpen's face. "Lord or no," he growled low, "I'll knock you out and carry you over my shoulder if I need to."

Halpen flushed and opened his mouth to respond, but Rall put a hand on his lord's sleeve. Halpen turned on Rall, then quieted.

Metten stood near the edge of the plateau, looking down. Jaena crouched next to him on hands and knees, clutching the rough surface of the rock against the fear of falling. Dark, wet rocks gleamed in the frothing water far below, along with something manmade – coils of brown rope swaying from the bank until they vanished down under the surface of the stream.

Metten grinned. "I think we know how that guy got across the river."

"They use it as a structural concept." Mage Othane stood behind them on the rocky plateau. "To build the bridge over it, you know. It helps them keep it solid."

"Solid's good," Metten said.

"Time to go," Othane said. He wandered back toward the bulk of the column.

Jaena inched back from the edge before standing. She'd never been around heights much before – not like this, where the cold rock dropped away into air, and she could feel gravity pulling her over the edge.

The gray lines of bridge – fragile strokes in the air between the twin abutments – had thickened. They were rigid now, and the floor a stiffened grate. One of the mages on the near side put his feet on the thing and walked onto the bridge that had not been there an hour before.

Jaena flinched away, then looked back to see the man standing on the construct in midair, equidistant between the two sides. He crossed and took his place beside the other mage on the Cassahn side.

Goddess. I'm going to have to walk across that thing.

A familiar stocky figure waited at the edge of the cliff. Commander Sri stood between the two mages, a cluster of armed guardsmen behind her. Going first, Jaena thought, as an example to her people.

One of the mages turned and nodded to Sri, and she stepped onto the deck. There was no sign of instability from the magic bridge.

"You'll have to knock me out to get me across that thing," Halpen whispered to Metten.

The red-bearded guardsman, still shadowing them, smirked.

Commander Sri stepped onto the rocky plateau at the other side, and her guardsmen jogged across behind her. They fanned out into the rocks, weapons ready.

The line of armed men and women followed, crossing the bridge three abreast and vanishing into the rocks on the other side. The mounted rear guard stayed behind, keeping watch on the trail.

"The vanguard will clear the way on the other side. We need to hurry." Ael ushered them back into the crowd waiting to cross. "Sooner or later the Rivasha border guard will realize the assault on the bridge is a fake."

"And they'll start to look for other incursions," Metten said.

Jaena cast a quick look to either side as she approached the abutment. The two mages stared straight ahead, strands of magery like webbing between their fingers, wrapping around their bodies to sink into the earth. Their faces were flushed under their dark skin, streaming perspiration in spite of the cold air.

Another man and woman wrapped in gray cloaks sat on the rocks behind the mages, waiting. Jaena sensed their *taylen* pervading all the space around them. Maybe these two waited in reserve. She hoped so. The more reserves, as far as she was concerned, the better.

She shuffled onto the bridge deck.

It felt solid to her feet, but her eyes told her better. The huge gap between the rigid floor and the fuzzy pencil-lines that made up the handrail yawned at her. Below, water frothed.

Her knees locked. She grasped the handrail in terror, looking down and down and down.

Someone bumped into her from behind. She swayed, heart rising into her throat.

"Fool!" Halpen whispered. He looked almost as shaken as she did. He nudged her with one hand. "Move on, will you? The faster we're done with this idiocy, the better."

Jaena tried to unlock her knees. She tried to release her grip from the handrail. *Goddess, help me do this.* It wasn't as if she could stay there, or go back either.

Then Metten's arm was around her, anchoring her. She closed her eyes in relief as he pulled her closer.

"Go on, Hal, would you?" Metten's voice was reassuring and calm. "I'll help Jaena."

Halpen mumbled something that sounded either terrified or rude, and brushed past Jaena in a way that left her clutching at Metten's arm.

"Sorry," she gasped.

"It's all right. Look, all the support people and the rear-guard are behind us. Let's go. I'll walk with you."

Jaena looked over her shoulder to see people and horses queued up to cross the bridge. The mages still looked strained as they supported their energy construct. She felt ashamed at delaying the crossing.

She released the bridge handrail and grabbed Metten's sleeve instead. Through sheer force of will she unstuck her feet from the bridge deck and took a step: one, then two, tiny steps but movement all the same.

The mist seemed to be clearing down closer to the river.

"Don't look down," Metten said.

She kept her gaze on the mages at the Cassahn side of the bridge, standing like pillars. The grate flowed beneath her feet as if she walked on solid land.

"I'm sorry," she said. Her face heated.

"Nothing to be sorry for." Metten did not release her arm. "You handled it. It only delayed us a moment."

Jaena stepped onto the gritty rock of Cassahn and past the mages. Ael stood there, directing new arrivals into one of the paths away from the cliff. She followed the group down a root-tangled path similar to the one they'd climbed on the other side, then back up another rise.

At the top of the next rise was the ridge trail. The Ull-fasten troops were splitting there: some heading eastward, others heading back toward Rivasha, presumably to come at the defenders from the rear. Ael and two grim swordsmen surrounded Jaena's group.

"Go, go, faster." A guardsman pointed east, away from the Rivasha bridge.

They stumbled through the rocks for a few minutes before the ground started to slope down, off the ridge that roughly paralleled the river. The view from here was beautiful, now that the river-born mist was behind them; the narrow road winding down, a ribbon of brown that swung wide and then vanished around the shoulders of a wooded hill on fire with the colors of autumn. This trail would meet the main road, and then they would be able to go back the way they'd come -- back to Iryor to rescue Wiel and the Ull-fasten mages who'd been stolen, this time with the might and anger of Commander Sri and the Ull-fasten troops behind her.

"Off the road!"

Weapons clashed. A horse screamed from the front of the column. A man yelled orders that Jaena couldn't make out. Guardsmen raced to the front. The rocks were too far behind them to offer any useful concealment. Everything was a clutter of military action and noncombatants in a confused muddle, looking for a place to go.

"Crap, we ran into their reinforcements," Ael said. "All together now, all of you! As close as you can get!"

Guardsmen pushed them off the trail next to a knobby rise. They crushed close. The smell of sweat and horse enveloped them. Jaena tried to see past the wall of shoulders and their armed escort, but could only make out a confused melee.

Metten fumed in the cluster of support people and wounded troops. "Let me out," he demanded.

"Orders are you're to remain inside and under guard," the man said.

"My lord, your hand ... " Rall began.

"My hand is much better. If it's demons, I can fight them!" Metten argued.

"Seems to be people, not demons," the guard said. "Cassahni reinforcements, I think."

Jaena peered over the man's shoulder. A man was carried toward the rear, soaked with blood, an arrow embedded in his chest. Around her was the clash of weapons, and the shouts and grunts of fighting men and women.

"I think you should be glad you're not up there," Lord Halpen said. "If it's not demons, it's probably Herrein's border guard, or the First. We know these people, Met."

Jaena froze. These were their own people up ahead, soldiers from Cassahn. Maybe Erdo was among them, the man who had guarded Herrein's door when Jaena went for lessons. Maybe others she had seen in the street.

She supposed she was an enemy now, for all intents and purposes part of the invading force from Ull-fasten. The others might legitimately claim they were hostages, but Jaena, a priest, was a hostage in name only. Commander Sri's goal was to rescue the *taylenor* Herrein had kidnapped from Ull-fasten. Sri's goal marched with Jaena's own. Jaena would aid the Ull-fasten to the limit of her ability to save Weil. If Herrein were deposed, so much the better.

That didn't mean she couldn't still feel heartsick over the deaths of men and women from her own city. She hummed a prayer under her breath. *Goddess, embrace their souls. And forgive me please.*

She was pretty sure the other priests in the Temple, along with the people she knew in the little towns she had traveled to on her circuit, would call her traitor. And perhaps she was. Nothing mattered except saving Wiel, saving any other *taylenor* from being Herrein's victims.

She remembered her last talk with Tasa Wimar in the goddess' garden in the Temple. He had trusted her. It seemed he'd been wrong.

Thank the goddess that she wasn't called upon to fight.

A segment of Ull-fasten troops surged forward, a line of blue light before them. A mage shield, Jaena thought. This guess was confirmed when she saw an attacker slide off the blue surface and fall under the weapons of the Ull-fasten troops.

With mages on their side, it did not take long for the skirmish to be won. The Cassahn reinforcements retreated once they saw the effect of the shield. The sounds of battle died down to a jumble of shouted orders and the moans of the wounded. The guardsmen around their little group relaxed enough to let their charges move a few feet apart.

People carried stretchers toward the *cernen* in the rear. Most carried wounded men and women. One stretcher carried an older woman in a gray surcoat such as Othane had worn. Her pale skin showed her Cassahni ancestry. Perhaps she'd been one of the many *taylenor* the Ull-fasten had rescued from Cassahn through the years.

"Is that one of the mages? Is she all right?" Jaena craned her neck to see what was going on.

"Not wounded, I don't think," someone said.

"She's just ill and exhausted," Ael said. "Maintaining that shield takes a lot out of them."

"Surely you know what happens to a *taylenor* who uses magery," Halpen said. "You, a Seeker."

"We should have more mages," the red-bearded guard said. "It takes 'em at least a day to recover anytime we need 'em. Delicate creatures, ain't they? You can't run any kinda action with just one mage."

Commander Sri rode back to them. She rode a gray mare whose legs were splashed with red. Sri's face dripped with sweat. Her hand gripped the hilt of her sword as if she'd forgotten she was holding it. Blood smeared her knuckles, red on brown, but she didn't carry herself as if she had been wounded.

She paused to exchange a few words with her guardsmen, then continued on to their little group.

"You are all well?" she asked.

Jaena nodded.

"We've taken Rivasha," Sri continued. "And we've stopped these reinforcements your group ran into on the road, but more will come. You stay in the center."

"We have to get back to Iryor as soon as we can," Jaena said. "I don't know how long Wiel can last, we must hurry."

The gray mare shied as a blood-soaked guardsman was carried past on a stretcher. Sri gathered the reins, controlling her mount, but her face was grim. "I don't need your guilt to spur me on, Seeker. There are Ull-fasten mages in danger as well, but I will not lose more men and women than I must. We should have intelligence by midday on Herrein's whereabouts. Then I can tell you more."

"Holy Goddess!" someone yelled from the front line. There was a clamor of disjointed shouts.

"Down!" Ael snapped, and turned to face whatever danger threatened, hand on his sword.

Commander Sri pressed her mare forward. "What is it? Report!"

Jaena caught her breath as the troops settled into a horrified silence. There was no sign of any further attack; they had slain or driven off Herrein's reinforcements. Instead, shock froze them in their steps as a black cloud that must have been many leagues tall filled the sky. It obscured the peak of the tallest of the eastern mountains, a giant visible on the horizon even from their position days away.

More black smoke drifted from the mountain. The stiff winds that ruled at that elevation began to carry the mass of black towards the east. As it drifted slowly away in a surreal silence, Jaena saw what had caused the explosion.

The top of Mount Nimn had been blown completely away.

"That's the sign," Metten said. "The Eastern Mage has returned."

Commander Sri looked away from the blot in the eastern sky. Her eyes caught and held Jaena's for one moment. "This will change things. For Herrein, and for us."

CHAPTER SIXTEEN

The ruined peak of Mount Nimn stood before them like a beacon for days as they traveled.

The gout of smoke that blackened the sky drifted away, carried into the East like a malevolent banner that eventually shredded in the stiff winds. An ominous red tinged the Eastern sky.

Spies reported that Herrein himself was with the Cassahni army that raced toward ruined Mount Nimn, instead of safe in Iryor.

Commander Sri left a strong guard at Rivasha to protect Ull-fasten from any attempts to abduct more *taylenor* to feed Herrein's urgent need for more power. The rest of the army moved east, marching fast. Jaena, Halpen, Metten and Rall were carried along like flotsam in the current of their grim purpose.

Ael and the other guards stuck close, vigilant now that they followed Herrein and his people. Perhaps they feared that Jaena and the others might try to escape. For her part, Jaena wished they could travel faster. Commander Sri's intelligence said that Herrein's army was ahead of them, trying to reach the Saarnen Pass into the mountain plateau lands of the East.

Where Herrein went, Weil and the Ull-fasten *taylenor* would be.

That was where Jaena wanted to be, too.

She thought wistfully of the Temple, a place of music and serenity she was unlikely to see again. She missed Ears, too; she'd left the jennet safe in the Temple stables, but perhaps she'd been given to some other priest by now.

"You're fools," Halpen grumbled as they walked in the well-protected center. "We're all walking to our deaths."

Two days into Cassahn, they began meeting refugees heading west. Straggly groups of people, families from homesteads, some with dogs trailing beside them or valued livestock led on ropes.

Commander Sri sent an officer to question them while the main army moved on.

That evening, the Commander sent for Jaena. Metten tagged along with a stubborn tilt to his chin.

A middle-aged man in a leather surcoat over an embroidered tunic admitted them. "Commander. They're here."

"They?" Sri stepped out from behind the screen. "Ah, Lord Metten. There's no keeping you away."

Metten bowed.

"Strangely grim, aren't you? I swear I mean no harm to the priest."

The ringed middle-aged man bowed. "I'll take my leave then, Commander."

Sri waved him out. "Sit down. I've news for you. I am telling you this as a courtesy, Priest."

"It's about Wiel?"

"The *taylenor* boy? No. He's with Herrein, up ahead of us, with the people Herrein stole from Ull-fasten." Sri's jaw set. "Herrein's planning to have his resources ready if he must face down the Eastern Mage. Also, the demons are back. Many of those refugees have truly horrifying stories of demon attacks in their villages. There's no doubt that the Saarnen Pass must be open."

"What's the news, then?"

"There's a reward on your head."

"He sent guardsmen after me. I didn't know why, but now I know it's because I'm *taylenor*. He needs every one of us he can get."

"That last set of refugees was from Fathers-rest, a little settlement north and east of here on Herrein's army's path. Herrein summoned them all to search for any *taylenor*. He offered a reward for you -- and the mouthy lord you travel with as well."

Metten grimaced. "Stay away from any refugees you see, Jaena."

"You think one of those poor people would turn me in?"

Sri paced closer. "They've been forced out of house and home. Some of them don't even own a change of clothes. Some have seen terrible things or lost people to the demons. Plus, they have no reason to respect you. Why would they bypass a chance at a rich reward?"

"I see." Jaena felt oddly ashamed, though she didn't know why. "I will stay away."

"Guardsman Ael will have instructions to keep them away if we pass on the road. Listen to him. He's not just your friendly traveling companion."

"I like him," Metten said, drawing Sri's glare.

"I know full well you're not going to try to escape," Sri continued. "Whatever evil you've done in the past, I see you're willing to atone. In spite of that, you'll continue to be guarded. For your good as well as ours. And we have to keep your traveling companion from bolting. As far as I can see, he's got no reason to stay with us and every reason to run."

* * *

They rode eastward toward the Saarnen Pass. Another day closer to what Jaena considered would be her death, they stopped near the formerly-thriving town of Sunrise.

"It looks empty," Commander Sri told them as they looked down at the village. "I don't think there's a living thing left in there."

They sat astride the horses Commander Sri had assigned them, on a hill overlooking the valley where the town lay. There were no cattle grazing in the pastures above the town, and not even a chicken in the yards of the outlying homes. Not one person could be seen in the streets, but Jaena caught a faint whiff of ashes blown on the wind.

It reminded her of Uthen, where she and Metten had seen people piling demons on the fire, weeks ago. She told Commander Sri that.

"Yes, well, it's not as if we're going to avoid the place," the Commander said. "Reports had Mage Herrein here, on his way to the east, a day ago. Priest, I want you in the rear again, along with Lord Halpen. You may take your man with you, Halpen, since I know you can't tie your laces without him."

Rall cleared his throat.

"There's no need for insult," Halpen said.

"Lord Metten, come with us. You had something to show us about the demons?"

"Careful!" Jaena cautioned him, but Metten was grinning at the prospect of being able to do something other than ride and sit in tents. She and the others were escorted to the rear, where they sat playing dice with their guardsmen for the next hour.

Then Metten stood before her, leading his mare, looking unusually somber.

"Jaena," he said. "Come with me."

Their guard started to rise. "I'll call a man to accompany -- "

Metten raised a hand. "No. I'll do it. You know Hal's the one you've been ordered to watch, anyway."

Lord Halpen looked sour as the guardsman sat down again.

"I'm taking you into the town," Metten said.

She went with Metten to ask for her loaner horse. The animal pinned its ears back and bared its teeth at her. She missed Ears more than ever.

Soon they were riding down into the town. It was a beautiful view, crisp in the morning air, the autumn-browning grasses bowing and rising again in the breeze. From a distance the tile-roofed buildings looked clean and picturesque.

"I am sorry, dearest," Metten said. "They've found someone they think might be Wiel."

Jaena's heart sank. "Dead?"

Metten nodded. "I'm sorry. I hope it isn't him."

"Were there demons here?"

"Yes. They're all dead now, piled on a fire in town. That's not what killed this boy, though. There's nothing like that you'll have to see."

Jaena thanked Imn-ashu silently for that small mercy.

As they entered the town they saw Sri's men still checking each house one by one. The acrid stink from the fire pervaded the town. It was strange to see the shops and inns abandoned, and smears of blood here and there on the streets. The smoking heap of a fire stood in the square, next to the town's market bell. A man and a woman stood near the door of a two-story merchant's house, perhaps waiting to take a body away. But most of the citizens seemed to be gone, probably swelling the tide of refugees running from the demons, the Eastern Mage and Herrein alike.

Metten tied the horses to the post.

She stopped him at the door with a raised hand. "Wait for me here."

Jaena was grateful that he made no protestations. He nodded and let her go in alone.

The outer room was cluttered with candle stubs, charcoal and account scrolls. The dry remains of someone's lunch lay crusted on a wooden platter on the table. Whoever lived here had cleared out in a hurry – chased away by demons, Herrein's army, or the Ull-fasten force come to liberate the town, she couldn't tell. She pulled a window covering to the side to let in a dim light, and proceeded into the inner rooms.

The body lay on a straw mattress. It was a boy, thin beyond the awkwardness of his years, covered to the waist by a ragged blanket. She pulled another window covering aside so that she could see and went to the bedside.

It was not Wiel. She drew a ragged breath of relief.

The boy's hair hung long and greasy to his shoulders, and his cheeks were hollow. He stared up at her with dead eyes no one had bothered to close. She could see his bones under the skin, sharp as if he had not been regularly fed, or as if something had leached all the energy from him so he had had no strength for nourishing his body.

There was no mark on him of wound or illness. It looked as if he had died from wasting away. The feel of *taylen* lay close around the boy's body, just remnants of a stronger power, like a candle burned to a stub. Herrein had taken everything this boy had.

Jaena drew the blanket up over him.

Outside, there were voices; she could make out Metten's, conversing with one of the guardsmen. Beyond that, the slam of doors and shouts of Sri's people, looking for townspeople that weren't there. Something still burning in the huge pyre snapped.

It was very quiet in the room. Jaena closed her eyes and tried to sing the boy's soul to Imn-ashu, but when she tried to voice the first few notes they came out choked and stifled. Her flute was in its leather case, in her pack. She would play for him later.

She turned and called Metten into the house.

"It isn't Wiel," she said.

"I'm glad." He looked at the body on the bed and didn't look glad at all. "The Ull-fasten guards didn't know him either. I'll have him taken away. I assume you would like to sing his soul, later?"

She nodded. No one but the Goddess would ever know the boy's name. She wondered where Herrein had found him, this unknown dead *taylenor*.

Metten shifted his feet and frowned. "The villagers here, who died — "

"I'll sing them. Just ... give me an hour or so. How many, Metten?"

"Fifteen. All killed by demons. Some of them are Cassahni, from Herrein's force. Sri's scouts have reported Herrein's army up ahead half a day or so. They left, Jaena. Just left their dead in the streets, and abandoned their injured horses and pack animals."

"They're in a hurry. Herrein's going to try to reclose the Saarnen Pass against the Eastern Mage."

A woman in the green of a *cernen* was waiting by the door as they left the house. "Are you ready for us to take him, Priest?"

She nodded.

"We have laid all the dead out in the yard of the local priest's house. Will you go there now?"

"I need a few moments," she told the *cernen*. "Can you show me where that is?"

"I know where it is." Metten took her arm and led her away from the stink of burning. Down an alley fronted by tiny houses, right at another square, and they stood at a garden-yard with covered bodies lined up before it, all waiting for Jaena. Metten ushered her past them.

"This was the priest's house. He had a little chapel here – more like a shrine, I guess."

The priest must be among the dead laid in the front garden; surely he would not have left all these souls unsung, and fled.

She nodded. Metten brushed his lips across the top of her head, stirring the hair there, and left her alone.

The priest had made a goddess' circle on the tabletop, out of twigs and dried flowers. An unlit candle stood off to the side, its melted wax dripped into tortured shapes. Jaena stood near the table and prayed for strength. She tried to suppress the heat of anger that she felt melting the ice inside her; she wanted to kill Mage Herrein, but the goddess would not stand for that. The goddess did not kill.

* * *

They found the missing villagers. Some of them had clustered in a cellar beneath the tavern. One or two others in back rooms of houses. There were only a couple dozen of them that hadn't died or run away. They came out of their hiding places quietly, faces streaked with tears, a rigidity about their expressions that betrayed shock. Jaena pushed her own feelings to the back, and spent time with the survivors, comforting them as a priest should. Her voice grew hoarse from unshed tears. That evening she stood in front of an appallingly sizable row of the dead, and played her flute to sing them to the goddess.

The first notes hung in the air too shrill, too weak. Jaena reached inside herself, putting all her sorrow and love through her breath into the instrument. The notes grew and were strengthened by the music of Imn-ashu's voice. The souls of the dead wrapped themselves in the goddess' song, shedding what they no longer needed, becoming complete, then vanishing into the goddess' peace.

The little knot of villagers wept. The Ull-fasten guards stood silent. Commander Sri stood behind Jaena in a formal posture of respect for the dead. The goddess came and stood close behind Jaena. She could see that the people felt the goddess' comfort and strength – their hopelessness faded even as she played.

The souls long gone, the last notes of the flute faded into the emptiness of the village streets. The guards stirred, speaking softly amongst themselves, and began to carry away the bodies of the dead.

Sri cleared her throat. "Are you all right, Priest?"

"Yes, I'm fine."

"I owe you an apology." The Commander's chin went up. "It's clear Imn-ashu favors you. She was here with us as you sang, even I could tell that, and I am not a woman who feels the unseen. I have no idea why she would lend her favor to a Seeker, but she must see something in you that I do not."

"I have no idea what it could be." The deaths were too recent, and Jaena was bitter.

"Nor do I. All the same, you have my apologies. If there's anything I can do for you until we arrive at Saarnen Pass, tell me, and I'll do my best to see it done."

"Thank you."

"Now we must move on. Herrein still has our people, and time's wasting for your Wiel and my people too."

"Let's go, then. I won't rest until Herrein has paid what he owes."

The Commander snorted. "That's quite a lot," she said. "Then Priest, I will tell you straight up. No more stops to ease the bereaved. No more singing of the dead. We ride to save our mages before Herrein destroys them. He has demons to fight again, many of them. It's clear from what happened here, we have no time to spare."

"I'm ready," Jaena said. "But after Herrein's gone, what will keep the Eastern Mage from destroying everything?"

"The Eastern Mage is a mystery. Cassahni legends say she'll destroy the land and the people out of rage, that the demons are her harbinger.

I'm not sure. Our own priests tell me there are other possibilities. Either way, Priest, when Herrein is gone, Ull-fasten takes over the defense of this country. Years we've spent, sneaking around behind his back, taking every *taylenor* we can back to Ull-fasten. That's over now. We'll destroy Herrein, but we won't let innocents fall defenseless. We'll push back the demons when Herrein is gone. We're here now, and we stay."

"So I'm a traitor indeed," Jaena said. "Or so the Council will see it."

"I doubt your Goddess sees it that way, Priest." Sri frowned at her. "And after all, chances are you won't live to be brought before Council anyway."

Jaena's mouth quirked. A strange thing to find humor in. It was true: her future was bleak. She had offered to be exchanged for the *taylenor* held captive by Herrein. Nothing good could happen to her, after that.

CHAPTER SEVENTEEN

W*e're bargaining chips.* Rall had been matter-of-fact when he'd said it, but the words echoed inside Halpen's brain.

After his race to get as far away from Herrein as possible, he was back in Cassahn again. Carried along against his will, closer and closer to Mount Nimn, following Herrein on his desperate rush to re-close the ancient Saarnen Pass against the Eastern Mage. There, Sri would hand him over, and that bastard Herrein would drain his *taylen* until Halpen was dead. In exchange for a couple of Ull-fasten mages Halpen couldn't care less about.

Metten and his Seeker-Priest didn't seem to mind. Halpen decided they were fools. He would give Metten one more chance to escape his fate. After that he washed his hands of both of them.

It was dark now, but not peaceful. Now that the Ull-fasten army was on the march within Cassahn's borders, everyone was on constant alert. Halpen and Metten had been left to fend mostly for themselves, though always under guard. Rall had been ordered to help with the wounded. Halpen saw him once a day, at most.

They were permitted to have a shielded lantern in their tent, but no open fires were allowed; dinner was cold smoked meats and bread.

Halpen gnawed on his, wistfully remembering the soft white breads of Iryor.

After he finished eating, he dug out the tiny flask of *aum* he'd carried all this way. "Something to take your mind off the food?"

"What is it?" Metten looked up from his meat.

"*Aum*, from the Southern Islands. It was a gift from the Chartess, for escorting his daughter to Duscapi."

Metten snorted. "What happened to that poor girl?"

"I made arrangements. Did you think I abandoned her? I asked my brother to escort her the rest of the way."

Metten took a drink of the *aum*.

Halpen sipped. It was delicious stuff, one of the luxuries of the islands.

When Metten finished his, Halpen poured some more.

"This is good – and strong." Metten lifted an eyebrow at Halpen. "You should offer it as a gift to Commander Sri. If you present your case right, maybe she'll let you out of here."

"You're being intentionally obtuse. It's just like you. They intend to exchange me for one of their mages, so Herrein can consume my *taylen* like a midday snack."

The corner of Metten's mouth quirked up. "Vivid."

"I'm riding towards my death. I'd have to be stupid not to attempt an escape. But I can't do it on my own – we're in the middle of an army, after all."

Metten swirled the *aum* around in his mug, then looked up at Halpen. "Is that what this is all about? You thought if you gave me your *aum* I'd help you without thinking about it too much?"

Halpen shrugged. "It's good drink."

"Yes, and you've wasted it. You didn't need to go to all that trouble. Of course I'll help you, Hal. Would have even before you plied me with the contents of your flask."

Halpen shrugged. "Curse me if I'll ever understand you, Met."

Metten took another sip, humming in appreciation. "Goddess, this is good. – Halpen, I'll give you all the aid I can, anytime you need it, to get out of here. I won't sit by and watch anyone become Mage Herrein's next victim. Least of all one of my friends."

"Your priest won't like it."

Metten sat forward and rested his elbows on his knees. "Yes, I know it."

"Well, then. I should get out of here as soon as possible. If I wait any longer, we'll be surrounded by Herrein's troops and probably demons, for all I know. Tonight's the night."

"Have you spoken with Rall?"

Halpen stared at him. "What about? He'll do as he's told."

"He's been out and about more than either of us. He knows things you'll need to know."

"I'll tell the man we want to go and when, and he'll steal some horses and have them where I tell him to. We'll get past the guards somehow – there's no moon tonight, is there? – and find Rall, mount up and go. I'm thinking we'll parallel the Wall westward to the sea and try to buy passage away from there."

"I'm not going with you."

"Then you're a deluded fool, if you don't mind me saying so."

"How could I mind that?" Metten laughed. "So go talk to Rall. I'll wait for you and help you out."

* * *

Rall came and went, frowning in disapproval. Halpen fumed and tried to pace in the cramped tent until Metten lost his patience and swore at him.

After a while Metten turned the lamp down to a bare tongue of flame. Rall made another appearance, this time to whisper specifics about the plan, and left again. Halpen stuffed his few belongings back into his pack, including the flask that sloshed with the remaining sip or two of *aum*.

When Halpen heard the low mutter of voices outside the tent, he knew it was time. The guard was changing. He sat through the exchange of greetings and information, waited until one set of foot-steps led away, and nudged Metten.

Metten set his shoulders as if he were going into battle and stooped under the tent flap. He started complaining as soon as he was outside. "I need to see the Commander. Now."

"Lord Metten?" The guard sounded confused. "What's wrong? Can't it wait until the morning?"

"In the morning we'll be marching again, and she'll have no time for me. I demand to see her. Show me where her tent is!" Metten's voice was coming from a different direction, moving away from their tent.

"But, sir -- "

"Didn't you hear me the first time? I meant now!"

Halpen grimaced, because the whole thing was so unlike his friend, then poked his head out of the tent.

Metten stood in the mid distance, head turned back over his shoulder to talk to the guard. The guardsman himself stood, attention fully on Metten. Halpen seized the moment and ducked outside, his pack almost catching on the tent frame before pulling free. He bent low and slipped behind the cluster of tents, raised his head to make sure there were no Ull-fasten guardsmen in the vicinity, and found himself staring straight into the Seeker's penetrating eyes.

Shit. Of course it would have to be her. Halpen straightened up and began to speak in an ordinary voice, sure his plan had been foiled.

Jaena shook her head, a quick warning, and raised her finger to her lips to quiet him. She moved aside to let him pass.

His jaw dropped. Unbelieving, he edged past her. Past his shock he still heard Metten complaining, and the guard's irritated voice ordering his friend back into their tent. Metten would not get to see the Commander this midnight, and they would sharpen their watch on the hostages. It didn't matter. Halpen had a chance to escape.

That hope lasted just until Halpen crept past the end of the tent cluster to see what he still had to face. It was hard to see, but there didn't seem to be an end to the bedrolls that littered the ground. Some of them were occupied, and some were guarded by a man or woman who had remained wakeful. He was pretty sure there were at least three sentries between him and the tree line that marked the edge of the pasture where they'd camped. And it was dark – he'd known it was a moonless night, but never stopped to think how that would hinder him as well as the Ull-fasten guardsmen.

The Seeker was looking at him from her tent a few feet away. Her expression was almost impossible to read in the darkness. She began to hum, soft and husky.

Halpen started forward, wanting to stop the song that would wake the camp. Then he remembered Jaena's song on the way to Goddess-eyes, the soft crooning that shielded them from notice by Herrein's pursuing guards. The Seeker thought Imn-ashu had shielded them that day; Halpen had known better, *taylen* recognizing *taylen*.

He gave her a jerky nod that she might have been able to see in the darkness. Then he took the gift that was offered and threaded through the groups of bedrolls towards the edge of the camp.

The song faded behind him. He had no idea how it worked, if it would still work when the Seeker could no longer see him. He kept walking, quiet as he could but making no effort to crouch or hide. There was nowhere he could conceal himself if he were noticed.

Eventually the clusters of bedrolls thinned out. He smelled the horses off to his right, heard an occasional equine grunt. They would be well-guarded, so he stayed away. Jaena and her song were just a memory. Everything was still and dark, chilled with the night air.

He crouched, trying to minimize his profile. He inched forward, alert for the sentries he knew would be somewhere between here and the tree line.

"Hai, who's that?" A low, harsh challenge.

Halpen cursed to himself. He'd been found out. He peered around but saw no one. The trees loomed, somehow darker than the night. The wind died down, quelled by the near barrier of the woods.

"Hai, it's just me." A woman's voice. "Ginnither. Posted just west from you. Anything?"

Halpen's muscles quivered with tension. The sentries were close; he was surprised they couldn't hear his breathing.

"All's well."

They paced away from each other, grim and alert. No banter there. They were in enemy territory and knew Herrein's forces were near.

Halpen took a deep breath and crept onward. After a moment he threw dignity to the winds and dropped to his belly, inching past the perimeter line and the sentries who couldn't be that far away. He spared a thought for the state of his cloak, dragging through dirt and even horse droppings for all he knew. It would never be the same.

When he touched the bark of the first tree, he closed his eyes for a moment. He stood up and trudged on, surrounded by low-growing bushes, their leafless limbs scratching at his skin. Gnarled roots of larger trees reached across his path. He shouldered through the woods with one hand out before his face to avoid smacking into their trunks in the dark.

He hoped he was still going north, but it was too dark to tell. Rall was supposed to meet him somewhere around here, but Halpen had no idea how far he'd traveled, or even whether there might be sentries posted in the thickening woods.

The sky beyond the bare branches of the tallest trees was moonless. An occasional star glinted between heavy overcast. Some animal made a yowling noise, not too far away.

"My lord." The familiar whisper came from his left and slightly behind him.

"Thank the gods it's you." Halpen took a deep breath. "Where the hell are we? How far do we have to go to get to some horses?"

"No horses, my lord. We'll be walking for a spell."

Halpen shrugged out of his pack. "Here, take this, will you? The damned thing keeps catching on every twig."

Rall heaved the pack over his shoulders with his own. "This way, my lord. It'll be a bit of a walk to the road, I'm afraid."

"You lead the way." Halpen put a hand on Rall's shoulders so he wouldn't lose the man as he stumbled along behind him. His foot turned twice on an even bit of ground; he hoped he didn't end up with a sprained ankle out of all this.

"Stop," Halpen whispered. "Rall, I need some water."

Rall handed over a leather water bag. Halpen sucked at it and gagged; the warm water tasted of the sack it had been carried in. "Is this all?"

"It's all I had time to take, my lord."

Halpen gulped again. "It'll have to do. Lead on."

The trees began to thin out about the time the heavy overcast began to blow off to the east. As the clouds vanished, starlight gave some faint illumination. They walked until they saw a yellow light glowing in the distance – probably a lamp in a window, but after the hours of darkness it seemed almost a sun.

Halpen leaned up against a tree, resting his sore feet in their expensive boots, as Rall crept forward to investigate. He looked up at the clearing sky, trying to identify the few constellations he'd learned in school. The Wheel shone almost blue-white against the black velvet. The Daughters sat spinning beside the Wheel, he remembered that much – but Halpen had no idea which direction they pointed, if any at all. He heaved a disgruntled breath and waited for Rall. After a few minutes he dug out the little flask and finished his *aum*. There was no point in denying himself that much comfort.

Rall seemed to be gone a very long time. Curse the man, didn't he know Halpen was freezing and needed a warm fire or at least some shelter?

"Hold!"

Halpen jumped and swore. He turned to see three men and a woman approaching from his flank, the woman with a crossbow aimed in his direction.

"Stay where you are!"

Halpen held his hands out from his body. "I'm unarmed!"

Then the intruders were close around him, along with a strong smell of unwashed bodies.

Halpen wrinkled his nose. "Where's my man?"

"Wim, Sorab, you go look for this man." The one in the moss-green cloak waved, and the other two men nodded and jogged away. One went back into the forest, the other headed towards the source of the yellow light.

The woman kept the crossbow aimed at Halpen's heart. Her hair was put up in a messy knot, out of the way of her aim. She looked deadly.

"What's someone like you doin' out here?" Green-cloak asked.

"Do you know where I can find horses and supplies?" Halpen asked. "I've no money now, but I can repay you well when I get back to the capital. You both look as if you could use a few silvers."

"Do we now?" The man circled Halpen, looking him up and down with a glint in his eye.

Halpen was acutely aware of the smears of dirt on his cloak and the detritus that had caught in his hair during the half-blind hike through the woods. "I may not look it, but I can pay. Later, when I'm back in --"

"Sure, back in th' city." The man smirked. "Ya got anyone else with ya but this man of yours?"

Halpen started to answer, then closed his mouth. Would it be better to say he had others with him? Or would that make him more of a threat, and therefore more likely to be killed by Crossbow-woman? He stared mutely at Green-cloak, undecided.

"Looks to me like yer escapin' from that army," Green-cloak said. "Question is, which one."

"He's a nobleman." Crossbow-woman spat in the grass. "Seems to me either side would pay."

"I see." Halpen understood this motivation very well. "You're unwilling to wait for your ransom. I can tell you that neither one of these armed forces cares enough about me to pay even a stale loaf for me. If you would only have the strength of character to wait a while, you could earn a year's living."

Something scuffled in the brush. A moment later Rall was flung into the clearing. He struck the ground hard. His head snapped back, and he lay still. The bandit behind him dropped one pack to the ground and began rifling through the other.

"Hey! That's mine."

"Not any more. What's he got, Sorab?" Green-cloak turned to watch as his companion sorted through Halpen's belongings.

Sorab tossed Halpen's spare tunic and breeches to the ground. He pulled out the little pouch of tooth powder and smelled it before flinging it into the woods. Then the man pulled out a tied sheaf of papers: letters from Lord de Morn and from his bank, guaranteeing safe passage and support.

He passed the papers to Green-cloak, who began to scan them, holding them close to his unshaven face.

Halpen cursed to himself. It appeared the scum could read.

The other man – Wim? – let out a shout of triumph. He held Rall's pack in one hand, and a leather pouch in the other. He shook it, and it jingled.

Crossbow-woman grinned. "Coin!"

That was all Halpen's money, sufficient for what he'd thought would be a fast ride to Ull-fasten followed by money for lodging according to his station, and expenses until he could use his credit at the foreign merchants and banks. He watched as Wim opened the pouch and looked in.

The man's eyes rounded as he saw the coins in the pouch. "Silver!"

Green-cloak's eyes narrowed. "Who are you?"

"Look, there's more where that came from if you get me back to the city."

"Yeah, the city, the city. Who's to say we wouldn't be taken 'n imprisoned as soon as we set foot in the place? Yer clearly somebody." Green-cloak's gaze settled a little below Halpen's collarbone. Halpen looked down and saw the brooch his father had given him, emblazoned with the family's emblem.

Crossbow-woman said, "If he's a Cassahni noble, we should offer him to Herrein's army. They'll pay ransom. These other people – the mages – they won't give a used chamber pot for him."

Green-cloak held out his hand, and Wim dropped the coin pouch into it.

"No, no! I told you, they don't care about me. I'm – I'm not as valuable as you think." Halpen looked around at the four bandits, and at Rall still lying unconscious on the ground. He cursed to himself. No help from that quarter.

Sorab grinned. "He don' want to go back to Herrein's army, so I say that's the ones who want *him*."

Green-cloak nodded. He walked up into Halpen's space. Halpen stared into his narrowed eyes and felt the tug as Green-cloak ripped the brooch from his cloak.

"Bring him."

Green-cloak walked off toward the yellow light, which faded into insignificance as dawn touched the world.

Wim circled behind Halpen and gave him a push. "Ya run and yer shot," he growled.

Footsteps crunched in the dried leaves behind him. It seemed Sorab and Crossbow-woman were both following. He spun around, searching. "Where's my man?"

"Shut up and move," Wim said. "He's no good to us."

"But I need him! Look, I'll pay. When I get back to the -- "

Green-cloak spun and grabbed his cloak. "It's time ya shut up, me lord. There's not going to be no city for ya. And ya may as well forget yer man. He's worth nothing to us."

Something hard pushed into his back, sharp through the layers of cloth. A knife. Halpen closed his mouth. It was clearly every man for himself. He hoped Rall wasn't dead.

After a short walk they approached a rundown hut. The sagging door creaked open and they entered a room that seemed to have been abandoned for some time. Cold ashes spilled out of a hearth along with an overturned pail filled with what looked like an old birds' nest. Spider webs hung in each corner. Muddy tracks stained the center of the floor, telling Halpen that some animal had gotten in here since the inhabitants had fled, probably seeking food.

One corner of the place had been swept, and packs and blankets were piled there. A lamp sat on the windowsill. Its flame was low, but would have seemed a beacon to anyone outside on a moonless, over-cast night.

Halpen swore to himself. They had fallen into the trap.

"Down," Crossbow-woman said. Halpen sat on the filthy floor. The planks felt like iron to his backside. The woman bound his hands, her fingers deft and sure. Then she came around in front of him and frowned before kneeling to bind his ankles as well.

Halpen made a noise of protest, deep in his throat.

She smirked. "Don't worry. If ya have to piss, speak up. We're not monsters."

She unwrapped his cloak from around his shoulders, threw it over him and left.

Halpen heard them talking outside. They were making plans for turning him over to Herrein. The bonds were too tight around his wrists, he was covered in dirt, and his throat hurt. His coin was gone, and the precious letters intended to introduce him to the nobles of other lands and cushion his progress there were in the possession of fools who would turn them over to Herrein.

He was alone, without help from friend or servant. He had not even the most basic comfort that was suited to someone of his station. Perhaps those thieves were used to these conditions, but Lord Halpen de Morn was not.

He would shout out to them. He would make a few demands and tell them who his father was. Perhaps they would see the advantage of helping him back to Iryor.

But the voices faded away.

A long time passed. No one came to give him food or water. In spite of Crossbow-woman's words, no one came when he yelled that he needed the pisser. Between the pain of his bindings, his thirst and his screaming bladder, he was miserable. He slumped against the wall.

When he heard voices again, he shouted. "Hai! Somebody come in here!"

Crossbow-woman appeared in the doorway. Behind her, Sorab and Green-cloak lugged in bags that clanked when dropped on the floor. Someone's silver perhaps, stolen from one of the refugees fleeing the developing confrontation at Saarnen Pass.

"Wait!" Halpen said. "Don't leave! Look, I need the pisser, the sooner the better. And water."

Green-cloak jerked his head at Sorab. The big man crouched to unbind Halpen's feet and hands. "No runnin', now," he growled.

Pins and needles burned through Halpen's legs. He limped away, following Sorab to a shallow hole behind a clump of trees. At least there was no sign of rashweed around it. Sorab gave him a few strides of privacy, more than Halpen expected. When he was done he felt somewhat human again.

He turned and spoke in a desperate low voice. "Turn your back for a minute and I'll vanish in these woods. You can say you thought you heard someone – maybe my man Rall, come to rescue me. I'll pay you. You can meet me in the city, at Winternight maybe, and I'll pay you, I swear it on my father's title. You won't even have to split it between your friends – it'll be all yours."

Sorab cocked his head. "Don' know why yer so scared to go back to yer own people."

The man was an idiot. "Just turn your back." He squeezed his eyes shut and forced himself to say the next word. "Please."

"Sure." Sorab turned in a casual way, his broad back to Halpen. "At Winternight now."

"I swear it." Halpen clutched his cloak tight around him and dodged behind the big tree. There was a tangle of brush there, then the welcoming dimness of the autumn forest. He clutched his cloak tight around him and began to run – then something slammed into his head above his ear and everything went black.

* * *

Everything hurt. From the throbbing knot above his right ear to the stabbing pain in his wrists, Halpen was in agony. He tried to move his arms but they were held fast – tied together in front of him, he realized as he awakened and the world came crashing in.

He kept his eyes closed for a moment. He was lying on something soft – definitely not the rough wood planks of the bandits' hut. A pleasant aroma filled the air – sharp-smelling herbs, the kind *cernen* steamed in a pot to help clear the lungs. People conversed nearby – women's voices, low and melodious.

Halpen opened his eyes to see a thin face hanging over him.

Mother Thara smiled. "You're awake."

He sat up, ignoring his aching muscles and the pounding in his head where Sorab must have struck him. "Where am I?"

Thara stood. Her robes fell loosely about her thin form. "You're with Mage Herrein, who has paid well for you."

Dread gripped him. "What's – what's going to happen?"

Thara gestured to two men wearing the badge of the mage's hospital. They lugged a tub of water that steamed into the autumn air. One held an armful of cloths. "Clean him up, and get some salve on those wounds so he lives long enough to be of use," Thara directed. "Then Herrein will see him."

"Tell my father I'm here!" Halpen blustered as Thara left the room.

In other circumstances, he would've accepted the ministrations of the attendants as his due. They were respectful as they unbound his hands and offered him herb-scented water to wash off the grime of his escape and captivity. One of the men combed the snarls out of Halpen's hair and re-tied it, and the other dressed his wounds. A boy scurried to the door and dropped off a clean shirt and cloak; the attendants made faces over his old clothing and handed it off to the boy. As the pain receded, a slow lassitude crept through him.

That lasted until the attendants bowed their way out of the room and a red-cloaked figure stepped in.

Herrein had aged since Halpen had last seen him, a couple of seasons ago. His face was lined and his mouth drooped at the corners with ill-temper or exhaustion. There were bare spots on his scalp between locks of gray hair. It looked as if he'd been pulling his hair out.

A look of triumph glinted in the man's eyes. "Good. I need every *taylenor* I can get."

"What are you going to do?"

"I never really took your *taylen* away, you know," Herrein said. "It's buried, and the key to it is hidden. *Here.*"

Halpen's eyes were fixed on the old man's hand. It stretched out towards Halpen's forehead, gnarled and veined and glowing with magery. Halpen shrank back. He wanted to run. He looked wildly around for some way to escape.

"There's nowhere to go." Herrein's fingers pinched air, then touched his forehead.

Halpen yelped. It felt as if the old mage reached inside, as if his own skin and bone softened to let him in. He shut his eyes, trying to hold still against the urge to flee. Something dark and blunt shoved at his consciousness, then retreated.

In its place grew a kernel of something familiar.

He remembered this feeling from his adolescent years. It hadn't lasted long; his parents were horrified when they understood what was going on. They'd bundled him off to Herrein to have every vestige of the *taylen* eradicated, so their son's life and status would never be at risk.

A bright seed opened up in him. Wide-eyed and shaking, he searched around the corners of his own mind. Something was different, as if he perceived something he had no words or concepts to describe, even to himself. A corner of his mind expanded with an almost physical pang. It felt as if a door had opened.

Out the door of the room and in the cold stone hallways which he now understood were part of a fortress, he felt others like him. Other *taylenor*.

No wonder Jaena had been so stunned when they'd entered Ull-fasten and she detected the presence of many *taylenor*. Their potential made itself known to him, drifting through the building like a layer of mist. It even prickled against his skin.

"You are at Spar," Herrein said, naming the ruined fortress that guarded the blocked Saarnen Pass. "Now that you are able to, you'll help in the fight against the Eastern Mage."

"I don't have any magery."

"There is no need for you to have any training in magery." Herrein limped to the door. "I have hundreds of years of experience. All I need is -- "

"Fuel," Halpen spat.

"If you choose to call it that. You and the other *taylenor* will help to beat back the Eastern forces that are ready to pour through the Saarnen Pass."

"That's your job. Mage Defender, isn't it?"

Herrein's lips stretched. The mage looked his years, which Halpen thought was saying something. The old man should have been dead more than a hundred years ago.

Herrein spoke a sharp order, and two liveried guards stepped into the room. "Bring him."

"What, now?" Fear shot through his veins. "No, no. I have to eat, get rested. Can I send a message to -- "

"In the east tower, by dusk. They'll send demons again tonight, I think."

"Yes, my lord!" the senior guard snapped.

"But I can't help if I'm hungry! And thirsty! I've spent all day crawling through the weeds or tied up. I can't -- "

"Bring food and drink." Herrein turned and limped out the door.

Halpen yelled, "I know where your priest is!"

The shout echoed between the stone walls. It resonated in his own ears. There was no going back from what he'd just offered the half-mad old mage. He thought of Metten, who'd helped him escape the Ull-fasten army, then pushed the thought of his old friend away. He didn't dare think of how Jaena had hidden him from the guards.

Herrein edged back through the door. His eyes lost their exhausted look and were avid. "You refer to the Seeker."

"I'll tell you where she is. I'll even help you get her. Anything. Just let me go."

The mage's eyes narrowed. "You lie. The Seeker is long gone, across the border among those *drathen*."

The vulgarity shocked him. Nothing was as it had seemed, when the venerated Mage Defender spouted rude words and pulled his hair out in his insanity, and threatened to kill a noble of the land. "No, I do know where she is. I saw her last night."

The mage drew closer, until Halpen smelled body odor and exhaustion. He wondered, frantically, how long the old man had been using his magery, and whether he was sane enough to understand.

Herrein looked down at him as if he could seek out the truth. "And how will you deliver her to me?"

"I'll tell you exactly how to get to her. I'll tell you where the sentries are. Her lover, Metten de Rell – he's with her, I'll tell you how to overcome him. Just spare me." He quailed inside at the thought of what he was doing to Metten. But his own life was in danger here – nothing else could be allowed to matter.

Herrein waved at the guards. "Commander Argen! This man will tell you everything you want to know about how to find and capture the Seeker. Make sure he's telling the truth. If anything he says proves untrue, he'll die harder even than he imagined."

CHAPTER EIGHTEEN

They began to run across breakdowns from Herrein's army. A wagon with a broken wheel sagged on its corner in the middle of the trail. Ahead lay a dead horse, soaked with blood from a slashed jugular vein – most likely put down because it was sick or lame. A skittish set of runaway packhorses ran along the ridge still carrying drooping saddlebags. These were valuable animals, but Herrein must have given orders to leave them behind as he rushed to the Saarnen Pass.

Jaena trudged beside Metten up the ridge trail. There were few trees here, just brush and brown grasses. Water was not as plentiful, a fact that had to be built into the timing of their rest stops. The stream of refugees ceased. There were no villages so close to the feared Saarnen Pass. Only the footprints of Herrein's army marked the trail before them.

Returning from the central cookfire holding her bread and tea, Jaena heard a donkey's bray.

Unbelieving, she stopped. The Ull-fasten army had horses and some mules, but that was clearly a donkey's bray – and it had a familiar hiccup she thought she recognized.

She spun around and headed toward the rear, where the pack animals were cared for.

"Priest?" A stocky groom stood up when she approached. The woman's bread and cheese slid off her lap to the ground. "Do ya need something? Are ya lost?"

"Did I hear a donkey?"

The groom grinned. "Ya, we picked two of them up today from Herrein's trail. Two jennets, both perfectly healthy and ornery as spit, if ya don't mind me sayin so."

"Really! Not injured or sick?"

"Nope. My guess is these two pitched some kinda fit and wouldn't go. So they got left. Lucky the bastards didn't kill 'em so we couldn't use 'em, is what I think."

"Someone in Herrein's force cares about animals. Where are they?"

"I'll show ya." The groom waved in the general direction of the supply wagons.

"Sorry about your lunch. I have bread and tea here if you'd like to have it."

"No thanks Priest. Look, here are yer donkeys."

Two donkeys munched from feedbags amid the other pack animals. Jaena gave a cry of delight to see Ears' familiar face with its white splash. The jennet pointed her ears at Jaena and hawed in welcome.

"No doubt that's yer donkey," the groom said. "Where'd ya lose her?"

"I had to leave her in the Temple stables – there was no way to get her out in time." Jaena stroked Ears' neck.

Ears bumped up against Jaena and nuzzled her. She nudged Jaena's arm. The tea slopped over the rim of the wooden mug.

"I'll stay with her a bit, if you don't mind," Jaena told the groom.

"We'll be headin' out again soon. This one'll have to stay with the pack train, but you can visit her when we're in camp. What's her real name, then?"

"Her name is Ears," Jaena said. "Thank you for taking care of her."

The donkey lipped some straw from the feedbag and gave Jaena a friendly shove. The groom grinned.

Jaena returned to the cookfire with a smile on her face.

People watched her as she went. Her smile was unusual; no one was feeling very cheerful lately, chasing the Mage Defender of Cassahn and his army in what could be a battle to their deaths, with dust and grit around them and possible demons just around every bend.

Metten took one look at her and broke out into a grin. "What happened?"

"Ears is here," she said. "Herrein was using her as a pack animal, but she must have refused to go fast enough. So they left her, and now she's here."

"And pretty safe – at least as safe as any of us is," Metten said. "She won't be in the fight."

"I'm glad of that." She took another cup of tea and sipped it slowly. It warmed her throat, and the grassy fragrance soothed her. For just that brief moment, everything seemed fine.

* * *

Spar Fortress perched above the Saarnen Pass like a bird of prey.

It glared down into the fall of tumbled boulders that had until recently blocked the pass, a brooding sentry waiting for the invasion from the East. The ancients who defeated the Eastern Mage had closed Saarnen hundreds of years ago, but the destruction of Mount Nimn had reopened it.

Now, anything could get through.

The Ull-fasten army stopped midday while Sri sent out patrols. Jaena waited with Metten by the side of the ancient broken road, with the boot prints of Herrein's army leading around the curve ahead of them. They were temporarily hidden from any sentries at Spar, but Jaena knew Herrein was well aware he was being pursued.

The guardsman Ael set a saddle blanket out on the roadside for her to sit on. It was the first sign that his temper might be thawing a little; he'd been angry ever since she and Metten had helped Halpen escape the camp.

"Thank you," she said.

Metten eased down onto the blanket beside Jaena. His elbows nudged her ribs, but she made room for him.

"Thank you, Ael. It's been a long, dusty walk." Metten smiled as if he hadn't noticed Ael's frown.

The guardsman didn't smile back. "Why'd you help him?" he asked.

"Had to." Metten nudged closer to Jaena. "He's *taylenor*, you know. Fodder for Herrein."

"I couldn't allow him to be traded to Herrein," Jaena said. "I won't send anyone else to die like that."

"You'll notice we didn't go with him," Metten added. His smile left his face, and he gave the guardsman a level look. "I assume you took note of that."

"I did that." The set of Ael's shoulders softened. "D'ya want some water before we move on?"

They sipped the leather-tasting water Ael brought them and watched one of the patrols come back around the curve ahead. A scout climbed over the rocks that separated this section of the old road from the cliff, and dropped to his feet almost in Jaena's lap. He gave them a grim nod and stalked off to report to Sri.

"I don't know that there's any way to attack that place," Metten said. "Of course, we do have mages." He looked doubtful.

Jaena's heart thumped. They must find a way to get in. Wiel was in there, presumably with the mages Herrein had abducted from Ull-fasten.

Sri called for Jaena as the day crawled on past noon. The Commander sat on a bench that her people had set up for her. Road dust dulled her steel-gray hair. Her second, Hashu, stood beside her. He was an older man striped with battle-scars on his dark cheekbones. His face was as hard as granite.

"Herrein's in there," Sri said. "No knowing for sure, but all the *taylenor* are probably in there with him."

"Wiel?" Jaena said.

"All of them." Sri's mouth set in a grim line. "We were too late to stop him. Now he's inside a fortress."

"Can we get in?"

"Not without losses I'm not prepared to incur right now. That's why I've called for you. Herrein has sent a messenger. He knows you're here."

A chill swept through her. "I guess we know what happened to Lord Halpen, then."

"He was probably captured before he even got to the main road. No telling if he's still alive." Sri frowned and looked away from Jaena, down the road at the army waiting for her orders. "I've more bad news. Apparently Herrein holds Lord Metten's brother."

Jaena hadn't known Metten had a brother. "I'll tell him."

Sri nodded. "No threats were made against the boy. But the situation isn't good. We're working on a plan, but a frontal assault won't work against that fortress."

Jaena knew what Sri was about to say before the other woman opened her mouth. She spoke up: "I'll go."

Sri nodded, shoulders set under the mail. "I regret it."

"I've always been willing to offer myself in exchange. That's why I came with you in the first place. If that's the only way to do it, then … there it is. How many of the *taylenor* will he exchange for me?"

"We'll take any we can. But we won't give up quite so easily, Priest. Let me explain our plan." Sri waved her second forward. "Hashu has a plan to cut them off during the exchange."

Jaena thought about where the fortress stood on its tabletop of land. It stood beside the Saarnen Pass, guarding it from above. It was almost as inaccessible from its own country of Cassahn; the only access that Jaena knew of was the drawbridge across the mage-cut gorge that sliced through the road they waited on. Without cooperation from inside Spar, she saw no way of getting in.

"Herrein's people will demand to come across the drawbridge onto the end of our road to make the exchange," Hashu explained. "That way there's no risk of us finding a way in while their attention's distracted. But we can still make an attempt on the place to get you out of this, Priest."

Jaena shook her head. "How?"

"We send a unit to scale the rock," Hashu said. "It will be tricky, but I think the rockfall left over from the destruction of the mountain provides a path under Spar that was never there before. Our mages can enhance it, as long as we make sure Herrein doesn't detect the use of *taylen*."

Jaena remembered the scout climbing over the rocks, moving with grace and precision as he dropped onto the road.

"You'll rescue me?" That thought had not occurred to her as she planned her own exchange for the boy she'd unwittingly delivered into Herrein's hands.

"If we can." Sri emphasized the last word. "We'd prefer not to leave any *taylenor* in Herrein's hands. But there are no certainties, Priest."

"No, of course not." Jaena felt a little stunned. "Thank you."

Sri continued. "While we're making the exchange, Hashu's climbers will already be on their way. We'll signal --"

"Not you, Commander." Hashu's voice held a note of weariness, as if he'd said this many times before.

"No more of that, Hashu. I won't wait in safety while my people risk their lives." The man opened his mouth again and Sri held up her hand, forestalling him. "No more, I said."

Hashu's chin went up, but he held his tongue.

An hour later, with plans muddling around in her head and the unfamiliar weight of a borrowed dagger in a sheath under her arm, Jaena returned to talk to Metten.

Ael shadowed her, tense with watchfulness. Maybe he thought she would try to run away. She waved him away as she sat on the blanket next to Metten, but he stayed close.

Metten reclined on his elbows, staring out at the military preparations in a deceptively relaxed manner. His foot tapped. "Well?"

"Bad news I'm afraid, my love. It seems Lord Halpen was captured and gave our presence away. And Herrein has your brother in the fortress."

He sat up fast. "What?"

"Your brother? Sri says Herrein's holding him safe for now."

"How in the hells did he get his hands on Faran?" Metten jumped to his feet. "He's still at school! How could that bastard get his hands on him?"

"And I wonder why," Jaena said, watching Metten closely.

"Who knows? The man's a monster. I don't understand it." Metten took a few short, sharp steps away, then back, as if he wanted to do something *now* and couldn't figure out what.

"Herrein has sent a messenger under a white flag. He's offering an exchange."

He was silent for a moment. "You agreed?"

"Yes. There's a plan." She went over it with him, everything Sri had explained to her, about what the Ull-fasten army was going to do during the exchange.

When she finished, he nodded. "I'm going, too."

Tears threatened to escape her control. She cleared her throat. "Thank you."

His eyebrows went up. "I thought you'd object."

"Oh, I do." She smiled, eyes still watering. "Thank you anyway."

"Is the Commander going to try to stop me?"

"I don't think so."

"Are you?"

She shook her head.

"Well, then." He grinned at her. "How soon can we get started?"

She took a deep breath and quelled her emotion. Sri's plan might fail; they could die during this action. Something could go wrong with the hostage exchange. She wished she could keep Metten from accompanying her on what was likely to be a doomed operation; but she knew there was no way to keep him safe short of asking Sri to keep him under guard. She would not be responsible for humiliating him that way.

And he would be a comfort. She couldn't deny herself that.

* * *

They rounded the bend before the last approach to the fortress. Herrein's representatives were already in place.

A drawbridge spanned the narrow gorge from the end of the approach road to the edge of the tabletop plateau Spar occupied. The bridge looked strong enough to bear the weight of a loaded wagon and four horses.

Herrein's guardsmen had already crossed and were stationed on the end of the approach road, guarding access to the bridge. There was no cover here for the Ull-fasten army.

On Herrein's side, the crumbling fortress at the end of the bridge could have concealed a hundred guards. Armed men flanked the fortress entrance. The portcullis was up and the huge wooden door was open. Pale faces peered out of the interior. Jaena squinted into the dimness, trying to identify Wiel.

Two emissaries stepped off the bridge onto the approach road, their hands held open in front of them. Sri's second in command and Mage Othane, the Ull-fasten representatives, went forward to meet them. The facing armies stood still, autumn sunlight reflecting from swords and mail on both sides.

"Where's Herrein?" Metten asked.

"No doubt he listened to counsel and stayed inside." Commander Sri's mouth stretched in a predatory smile. "Wise counsel indeed."

The emissaries concluded their arrangements and withdrew, each to his own side. Hashu and Othane looked in Jaena's direction. Hashu nodded at Commander Sri. All of their terms for the exchange – who would be exchanged for whom, what representatives of each party would be present, and so on – were as they'd agreed with Herrein's side in earlier parleys.

"It's time," Sri said. "Goddess be with you both."

"We'll need her," Metten said.

Jaena reached for Imn-ashu's presence. She hummed a soft prayer, an echo of the eternal song from the Temple. There was no response, but Jaena felt strengthened nonetheless. Imn-ashu would help her right the wrong Jaena had done when she took Wiel from his family. As for the wrongs Herrein and the mothers had done – she shook her head, putting that resolutely out of her mind. One thing at a time.

Jaena and Metten began walking, accompanied by Sri and four

guardsmen. The dagger bumped against Jaena's side, awkward in spite of its carefully disguised underarm sheath. She thought about Hashu's climbers lying in wait in the rocks below Spar. She fought the urge to look down and try to see them. They were to attempt the fortress from beneath while the exchange was going on.

On the other side of the gorge, the knot of people waiting at the door of Spar Fortress emerged into the chill light, blinking. Four guardsmen advanced before them, wary of any variation from the agreed-upon plan of exchange.

"Bowmen," Metten hissed.

Jaena glanced upward to see the bristle of arrows poking out from arrow slits in the upper floors of Spar Fortress. Meanwhile she could almost feel the dozens of swords at her back from her own guardsmen, and the restrained *taylen* of the mages.

"Ignore them," Sri muttered.

Women in belted robes carried a stretcher across the bridge. One of them looked like Mother Rhody, her strong arms, reddened from work, supporting the end of the stretcher. The one they carried was familiar, with shiny, dark hair and a pale face.

"That's Wiel," Jaena said. Her heart stuttered. He wasn't moving.

"I see another of our *taylenor*," Sri said. "Damn it. He said there would be three."

"Don't stop the exchange," Jaena begged. "I need to get Wiel out of there."

"There's no stopping it now, Priest."

The cluster of Herrein's guardsmen and the stretcher-bearing mothers stopped. Ahead of them in a tense semicircle stood more armed Cassahni. The short, bearded man at the apex of the semicircle was Herrein's representative, a Commander Argen. Metten made a noise at the back of his throat, his eyes fixed on the man; apparently he recognized him.

Othane and Hashu withdrew, dropping behind the front line of their own guardsmen.

"Let's go," Sri ordered.

Jaena stepped forward. Metten and Sri were a solid presence next to her, the hyper-vigilant Ull-fasten unit looming behind. The dust of the road slipped under her boots and the chilly sun shone down, giving no warmth. Her eyes were fixed on the still form on the stretcher.

They came within reach of the Cassahni contingent.

"Here are the priest and the Cassahni lord, as promised," Sri said to Herrein's representative. "Give us our *taylenor*."

A Cassahni guardswoman stepped forward to take Jaena's arm, drawing her away from Sri. Jaena cast a quick look down at the stretcher, trying to see that Wiel was alive before he was taken to safety. His eyes were closed, and his face was turned away, and there was too much happening for her to see if his chest rose and fell.

Another person – a *taylenor*, she could feel it – stumbled forward as if pushed into the ranks of Sri's people. The other hostage.

Hands reached out to take the stretcher from the mothers and carry it to safety. Jaena stepped toward Spar, toward the fate she'd traded for.

The mothers stepped away, suddenly holding nothing. The stretcher bumped, yanked away from friendly hands. Herrein's guardsmen pulled the stretcher back, back, toward the bridge – armed men, hurrying Wiel back into the fortress.

A howl of rage went up from the Ull-fasten ranks. Swords clashed. A strange Cassahni guard grabbed Jaena around her waist and lifted her up, over a fallen guard with blood-soaked hair. Her captor carried her toward the bridge and the yawning door of the fortress.

"Jaena!" Metten shouted.

Blue light flared, along with a crackle of violent energy. Battle magery, from which side Jaena couldn't tell. She kicked out, striking nothing but air. She flung all of her weight against her captor's arm, and fell hard onto her knees on the rocky apron just before the bridge.

The warrior lifted her again. His mailed arm crushed the breath out of her. She struggled against his chest, kicking backwards. She struck upward, aiming for the man's neck and chin, but he seemed to be encased in leather and steel. Her blows had no effect but to send pain arcing through her own hands.

Something nearby was on fire. Smoke obscured her view. All she could see was the black open door to Spar Fortress.

A hard shape bumped against her side; it was the dagger Sri had insisted she carry, that she had forgotten as Herrein's man had clamped her arm to her side and carried her. She fumbled for it, fingers tangling in the cloth of her tunic.

Her captor tripped on something and fell forward. She slammed the blade upward. It found the gap in his mail and slid into the flesh. Blood spurted from the man's neck. Jaena rolled away, tried to keep rolling but slammed up against the lip of the bridge. Empty air opened under her gaze as she stared down into the gorge. Panic gripped her.

She had killed a man. *Imn-ashu, forgive me.*

"To me!" The voice was hoarse with smoke and fury; it took Jaena a moment to realize it was Commander Sri.

Jaena scrambled away from the edge and climbed over the motionless form of the warrior who had been carrying her. Her feet slid in the pool of blood around him. Her stomach roiled. She stumbled back toward the road, searching for Metten's black curls in the melee.

"Metten!"

There was no reply. Fear rushed through her. All around her was steel and mail and dust and blood, and no sign of Metten anywhere. After a moment she distinguished Commander Sri's steel-gray hair and forced her way toward her.

Sri was bareheaded, her helm lost somewhere. She and one of her guards were besieged by three of Herrein's men, striking in all directions. As Jaena watched, one of the attackers won through Sri's guard. The man brought his sword down hard.

Sri ducked, but the blow struck true. It cleaved through the top of her head and down through her face and neck. Blood spurted horribly as the commander's lifeless body fell.

Jaena screamed and turned aside. Sound crashed against her: the roar and crackle of magery, the clang of blades, and shouts. A Cassahni guard charged at her. Without thought she threw herself low and struck out with the dagger. The blade sliced through leather into the meat of the woman's calf. Jaena looked around for a place to run, looked for Metten, but she could see nothing familiar.

Something pulled at her leg, hard. Whatever it was, it dragged her away from the center of the melee.

She kicked out, trying to roll up and strike out with the bloody dagger she still clutched. She was pulled as if being dragged by a horse, dirt and stone abrading her palms as she tried to slow her progress.

She looked down at whatever was dragging her away and saw nothing at all.

Goddess aid me! Jaena squirmed against the ground, trying for purchase against something that wasn't there. The fight flew by her. Ull-fasten guardsmen grabbed for her, hands slamming into a crystal wall of shield that had not been there a second before.

With a last burst of energy she dug her heels in, hard. They dragged against the dry stone to no avail. The battle vanished above her as she fell into scrubby gray-green bushes and blue sky.

CHAPTER NINETEEN

"Let me out!"

Jaena peered through the opening in the wooden door. It was wide enough for a guard to check on her, wide enough for her to put her hands through up to her forearms. It looked out onto a narrow street and crooked steps leading up to a hut across the way. The hut's roof was hung with bright banners that fluttered in the chill air.

Jaena shivered as she drew her arms back inside.

The room itself was tiny, with a bench along one wall and a chamber pot covered in one corner. The quilt that had been thrown over her when she awakened was now crumpled up on the bench.

The room she was in had the feel of a living area. There was a mark on the wall where a picture had been hung, and a rag rug on the floor. There was a door in the wall behind the bench, but it was barred from the other side. This place had been converted into a cell to hold prisoners; maybe just to hold Jaena.

Her head ached, and she seemed to have lost time. Maybe she'd struck her head when she'd fallen off the cliff. She wondered who had caught her.

There were voices outside the walls. Jaena shouted out again.

A moment later the door swung wide. The young man who stood outside glowered at her. "Come. She wants you."

Jaena stepped out the door and pulled her cloak tighter against a wind so cold it seemed to have teeth. A barrier of snow-covered peaks towered into the sky. "Where am I?"

"She'll tell you." The man didn't seem much concerned with guarding her. He walked beside her, apparently weaponless – though he could have concealed almost anything behind his impressive beard.

They passed two tiny houses down the rutted street and began to climb steps carved into rock. There were only a few. The steps ended in a jumble of debris and crumbled stone.

A dirt path branched off this one to the north, clinging close to the almost-vertical cliff face that formed the mountainside. In the other direction, a wider path, scuffed with the prints of people and horses, led past jumbled rocks so sharp they looked to be newly-fallen. This wider trail was guarded by men in mail and quilted coats, one of them mounted on a stocky mountain horse. A rope-bound torch stood jammed into a makeshift iron bracket in the ground, burning even though it was daylight.

A boulder the size of a small hill blocked the segment of path directly ahead of them. Black-bristled demon heads on pikes glared at Jaena with the red gone out of their eyes. The rock below the heads was pocked as if from acid from the draining of the severed heads.

Jaena looked up and up, reorienting herself. The side of the mountain broke apart into air above them.

This must be Mount Nimn.

Fear shivered through her. Legend said this was the stronghold of the Eastern Mage. She'd seen the top blow off this peak a few days ago, black smoke like a banner streaming into the heavens. The wide, guarded path must lead down into the now-open Saarnen Pass and from there into Cassahn.

Her escort led the way around the fallen boulders into the remains of a huge cavern, now open to the sky.

There were others there – women and men in quilted wraps. The men were all bearded, and the women's chins dipped into bright scarves around their necks. They nodded at her. She nodded back, more confused than ever.

The woman who stood near the cavern wall had dark red hair that swung in two thick braids down to her waist. She wore black breeches and a mail shirt, glittering over the same quilted coat the others wore. A sword hung sheathed at her side.

A necklace of teeth dripped from her shoulders. They were fangs, tipped in black and red. As the woman turned toward her, Jaena saw the spikes of a demon's coat and realized this woman wore a fur made out of the skins of demons. She had no idea how anyone would obtain such a thing from demons who, as far as she knew, could only be killed by fire – or why anyone would want to wear such an obscene decoration.

The woman's eyes swept over her. "Imn-ashu's priest."

"Yes."

"I am Ark-amne. I will outfit you with supplies and a guide. Go where you will, as long as it's east or north from here, away from the battle."

"But I have to go back. Was it you who took me from Spar Fortress?"

Ark-amne nodded. "You would have come to a quick end there."

"I don't understand. I don't even know you." Jaena felt lost, and not a little intimidated.

Jaena looked around at the men and women who watched. For the first time she noticed that many were scarred or wounded. One woman, silver-haired and plump-cheeked like a grandmother, held her arm in a quilted sling. Beside her, a man leaned on a crutch. The teenager next to him was missing an eye. A red keloid scar wrapped around his neck.

"You don't have to know me. I saved you for my sister's uses. Go back with Mkot, he will show you the way between the mountains. The nearest town is several days' travel east, and there's a Temple of Imn-ashu there."

"May I speak to you alone, if you don't mind?"

The crowd murmured in disapproval at this request. Mkot, the young man who had escorted her here, growled at her under his breath. Jaena turned, startled at this response.

Fire sparked in Ark-amne's eyes. Jaena took a step back.

"I will grant you the honor," Ark-amne said. "For my sister's sake."

The crowd filtered away out the entrance to the cavern. Even Mkot left her; Jaena wondered at that, since it left the red-braided woman without a guard.

When she and Ark-amne were alone in the echoing space, Jaena said: "Thank you. But I'm afraid I don't understand at all."

"And it is my task to enlighten you?"

Jaena felt ashamed, as if she asked something she had no right to. "Thank you for your care for me. But I didn't wish to be saved."

"I saved you for Imn-ashu. You are special to her. Because of that, I intervened where I usually do not."

Jaena's knees shook. "Imn-ashu, your sister?"

Fire licked around the woman's face and struck sparks from her sword and mail. "You don't know me."

"No. I'm sorry."

"It's irrelevant. You grew in ignorance, under the tutelage of that monster Herrein. Against all my sister's usual creeds, she cares for you. Take this gift and go – it won't be offered again."

"I – I thank you. But I can't go. There's someone in Spar Fortress I have to save. I put him there, and now I need to get him out. It was a sin I want to atone for. If you won't help me get back, maybe blessed Imn-ashu will."

"You, her priest, believe she will intervene? You'll have to do without her. She will comfort, she will take your soul at the end, but she won't show herself in the world. I am the only one who does that, even after the half millennium I've been smothered in sleep beneath this mountain." Lightning arced from the red-haired woman, tinged red like blood.

This was the Eastern Mage. Jaena's heart pounded. Imn-ashu's sister was the Eastern Mage. Not peaceful at all, this woman, but full of fire and war, as far opposed from Imn-ashu's music as possible. Legends said she came with the demons, following their death and destruction into Cassahn. But demon's heads adorned her hall, and she wore their teeth around her neck.

She smelled the soft aroma of *hibon*, felt warmth behind her even in the chill of blasted Mount Nimn. *Imn-ashu.*

Ark-amne laughed. Her hair in its fiery braids seemed to twist and move of itself. "Sister, I see you."

Now, now Imn-ashu would speak. Jaena squeezed her eyes shut, praying for that and afraid of it all at once. Something touched her shoulder in comfort. But the goddess did not speak.

"She plays her role, as I play mine. Mine is harder." Ark-amne shone like sunlight glaring on metal, just for a moment. Jaena saw the brilliance of it even behind closed eyelids. "Open your eyes. Your goddess is gone."

Jaena gasped as the warmth of Imn-ashu's comfort vanished, leaving her chilled to the bone. She opened her eyes. Ark-amne's brilliance had dimmed, though the wildness in her eyes remained.

"Go, while I'm still in a humor to please my sister. I have my own task to do, though I'm weak from these many years of slumber, and there are few *taylenor* here to lend their aid. The demons are loosed. I intend to send them back to the pit of hell they come from."

Jaena felt as if the world had been turned inside out. Nothing was as it had seemed. Blessed Imn-ashu, source of endless comfort, would do nothing to intervene in the battle, but the Eastern Mage, full of fire and death, was perhaps their savior after all. She had no idea what to say.

But she knew that Imn-ashu had been with her long ago, when she'd survived that brutal winter of plague in her family's homestead, and again when she'd fled Herrein's imprisonment. Why did Imn-ashu not show her hand against the evil in this world? Was there something Jaena still didn't understand?

A guard's challenge rang out, outside the roofless cavern where the demons' heads bled acid into the rock. Ark-amne turned away towards a man who came half-limping, half-running into the cavern. Others streamed in after him, including the bearded young man Mkot.

Questions clamored in Jaena's mind. But more important than her confusion was the fact that Jaena was being forced ever further away from her goal.

She stepped forward. "Wait! I need to get back to Spar Fortress."

"Enough!" Mkot took her arm. "Come with me. You're fortunate she's told you so much already."

"But -- "

The limping man had dropped to his knees before Ark-amne. The back of his quilted coat was eaten through to the skin, and the skin beneath blistered and blackened. "They're in the pass," the man choked out.

A shout went up from the people in the cavern – a long collective cry that echoed around the walls. Ark-amne grabbed a branch from a pile near the walls. Its tip blossomed into flame.

She put her other hand on the messenger's shoulder. A sleeve of golden light coated her arm. The man swayed into her hand. Jaena felt a twist in her gut, felt the distinctive pull.

Her senses woke. Reaching out, she felt it: *taylen*, lying thick throughout the blasted cavern.

The messenger reached forward, put both his hands on Ark-amne's glowing ones as if for support. The rip in his coat gaped, exposing more of the blistered skin on his back. He cried out in pain.

"Wait," Jaena said.

"Away with you, now, or the mage's work will have been for nothing," Mkot hissed. He dragged her through the debris that littered the floor and around the huge boulder outside the cavern. Jaena tried to keep her feet under her; Mkot moved fast.

"Just let me go," Jaena said. "I need to go back to Spar Fortress!" Wiel was there, depending on her. Maybe Metten was there, too, captured during the aborted hostage-exchange. Panic crawled along her nerves. She'd sworn to the goddess to right the wrong she'd done when she'd given Wiel to Herrein. It might already be too late to save him, but she would not give up.

Ark-amne was fighting the demons too. *I intend to send them back to the pit of hell they come from*, she'd said. Maybe Herrein would listen to that.

"The mage said anywhere but there. She wants you saved for Imnashu." Mkot kept pulling. He was powerful with the strength of someone who trained in arms; Jaena was no match for him.

They passed down the steps and veered away from the rutted street. Mkot picked up a cloth bundle as they passed a black pillar and thrust it at her. "Supplies."

Behind them, people streamed out of the cavern, armed with swords and torches. Jaena turned to watch them. Mkot yanked her away, towards the path that curved around the rock wall that formed the side of Mount Nimn.

Something black and spiky barreled out of a crevice. Jaena recognized the red eyes and hump-shouldered run. The demon ignored the people and ran the other way, toward the gap that was the Saarnen Pass and Spar Fortress. Toward Cassahn.

The guards grabbed for the flaming torches. The first demon caught fire like a ball of pitch, yowling as it burned. But the others kept coming. The guards and the horseman who barred the way were overcome in seconds.

Shadows moved, squirming black-on-black. Dozens of demons moved through the gap in the stone.

"Faster!" Mkot shoved her onward, away from the demons. She stumbled down the path. Shouts echoed behind her as Ark-amne's people raced after the demons.

She stumbled on the steep slope and fell. Her knees slammed hard against the rock. Mkot lifted her with a hand under her shoulder and propelled her onward.

"What's happening?" Jaena reached a level space on the path and turned to him.

"Can't you tell?" For the first time he looked as panicky as Jaena felt. "What do you think's happening? The demons are returning, the Eastern Mage after them as was foretold. Now *go!*"

Jaena moved. The sounds behind her were getting louder and yet seemed to be moving away. The battle must be moving toward Spar, toward Wiel and Metten and the *taylenor* held by Herrein for use in this battle. Her time was running out.

She spun and dashed past Mkot, back up the trail toward the cavern.

"Stupid woman!" Mkot howled. "You don't understand!" He barreled up the path after her, fast with the liquid ease of youth, familiar enough with the terrain not to stumble on every stone.

Jaena felt the distance between them closing. She remembered being chased by Herrein's people on the way to Rivasha, remembered calling on Imn-ashu to hide them, remembered them crouching in the autumn-leafed woods while their pursuers passed below them. She remembered the prayer she had sung.

Maybe the goddess would answer again.

She tried to form the notes, but her run snatched them away from her as she gasped for breath. Mkot's feet scraped on stone behind her, the sound growing nearer. She reached for the prayer again, began to hum, calling for aid. Her labored breathing broke the song, the prayer incomplete. The goddess was as far away as she had ever been.

I have to get away.

Something spun out of her, strength unwinding from her core like thread from a spool. *Taylen.* She *pulled*, hard. It was the first thing most *taylenor* could do, and Jaena began to realize she'd done it before, all unknowing.

Silence pulled about her like a curtain.

Jaena's fingers slid on rock. Everything looked soft, as if there was a film between her and the world around her. The sounds of battle from the pass seemed muffled, and the breeze died. She pushed a scraped hand out before her and felt nothing but a change in temperature, a warm downy feeling before her hand plunged again into the cold mountain air.

"What!" Mkot stopped and stared, his eyes somehow not meeting hers.

Jaena stared back for one frozen second before she collected herself.

Just as she moved, Mkot swore – "Damned *taylenor*" -- and threw himself up the path where she had just been standing, arms out.

She gasped in surprise and scrambled out of his way. She couldn't get far; the path edged the side of the cliff face. His outstretched arms bumped against her arm. She wrenched her arm away and grasped for handholds on the steep slope. She pulled herself up out of Mkot's way. Dirt sifted down on her pursuer.

Mkot climbed after her. Without being able to conceal her sound, she'd never elude him.

Jaena reached to her right, found a handhold that would take her laterally across the escarpment. Her boots slipped on the dry rock.

Mkot's eyes followed the scraping sound of her boots.

Jaena moved sideways, fingers digging into cracks in the rock. Fast as she could, she dropped the few feet back to the trail. A low grunt escaped as she landed hard.

Mkot looked after her. In spite of the blurring effect of her concealment, he could still hear her well enough.

She ran back up the path toward the pass, back toward the crevice that had vomited the demons out into the daylight. It was clear now; all the demons had streamed down the big trail into Saarnen Pass. Bodies of guardsmen and horses lay dumped like broken toys in the path. The stench of demons still hung in the air. Ark-amne's scarred and wounded warriors had followed the demons, either to fight them or follow them like a spearhead into Cassahn, Jaena still wasn't sure.

When Jaena reached the big boulder that blocked the entrance to the cavern, she dodged around it and stopped.

In the back of her mind she still marveled at the soft edges of her concealment. She hoped it held.

Mkot's running footsteps followed her. He stopped at the top of the shallow steps and looked around. She heard him calm his breathing, no doubt listening for any sound that would betray her.

"Ark-amne means you no harm, Priest. She saved you. Why are you running?"

She stepped away, soft as she could. The cavern was empty now. She slid past one of the speared demon-heads and behind another rock. The clear sky opened above ruined Mount Nimn, a beam of sunlight brightening the rocks around her. A jumble of sounds echoed from the pass: shouts, the clash of metal, a rumble of something falling. Sounds of violence.

Goddess, let me get back to help Wiel. Stay with them all, please. But there was no song on Jaena's lips, and no touch or fragrance to signify the presence of Imn-ashu. Jaena knew what it felt like when the Goddess was with her; she wasn't here.

This shield around her was *taylen*, nothing else. She could feel the drain. The pull from her gut, the dizziness. Past the dim amazement at being able to do such a thing at all, she knew she wouldn't be able to keep this up much longer. *Thank you, Imn-ashu, for teaching me this.*

Mkot was in the cavern, on the other side of the boulder that blocked the entrance.

The cavern tilted and spun. Jaena let go of the *taylen*, just a little, trying to ease the discomfort. The shroud around her thinned.

She slid her boots off, quiet as she could, and shoved them under her arm.

Jaena gathered all her strength and dashed away, past the spitted demon-heads and the acid-pitted crevice that spawned the demons. Her cloth-bound feet made no sound on the rock. She pulled the remains of her concealment about her like a cloak. Her gut rebelled against the use of so much *taylen*, but she pressed one hand into her stomach and stumbled on.

She followed the curve of the mountain wall, avoiding the wide path Ark-amne and her warriors had taken, with Mkot nowhere behind her. Her heart hammered.

Jaena dashed farther around the bend, where there was no trail. She stumbled up a slope made of fallen rock. She let go the *taylen* and felt the blurry edges of her concealment fall. Her stomach spasmed. She bent over and lost her last meal, hanging helpless over the ground while the brown stone whirled around her.

After a moment she moved away. Her feet stung. She slipped her boots on again, over torn cloth and abraded skin.

She looked around, trying to figure another way back to Spar Fortress, back to Wiel and Metten. Ark-amne cared nothing for them.

But with her new information about Ark-amne's goals in this battle, Jaena thought she saw a way to save them.

The wide trail into the pass lay below her position. The mage and her people had left few marks on the path, but there were little pockmarks here and there, holes dripped into the stone by the demons as they ran. If Jaena went that way, she would run into a wall of Easterners and demons.

She looked up. All she could see was the immense fall of rock from the destroyed peak of Mount Nimn. The debris towered over her head, slabs of rock mingled with a scree of pulverized stone. There must be a way around this barrier, but Jaena didn't see it.

A wail – or a battle cry – echoed from the direction of Spar Fortress.

Jaena flung herself at the fallen rock. She climbed as fast as she could, her hands clutching at newly-fractured, sharp stone. Smaller stones rolled under her boots; she bumped to her knees, pain rolling up through her leg to her hips.

"Stop!" Mkot had seen her. "You're running into the middle of the battle, woman!"

A new rush of energy spiked through her. A few more handholds, rough under her scraped skin. More pebbles rolled under her boots. Below her, Mkot swore as the dislodged rubble showered his head.

The top of the fall was within reach. Jaena stretched out and pulled herself up. A few more steps across the width of the fall and the Saarnen Pass spread out below her like a toy battlefield.

A black wave of demons struggled toward Spar Fortress where it sat on its pillar in the middle of the Pass. Behind them rode the Easterners, following the demons as the shaft follows the point of the arrow. A muted blaze of red hair betrayed the position of Ark-Amne in the front of the group. Weapons gleamed in the sun, and another battle-cry broke the chill air.

The way into Cassahn was defended only by Spar Fortress, with its garrison of Herrein, his store of *taylenor*, and the unit of guardsmen he had brought with him. The light of a mage shield glimmered into existence, barring the gap.

Right now, as she watched from the rubble of Mount Nimn, Herrein drew on one of the *taylenor* to feed this shield. It glowed blue in the sunlight. The first demons flung themselves against it, scrabbling against its glasslike smoothness and finding no purchase.

Mkot reached the top of the rock fall and threw himself at her. He slammed into her so hard she nearly stumbled down the drop. "Where are you going?" he hissed. "Can't you see this way isn't safe?"

Rock scraped her arms. "Let me go! I have to get back to Spar before it's too late."

"What in the hells do you think you can do?" Mkot's hand clutched her forearm. "You're just one person! Not even armed!"

"There's someone I have to rescue from that fortress."

"Well, forget it. The mage said you're to be saved."

"I don't want to be saved. I betrayed someone into Herrein's power, and now I'll get him out. I swore to Imn-ashu I would do it. Don't stop me!"

The man's eyes showed white. "You swore to Imn-ashu?"

"Yes!" She yanked her arm from his grip. "I'm a Seeker, and I gave another *taylenor* to the mage!"

"You're a Seeker!" His expression betrayed his shock and distaste. "Imn-ashu allows this?"

"Let me go. I have to get back there and try to make good what I've done."

"Ark-amne said -- "

"I know what she said, but I swore to Imn-ashu." Jaena turned away and watched the battle break against the shield. Ark-amne's red hair was visible in the jumble of people catching up to the demons. She raised a spear that seemed made of nothing but flame and spitted one of the demons. The thing crawled up the shaft of the weapon toward her, leaving a coating of black ichor visible even from this distance.

"You can't get in, even if you get to Spar," objected Mkot. He sounded younger now, and uncertain.

"All I need is to get close enough for Herrein to know I'm there. He'll get me in."

"You're one woman, not even trained in arms. You'll be killed before you can sing one prayer."

Jaena shook her head. "Herrein wants me alive. That's my chance – and I'll take it. There are many *taylenor* in there who can help me. I have a plan. It's a slim chance, but I swore it and I'll keep my oath."

"An oath to Imn-ashu. If Ark-amne knew -- " Mkot tugged at his beard. "They're kin, you know. The stories say Ark-amne ever guards Imn-ashu's back, and burns *hibon* for her every full moon."

"Then for Imn-ashu's sake, help get me back to the fortress."

Mkot groaned. "Goddesses. My luck to be born in the end times, I will never be forgiven. All right, Seeker, I will get you as close as I can to Spar Fortress. Getting inside will be up to you."

Hope flared. "Oh, thank you. But what will happen to you when the mage finds out?"

"What will that even matter, if I don't survive the battle?" He cast a last look back at the roiling mass of demons at the foot of the mage-shield. Ark-amne's people struggled around the edges of the mass, striking out at the demons with flaming torches. Some had already fallen and lay here and there amid the rocks, forgotten.

The mage herself glowed with *taylen*, burning demons with her power. She had cleared a path before her. Now she stalked toward the massive fall of rock that was the remnants of the ancient barrier of Saarnen Pass.

Spar Fortress stood above the carnage, black windows looking out over the Pass. Jaena knew Herrein stood behind one of those windows, pulling energy from one of the captured *taylenor*.

"Let's go!" Jaena tugged at Mkot's sleeve. "Where to?"

"Follow me."

He slid back down the rockfall she had struggled up with so much difficulty. Halfway down, he traversed the pile of rubble and stopped near a tilted slab.

Jaena climbed next to him. Her hands burned from the friction against the rocks.

"There was a gap here, where this big rock fell across smaller ones." Mkot hunched down and stared into shadows. "We worked on it, and now a tunnel goes all the way through the rockfall. This is what our sentries have been using – it's not big enough for riders, of course."

"Of course." Jaena swallowed. "I suppose the roof won't fall in on us when we're halfway through?"

Mkot tilted his head. "Pray it doesn't, Priest. It's been sturdy so far." He crawled into the gap.

It seemed to take forever to crawl through the tunnel. Jaena's knees scraped on the rock, and her hands bled. Before her, Mkot's broader shoulders sometimes filled the confines of the tunnel. Soon it grew so dark Jaena could not see Mkot at all, though she could hear his boots scraping across the rock and his occasional mumbled curse.

Jaena prayed they would not get stuck in here. The air was close and dry. The weight of tons of rock pressed close, groaning in a way Jaena could almost hear.

Eventually the floor of the passageway seemed smoother, and the walls a little wider. Jaena lifted her head. Dim light came from somewhere ahead of them, showing her the outline of Mkot rolling his shoulders in the additional space.

Jaena gasped in air that seemed a trifle fresher.

Rays of sunlight stabbed into the tunnel. Mkot pushed himself out, then crawled to the side. Jaena used her elbows to lever herself out from under the roof of the tunnel as Mkot had done.

"Stay down," Mkot whispered.

Clear blue light filled Jaena's vision. She craned her neck, looking up and up at the expanse of shield that Herrein had created. The shield glowed, either from within or from the brilliant sunlight that filled the rock-strewn valley. It towered over them, extending from the floor of the Pass to where Spar Fortress sat on its pillar guarding the gateway to Cassahn.

Herrein must have needed incredible power to maintain it. Jaena's fear for the *taylenor* captives grew.

"Look." Mkot nudged her. Jaena followed his gaze to the melee of easterners and demons at the foot of the shield. Ark-amne's hands were filled with fire as she used her mage power to burn demon after demon. Torches glittered at the front of the battle. An awful stink filled the closed pass, the reek of burning demons.

But there seemed no end to the demons. And Ark-amne's people were fewer and fewer as they fought, bright specks of quilted coats and chain mail in the mass of blackness.

"This is the last battle." Mkot's voice was strained. "We learned it when we were children. I should be down there with my friends."

Jaena yanked on his arm. "There's nothing you can do down there except die. Ark-amne sent you with me, remember? Help me get closer to the fortress."

Mkot swore. He wiped away tears with the back of his hand, leaving smears of dirt on his cheekbones above the beard. He slid down the slope from the mouth of the tunnel.

Jaena followed him, ignoring the sounds of battle. They half-ran across the floor of the pass, approaching the wall of shield from its furthest edge where it melded seamlessly into the rock of the cliff face. Scrubby branches and gray-green grasses stuck out from the sheer drop. Jaena looked up again; this was the cliff she'd been pulled down during the hostage exchange. At the top of this cliff lay a way into Spar Fortress.

Mkot glanced at Jaena, then up. He shook his head. "There's no way. The demons can't even get up there."

"We don't need to. All we have to do is wait." Something shifted in the air, a warning along with a fragrance of *hibon*. Imn-ashu was back with her again. Jaena took a deep breath of relief.

Mkot pulled at his hair. "How long? My friends are dying, just over there. I need to go help them."

"Go." She pushed him away. "It won't be long. Herrein knows I'm here."

Mkot frowned at her, then looked toward the battle.

"Go! Imn-ashu keep you safe."

He gave a jerky nod and was gone. Maybe he would last out the hour, down there amid the demons. She sang a soft prayer to Imn-ashu for him.

The cliff loomed above her, impassable, and the glowing blue of Herrein's shield began only a few feet away. Jaena's nerves prickled.

Then something invisible grabbed her and hauled her back up the cliff face, fast and desperate. The turmoil in the pass vanished below her as Herrein's pull dragged her up and dropped her, hard, before the gates of Spar Fortress.

Her head spun. The doors of the fortress creaked open and guardsmen were all around her. Her hands were forced behind her and tied, and Jaena walked into the fortress of Mage Herrein the Strong.

CHAPTER TWENTY

Halpen paced back and forth in front of the arrow slit that was his only source of fresh air. What was the delay? Surely Herrein had found the Seeker by now.

Unless she'd evaded the old mage somehow. That didn't bear thinking about.

"Sit down, would you?" The plaintive demand came from one of the three other *taylenor* imprisoned in this room. This one had been taken away in the night, presumably to feed the old mage's hunger for *taylen* to fight his magical battle against the Eastern hordes. Now she huddled on her cot, curled against the wall. She'd thrown up her food twice now. Likely she'd lost the will to stand. The sour smell filled the room in spite of the air wafting through the arrow slits.

Halpen ignored the woman. He waited for Mother Thara or someone else in authority to come and release him.

After he'd told Herrein where the Seeker was, they'd given him back his boots and cloak, and provided him fresh water and bread. Mother Thara had checked in on him twice, offering no information in response to his demands but at least showing proper respect by her presence.

Halpen peered through the arrow slit. He could see only a little of the confrontation going on in the pass. Demons threw themselves against the blue shield that blocked the way into Cassahn. The sooner he got out of here, the better.

A muffled groan came from the cot directly under the other arrow slit. Thara had ordered the boy moved there last night; maybe she hoped the cool air would help him last a little longer. The boy's left wrist stuck out from under the cover, so thin his bones stuck out like knobs from his sticklike forearm. He raised his voice in feverish rambling, but his words were nonsense.

Thara had said the boy's name: Wiel. Halpen knew that name. He avoided looking in Wiel's direction. He had other things to worry about.

The wooden door creaked open. Halpen turned, lifting his head.

"My lord." One of Herrein's men nodded at him. This one wore the badge of a commander.

"At last." Halpen clutched his cloak about him. "Do you have my pouch of documents?" Surely Green-cloak and Crossbow-woman had been as eager to sell those to Herrein as they'd been to sell Halpen himself.

"That will all be seen to, my lord."

"Good." Halpen left the reek of the tower room. He felt the others, all except for the delirious Wiel, watching him go. He didn't turn to look back at them or say anything to them; he knew they didn't have long to live, here in the tower as Herrein fought the last battle against the Eastern Mage.

All the doors on this level were closed. At least one must lead to the stairs.

"Second door on the right, my lord," said the commander from behind.

Halpen beelined for the second door. He wanted his sword and his documents, and preferably an apology from Mage Herrein, before he shook the dust of this place from his feet and headed for the border. He heard a cry from behind one of the closed doors and ignored it, pushing ahead.

A strangled gasp stopped him in his tracks. He spun around.

The Commander gurgled blood through the gaping hole in his throat. Halpen jumped back as red sprayed the walls. A hooded figure lowered the jerking body to the floor.

"What the -- " Halpen blurted, and was stopped by a hiss of warning from the figure who'd slit the Commander's throat.

A red-stained hand put back the hood, showing a familiar, though heavily-bruised face.

"*Rall?*"

Rall hushed him, fingers to his lips. "Come on, my lord."

"But I – I need my documents! Herrein is going to release me --"

Rall rolled his eyes. "Herrein was never going to release you. Come *on*, before we're discovered."

Halpen turned and followed Rall. His mind spun. "I thought you were dead."

"Please hush!" Rall went back along the hall, past the barred room where the other *taylenor* were being held. He pushed a door open. Worn stairs led downward along the curved inside wall of the fortress.

Halpen brushed past Rall and down the first two steps. Then he stopped.

"My lord! Go!"

"Wait." A shout came from the room he'd just been held in, Wiel's hoarse voice echoing from the stone walls. "That boy's in there."

"Which boy? The one the priest was looking for?"

"That one." Halpen put a foot forward and found he couldn't continue down the stairs toward his freedom. He remembered the priest, curse her, standing aside to let him pass as he escaped the Ull-fasten camp. She'd protected him with her *taylen* magic. And he'd betrayed her for his own safety – perfectly understandable, and he'd do it again, but still ... "Hell. Rall, go and get him."

"My lord?"

"Go! You'll have to carry him down the stairs. Hurry!"

Rall said something under his breath and backtracked to the room Halpen had been held in. He lifted the bar, went in and a moment later appeared with a slight form draped over his shoulder. He left the door ajar behind him.

"Let's go," the manservant hissed. "They'll all be in the halls in a moment."

Halpen found his gaze caught by Wiel's face as Rall proceeded ahead of him. The boy looked ancient, sweat-soaked black hair stuck to his forehead, closed eyes sunken in a sickly-white face. If the boy started making noise again, they'd have to leave him. That was all there was to it. Obligation be damned.

They crept downward, Halpen trying to soften the hollow sound of his boots on the stone.

The last steps ended before two doors. The large one undoubtedly entered on the first-floor hall and from there out to the main doors that led across the drawbridge. There would be guards there barring the way out.

Shouts echoed down the stairs from the upper level, and a hollow thud as of a door being flung open. Someone wailed. The *taylenor* escapees had been discovered.

There was a sound of running feet coming down the stairwell.

The smaller door looked rusted shut, but it swung open with a protesting squeal. They crowded into a cramped passageway. Rall pulled the door closed behind them. Darkness swallowed them.

The alarm had been raised. There was a clamor in the hallway outside as guardsmen stationed in the big hall joined the others on the *taylenor* floor. They must be running right past the smaller door.

"Go, my lord, fast."

"But I can't -- "

"Go!"

Halpen stuck one hand out in front of him and grabbed the wall with the other. He moved as fast as he could down the pitch-black passageway. The way curved, probably following the outer wall of the fortress, and dropped into a staircase that Halpen only discovered by missing the first step and falling. His knees hit the stairs, and he caught himself on one elbow and the other hand. Pain stabbed up his left arm. He stifled a curse as Rall crowded close to him, trying to get out of the line of sight from the door.

Behind them and around the curve of the wall, the door squealed open. Light from the fortress' first-floor lamps lit the back wall.

"Looks clear," said a voice. "All dark, none of the torches are missing. I want two guards here, just in case."

The door closed. All light was extinguished for several terrifying moments. Halpen heard clumsy movement and the snick of a fire-steel until a small flame blossomed in a wad of charcloth. Rall dipped the pitch-end of a small torch into the flames, and they had a fitful, wavering light.

"Since my arms are full, you must carry this, my lord. Hold it high and please follow me." Rall bent to pick up the *taylenor* boy, who was slumped against the wall.

Halpen gritted his teeth against the pain of his injured arm and held the torch as high as he could.

This must be the way to the part of the fortress that extended underground, to supply rooms and other facilities for use in a siege. Herrein's men would not have been so stupid as to leave it unguarded. Halpen hissed at Rall: "What did you do with the guards?"

Rall ignored him.

The torchlight illuminated walls lined with empty hooks. An occasional alcove held sealed jugs for vinegar, oil or wine. Midway down, a barred door led to the cellars. On the right, an opening yawned into a dark space: a storeroom or even ancient cells of some sort. Halpen shivered, glad that Mage Herrein's madness hadn't led him to keep his captives down here.

On the other side of the space, an iron grate covered a hole in the floor. The torch illuminated walls lined with bundles of supplies. A couple of the bundles were torn open, and grain scattered on the floor. Someone had been raiding the supplies.

At the end of the passageway, a body was shoved up against the door like a doorstop. Blood drained from the guardswoman's body into a puddle that filled the hollows on the stone floor. Her key-belt was empty.

Halpen exhaled a long breath, impressed. "Did you do that?"

"Please hush, my lord."

Halpen ignored the disrespect and followed.

As they went down and down, the air grew damp. Halpen saw no more supplies stored here; no doubt they would have spoiled fast in the increasing moisture. The way ended in a pile of heavy stone, sitting stacked before an unfinished-looking wall.

"Rall, stop! Where in the hells are you taking us?" Halpen began to panic. What kind of rescue was this? They were at a dead end.

"It's all right, my lord." Rall walked over to the stone wall, turned slightly to be sure Halpen was watching, and stuck his arm right through the stone wall up to his elbow.

Halpen pursed his lips and breathed out a long breath. "It's magework."

"Yes. An artificial construct, like the bridge we took to get into Cassahn. We can go right through it and come out in a tunnel that will lead us to the Cassahni side of the pass. Drops us almost in the Ull-fasten army's laps, my lord. I'm sure they'll be glad to hear about this way in."

"Imn-ashu's eyes. I've underestimated you, Rall." Halpen reached out and put his own hand through the wall. It was jarring; he could almost feel the rasp of stone, and half-expected to be stuck there forever. He pulled his arm out, fast.

"Let us go, my lord." Rall bent over, rearranging Wiel's weight on his shoulders.

"But – it's not guarded? Herrein doesn't know about this?"

"The thief who told me of this place is dead. He and his companions used this as a base when it was empty. They've been coming back to steal provisions and armor, but they'd be stupid to come here just as the demons are about to enter Cassahn."

"Who did tell you?"

Rall gave an odd half-smile that was not amused at all. "Do you remember Cherik, by any chance?" At Halpen's blank look, he continued. "The man who captured you and sold you to the Mage Defender?"

Green-cloak. Halpen took a deep breath. "He's dead, you say."

"He was anxious to tell me everything he could, but in the end it wasn't enough." Rall led the way through the wall, his form distorted as the stone closed about his back and shoulders. Halpen took a deep breath and followed.

Enclosed by stone, he held his breath. Was there air in here? Moving his legs took extra effort, as if he indeed forced himself through rock. Rall in front of him was invisible. All he could see was gray and brown and occasional fractures in the rock. He thought he felt the pressure of tons of stone against his eyes, so he closed them tight. His heart raced. He assumed this was very much like being buried alive.

Then, as if something almost shoved him, he fell forward and out of the mage barrier and stumbled into Rall and Wiel.

"Why do you have to stop so fast?" he complained. "I almost fell, and my arm's already broken."

There was no reply. He looked past Rall's back, focusing on the passageway ahead of them.

Staring back at him were familiar faces: a pointy face wearing a snarl, and a woman with her dark hair wrapped in a messy knot. The bandit Wim, and Crossbow-woman. Halpen went for his sword then remembered it wasn't there. Pain shot into his shoulder.

Behind the bandits loomed armed men and women, wearing mail and the Ull-fasten colors. A vanguard of them clustered in the small corridor, illuminated by a diffuse light that seemed to come from no definite source. Halpen felt *taylen* like a cloud amidst the people; there were mages here.

"What's the delay?" A tall form pushed through the group of armed people. A harsh face striped with scars looked in Halpen's direction. Hashu, Sri's second in command, led this company through the bowels of Spar Fortress.

It seemed that after their leader's death, Green-cloak's bandits had sold the location of the secret passage to the Ull-fasten army. Too bad they hadn't waited until Halpen had made his escape.

CHAPTER TWENTY-ONE

Herrein waited for her just inside the great hall.

She'd expected him to be managing the mage shield and the defense against the demons from high in the tower. Instead, he stared at her with red-rimmed eyes from just a few feet away.

Jaena shivered. This was not the Mage Defender she'd known in Iryor. This man was on the edge of exhaustion. His bony hands shook, and his scalp showed large bald patches. His mouth stretched in a distorted smile.

Herrein didn't look like a man willing to listen to reason. Jaena had given herself back into this man's power so she could try to persuade him to ally with Ark-amne against the demons – the Eastern Mage not the threat of legend, but instead a potential ally. Now she feared her plan wouldn't work.

She tried to speak up anyway. Her guardswoman's elbow jammed up into Jaena's jaw, stunning her into silence.

"Foolish to venture so close to the fortress," Herrein said.

Jaena's nose wrinkled. A strong unwashed odor emanated from Herrein. "Mage Defender, I've come with news. The Eastern Mage is working to kill the demons; she's battling them over there, fighting the same battle you -- "

The guardswoman's hand slammed into Jaena's cheekbone. "Shut it."

Herrein cackled.

Two armed guardsmen stood between her and the old mage, protecting him. Their faces were expressionless, their bodies oddly rigid. *Distaste? Disapproval?*

Jaena recognized one of the guardsmen from Herrein's house in the city. Erdo looked older now, much older than accounted for by the three years that had passed since he last escorted her to Herrein's house for training. Those days seemed a lifetime away – the days when she'd trusted Herrein, believed that when she searched for the *taylenor* she was saving them from a miserable death from the Dark Twin.

She glanced up at Erdo, but he looked straight over her head and would not meet her eyes. She couldn't count on any help from that quarter.

She made a silent prayer for strength, humming the sacred song deep inside her head. Something wavered in front of her like a heat mirage on a sweltering day, and then she gasped as her song was swatted aside with a force that staggered her.

Herrein laughed. "So you have discovered your *taylen*. A good thing, Seeker. But I'm ancient, and strong, and you're a child before me."

Mother Thara emerged from the stairwell, the hem of her robe brushing the stone floor. "Mage Herrein, the shield is failing."

"Duty calls," Herrein said. "Constant vigilance is needed, and all the *taylen* I can get. This one is fresh and strong. Erdo! Put her with the others!"

"Wait! Mage Herrein, the Easterners are fighting the demons too. If you send reinforcements, maybe you can beat them back together!" She rushed the words, hoping they would penetrate Herrein's mania.

Herrein vanished up the stairwell after Thara.

"Come." Erdo jerked his head toward the other guard, who led the way out of the hall. Every guard in the unit defending the entryway looked away from Jaena as she passed.

Just outside the hall, to Jaena's right, was a door that looked rusted shut. Erdo gestured toward the stone steps before her. "To the top."

Jaena trudged up the spiral steps. At the top of the stairwell was a hallway that stretched from one end of the upper floor to the other. Armed guards stood before one of the doors that lined the hall. Like the other troops downstairs, they looked away from Jaena's face as she passed.

Erdo opened a door further down the hallway and stood aside for her to enter.

"Is Wiel still here?" she asked him. "Tell me that at least, before you lock me up."

The other guardsman snarled at her. "Get in."

Erdo cast her an unreadable look. "Sorry, Priest. He's gone."

It hit her like a shock of cold water. She gasped. She allowed herself to be pushed into the room, and stood with the world narrowed down to a black tunnel as the bar dropped over the door behind her. Footsteps moved away down the hallway.

Jaena sank to the floor. Her eyes were dry; no tears would come, just an immense shattered grief that weakened her muscles until she lay down on the stone floor and stared blindly at nothing.

"Excuse me." A low voice came from somewhere nearby.

Jaena closed her eyes and ignored the bid for her attention. She had failed, and the boy she'd stolen from his peaceful life in his own village was dead. Guilt wrapped around her like a shroud. She would never be free of it again.

"He's not dead." The low whisper insinuated itself into her little world of grief.

"How do you know?" Her voice sounded hollow in her ears. She levered herself up from the floor to a sitting position, her legs curled under her as she finally looked around her.

She had an impression of dim light and stone and other people. Someone knelt beside her. She forced herself to focus.

"He was taken away. Maybe rescued."

The boy had a thin face and a riot of dark curls. He looked familiar, yet she didn't think she'd ever seen him before. She shook her head, trying to clear away her grief and shock.

Someone else crouched near her, a familiar, angular form with gray hair brushing the top of his shoulders.

"Othane." Relief swept through her. "You're well."

"As well as possible. You're unhurt?"

"Yes. Just ... they said Wiel was gone."

"Ah." Othane sat back on his heels, then pushed himself up with the help of a palm flat on the floor. In the dim light she saw new lines in his face, and a droop to his shoulders as if he fought weakness. "He is gone, taken by your friend Halpen and his man."

"Taken. That means?"

Othane shrugged. "Rescued, it appeared to us. We saw them rush into the sickroom next to us and emerge with Wiel thrown over Rall's shoulders. They ran for the stairs. What happened after that ...?" He shrugged again.

All is not lost. Jaena took a deep breath.

"He was very ill, Priest. Herrein has been using his *taylenor* hard, fighting the Eastern Mage. Wiel may have been too sick to survive being carried so roughly."

"I'm going to assume he made it." She stood up, noticing the blue cast to the light that made its way through the arrow slits. That must be from Herrein's shield, turning the air blue as it forced back demons into the spears and torches of Ark-amne's army.

The arrow slits were cut through the thick stone walls, tall, narrow gaps but still wider than they had seemed from below. The room was cold, but there were rush mats on the floor, a single chair and a single pallet shoved against the wall. A torn screen angled across the back corner; Jaena assumed there was a bucket or similar convenience behind it. She sighed.

Jaena didn't recognize the other people sitting up against the walls of the cell. Two men and a very young woman, all wearing the Ull-fasten badge of magery, watched her. They barely moved. Their half-lidded eyes were dull.

"Celophe," Othane introduced the young woman. He turned to the men. "This is Ewen, and Ishen, who was personal courier to the Commander."

Jaena looked down at her feet. The memory of Sri fallen, hair dabbled in blood, was too vivid behind her eyes.

"Since you're here, I'm guessing there's no army coming to rescue us," Celophe said. She coughed, hard, and sank back against the wall. The bones in her face were sharp, as if she had not been eating. Othane went to her, murmuring a question so low his words were indistinguishable.

"I'm Faran," said the boy with the dark curls.

Now she knew why the boy looked so familiar. Her heart sank to find him here. "Greetings," Jaena said. "You brother's told me about you, a little."

He favored her with a frightened smile. He seemed in better shape than the rest. His *taylen* loomed like a huge presence in the room, new and unscathed. It overpowered the sense of *taylen* she felt from the others in the room.

"Are you all right?" Jaena asked.

"I just got here," the boy said. He looked up at her through dark curls. "Herrein's men took me from home and brought me here with the supply train. I'm to serve Mage Herrein, they said – help get rid of the demons."

"I see."

"These other people are very sick," the boy said, his dark eyes wandering from person to person around the room.

"They've been giving their energy to the Mage Defender," Jaena said. "It's not an easy thing to do."

Jaena felt sick. All these people, here to feed their energy to Mage Herrein, might be able to rid the land of the advancing demons. With Ark-amne fighting the same battle from the other side of the pass, if Herrein sent reinforcements they stood a chance of sending the demons back to the pit of hell they'd sprung from. But these *taylenor* would die, and Mage Herrein would live, nourished in his magery by the energy of those in this room. He would consume the lives of others and live on and on, half insane if she interpreted the signs right, a parody of life.

Why must this battle be fueled by the *taylen* of innocents?

There was a clatter in the hallway. Raised voices echoed down the corridor. A moment later something slammed into the other side of the door.

The door creaked open and one of the guardsmen threw someone new into the room. Jaena knew who it was as soon as she saw his dark hair. Metten hit the floor hard, on his left side, and lay there a moment gasping.

"Stay there, then, if you want in so bad," Erdo said. The door slammed closed again.

Jaena kneeled down next to him. Bruises stood out on his pale skin, and he clutched his left side. He turned his dark eyes to her face, grimaced in pain and then grinned.

"Metten!" Faran threw himself on his knees next to Metten. "It's you!"

"It's me, Faran. I'm here to give you what help I can," Metten gasped, still lying on the floor.

"And a lot of help that will be, locked up here with the rest of us, with a broken rib most likely." Jaena stood up, exasperated at this turn of events. Metten had the common sense of a flea. In spite of her annoyance, the weight on her shoulders lightened. Metten was still alive.

"It's not as if I asked to be captured," Metten responded.

"Do you have a broken rib?" Faran asked.

Metten groaned, sitting upright on the floor. "Goddess knows, Faran. Feels like a horse stomped on me in the battle, which is very likely what happened by the way. Jaena, this is my brother. I told you about him, remember?"

"I see the resemblance." Faran looked like a younger Metten, about ten years younger if she had to guess. "And his *taylen* is the strongest I've ever sensed."

"*Taylen?*"

"I guess that's why I'm here," Faran said.

"When did that happen?" Metten shook his head. "Has that bastard been using you for your *taylen*? Are you all right?"

Metten gasped with pain as he tried to push himself up from the floor. Failing, he held out one arm to Jaena and raised his eyebrows in question.

She helped him up. He wavered on his feet for a moment. Faran stood against his brother's side and propped him up as Metten gasped for breath, then steadied.

"I'm fine." Faran frowned at the others in the cell. "I don't know why he's saving me?"

"Couldn't Father get you out of the country when he found out you were *taylenor*? I assume the stubborn idiot knows about – all this." Metten waved his hand around at the suffering *taylenor* in the cell, the stone walls, the flush of blue light outside the arrow slits.

"Aunt Rai offered to get me out of the country. To Duscapi, maybe. Papa wanted me here, to be Lord de Rell after him."

"You're the oldest, though," Jaena said to Metten.

"I told you they cast me off," Metten said.

"I thought you exaggerated. They actually disinherited you? Then they had only Faran to be Lord de Rell after your father, and were surprised when he showed *taylen* ..."

Metten shrugged, then paled again.

She came closer, drew her hand gently down the side of his face. "Let's get you to a chair. Othane is here. He'll take a look at you once he's done with Celophe."

With Faran on one side and Jaena on the other, they gave Metten more assistance than he required to the only chair. The Ull-fasten mages sat against the wall and watched silently.

"Look," Metten protested. "I'm not an invalid."

"You're banged up, though," Faran said. "Nurse would scold you." His dark eyes gleamed with humor, just like Metten's.

"It's been many years since I was under Nurse's thumb," Metten said. He coughed. "Faran, is there water here?"

Faran ran off to the table to pour water from the jug. He was so young and alive, compared to all the other *taylenor* in the room. Jaena felt sick to know what would happen to him.

"Do you want to share why you were cast off?" Jaena said.

Metten shrugged with his good shoulder. "It's of no importance to anyone but me and my family. There was -- an affair, just once, when my mother was feeling neglected. No one but my mother knew about it until recently. My real father wrote letters before he died, apologizing to everyone he'd wronged in his life."

"You and Faran look alike," Jaena said.

"My father would never have discovered it without those letters. We both resemble my mother, Faran and I. I had no idea either, not until he came raging into my room and told me I was no son of his."

Jaena waited until Metten sipped some of the water Faran presented in a stoneware mug. It took him a minute; he paled after he had sipped it, and wavered a little on the chair. Faran went to get more water.

"You aren't bitter," Jaena said.

"Well, I miss my mother and Faran, of course. But I was never cut out for being a lord and managing things, Jaena. My father used to throw up his hands and wonder how I could possibly be his son. Funny how it eventually turned out."

"Yes, very funny." She took his hand. "So you had to fling yourself into captivity to make sure you could protect Faran."

"I didn't fling myself. We were captured. The rest of my unit is in manacles. I asked to be treated according to my station, and they threw me in with you. What could I do from out there?"

"Or in here either," Othane said. He had turned away from his countrymen and knelt on the floor next to Metten. "You and the priest are equally foolish in that regard."

"I thought if I explained to Herrein about the Eastern Mage, he would change his plans," Jaena explained.

"Have you seen your Mage Defender recently?" Scorn dripped from Othane's usually-kind voice.

"Just now." Jaena sighed. "He's unlikely to be reasonable."

Othane waved her away from Metten. "Let me look at you. Here, my lord, let me see your ribs."

Jaena turned away to afford them some privacy. She drew Faran with her. Behind them, Othane and Metten murmured, and Metten gasped as pressure was put on a tender area.

"It's as I thought," Othane said after a moment. "You have a cracked rib, my lord. Or broken, possibly – I can't tell." The mage sat back on his heels and looked Metten in the face. "I don't have the strength to heal this. You must be careful not to be too active. You could worsen the injury."

"Yes, well," Metten said. "I'll be sure to stay in bed and sleep until noon."

The door creaked open and Erdo stepped in. "I need Celophe and the boy."

"No!" Metten said.

Erdo shrugged. "Herrein needs what he needs, my lord. If we deny him that, the easterners will overrun us within a day, demons and all."

"I want to see Mage Herrein," Jaena said. "I have to explain about the easterners. He wouldn't listen, but he has to! Please, Erdo, you know me. Leave the others here until after I speak to Mage Herrein."

Erdo shook his head. "He'll just send me back. Or worse yet, slay me where I stand and send one of my subordinates. Priest, I can't."

"What is the delay?"

Jaena knew that voice. In spite of their dire circumstances, hope flickered. "Mother Thara, please listen to me."

Thara drifted in from the corridor. She was as severe and beautiful as Jaena remembered. Of course Thara knew all about Herrein's deception regarding the *taylenor* children in the hospital. Of course she was complicit in the evil Herrein did. She had stood in the hallway in the hospital as Wiel was taken away, saying to Jaena: "You belong to us, Jaena. You are all Herrein's."

But the woman had been her guide since Jaena was brought in at the age of six, cold and shaking with fear from the house of death her family home had become. From a distance Thara had watched over Jaena, planned her studies, assigned her a teacher from the ranks of the other mothers. Never warm and nurturing, Thara had nonetheless been like a rock of stability in Jaena's uprooted life.

Thara was a mother, sworn to care for the sick and abandoned. There must be some compassion left in her heart.

Surely she would listen now.

"Mother Thara, please listen. The Eastern Mage fights the same battle we do, from the other side of Herrein's shield. I was there. She tried to save me, but I came back to tell you they aren't the enemy. Her name is --"

"Ark-amne, sister to your Goddess," Thara said.

Jaena stared.

"I know who she is. Imprisoned in Mount Nimn hundreds of years ago. She should have slept forever."

"Does Mage Herrein know? We are both fighting the same battle! If we join forces, we can destroy the demons. There's no need to hurt more of the *taylenor*, or continue this senseless bloodshed!"

Thara turned away. "The Mage Defender needs the Ull-fasten woman, and the new boy. No more delays, Erdo."

Erdo paled and prodded Celophe until the woman wavered up from her place on the floor.

"Mother Thara, please listen," Jaena said.

"To what? The whining of a child who doesn't understand her elders? Mage Herrein knows full well what he does."

"But he can't! She's Imn-ashu's sister!"

"And she's the Eastern Mage." Thara pulled her shawl close around her against the chill of the stone walls. Her pale eyes did not leave Jaena's face. "Demons or no, she won't stop until Herrein is bones and dust, and Cassahn is hers again. *That* is what the stakes are. That's what he fights. Guardsmen – *now*!"

Erdo jumped. "Yes, Mother Thara!"

"How could you?" Faced with Thara's opposition, Jaena cast tact aside. "You, who swore to care for the sick! You lied about the Dark Twin, you lied to me!"

Erdo pushed Jaena back into the cell. Her shoulder scraped against the stone wall. The other guardsman wrapped a cord around Faran's wrists behind the boy's back. Celophe stumbled. Erdo grabbed the woman's arm and half-dragged her behind him.

"You're not taking my brother," Metten growled. He stood with a guardsman's arm at his chest, holding him off.

Thara laughed. "You're worthless, Metten de Rell. You have no *taylen*. You aren't even entitled to the name you use. If you persist in obstructing Herrein's guards, you'll be executed. Now come!"

Metten dodged around the guardsman's arm and ran for the door. He slid around Thara, almost into the stone corridor. Erdo stopped him with a drawn short sword, held ready for the strike.

Metten stopped, panting. His arm curled at his side, bracing his ribs. His eyes went from the blade to Erdo's stare.

"We can save all these *taylenor* if Mage Herrein would just listen to me," Jaena said desperately.

"Don't you understand, idiot child?" Thara's face flushed. Her eyes glittered. "This is the Last Battle! Herrein fights to keep us secure from that witch and her demon minions on the other side of the pass! Sacrificing a few *taylenor* is nothing. Herrein must continue to live and rule."

Jaena drew back with horrified fascination. Thara was always composed, always restrained. To see her red-faced and spitting with anger was terrifying.

The light that sifted into the cell from outside shifted. The luminescent blue wavered, darkened. Thara's gaze went to the arrow slit.

"Now!" Thara spat to the guardsmen. "Herrein's magery fails. Now or we are defeated."

Erdo shoved the two *taylenor* out of the room. The door boomed shut and the wooden latch dropped. Jaena, Metten and the three Ull-fasten mages sat stunned in the darkening cell. The acrid smell of smoke blew in through the arrow slits.

Jaena felt as if the earth had been pulled out from beneath her feet.

Next to her, Metten cursed.

Othane said: "I'm sorry. This is what's been happening, right along. The fight against the demons is incidental. Herrein fights for his life and his rule."

Jaena took a deep breath. It quivered as her body shook. "I thought – I thought he didn't know Ark-amne was on our side."

"Ark-amne isn't on our side," Othane said. "If you mean the Eastern Mage." He went to the nearest arrow slit and leaned up against the thickness of the wall, trying to see out and down.

"How did you talk to her?" Metten asked.

Jaena ran through a quick explanation of how she'd been dragged away from the battle, and Ark-amne had tried to save her for Imn-ashu's sake.

"I'll thank her for that," Metten said. "If I ever see her."

"She fights the same enemy we do," Jaena said. "I saw her, with her people at Herrein's shield barrier. They're killing the demons, trying to drive them back." *I intend to send them back to the pit of hell they come from,* Ark-amne had said.

Othane looked grave. "We know of Ark-amne, in Ull-fasten. Though we had no idea she was the Eastern Mage. She may have tried to save you for her sister's sake, but make no mistake, Priest, Ark-amne is no friend to *taylenor*."

"What do you mean?"

"You said she drew *taylen* from one of her people."

Jaena remembered Ark-amne holding a burning torch with one hand, her other hand on that of the demon-burned Easterner. She'd leached *taylen* from the man. Jaena had sensed it, licking along the man's hands into the body of the Eastern Mage, feeding her power.

"He offered it," she said uncertainly.

"It doesn't matter. It's a crime." Othane turned away.

"How is it different from what I offered you?"

Othane's face flushed. "We won't speak of that. It was a mistake."

"It was not a mistake! It was my free will, and it saved a life."

Metten looked from one of them to the other. "What are you talking about?"

"Nothing." Othane turned away from all of them and stared out the arrow slit.

Jaena glowered at him.

"I know a little of Ull-fasten," Metten said carefully. "I asked Ael when he was guarding us in the tent. He said you mages, in Ull-fasten, use *taylen* in the service of your country. You work with the regular guardsmen, and some of you die young from it. I saw it myself, when we crossed the mage-bridge into Cassahn."

"No one has to serve," Othane said. "In Ull-fasten, our *taylen* is our own, to offer or not offer as we choose. You know nothing of it, my lord, so don't attempt to use it in argument against me."

Metten tilted his head, as if to say *fair enough*. Then his face grew clouded again. Jaena knew he was worrying about Faran, but instead he said: "What's happened to Wiel? Have you found out?"

Jaena explained what she'd been told about the boy she'd come to save. In the middle of her explanation, the clash of battle rising to their height from the struggle below stopped as if a lid had been dropped on it. The effervescent blue of Herrein's mage shield dimmed, leaving their tower cell pitched into gloom.

Jaena hoisted herself into the wider area built into the stone wall to allow archers access to the arrow slit. Othane and Metten craned to see into the other opening. Below, Ark-amne's forces streamed away from the pass in a disorganized retreat. There was no sign of Ark-amne's flame-red hair, or of her fiery spear. Herrein's shield was a weak-ened, muted glow barring the tumbled boulders that remained of Saarnen Pass.

Bodies littered the narrow ground in her limited field of view. Burned demons lay here and there; she saw no living ones. A few Eastern guards waited at the pass; she recognized their quilted coats from here, saw an occasional glint as the dim blue of Herrein's shield struck an eerie reflection from chain mail or sword.

"I don't understand," Jaena said. "What's happening?"

"I'd say your Eastern Mage has run out of people to assault the pass," Othane said. "And possibly run out of *taylenor* to feed her power. We will see what'll happen next."

Would this mean a reprieve for Faran and Celophe, hauled off to give their energy to feed the shield?

Jaena sang a hushed prayer. It felt strange, to call Imn-ashu in this prison. Imn-ashu would not intervene, Ark-amne had said – and who should know better than Imn-ashu's sister? Jaena wondered if she should feel bereft, as if the goddess she'd spent her life serving had abandoned her. Instead she felt comforted. Imn-ashu did not intrude on the affairs of humans, would not leech *taylen* from innocents so she could act in the real world. There was no chance Imn-ashu would start a war, or act to either sacrifice or save a human from the demons. Maybe because of this, the goddess' comfort and strength were worth far more.

The scent of *hibon* wafted through the room. The others sensed it; the two sick Ull-fasten mages slumped against the wall lifted their heads and sniffed. Metten smiled. Jaena hummed a few notes of prayer and gratitude.

Then the door opened, and Celophe and Faran were thrust back inside their crowded cell. They both stumbled and fell. Faran was crying. The Ull-fasten mage lay still, her wool coat tangled around her legs, and did not get back up at all.

CHAPTER TWENTY-TWO

Othane and Jaena pulled the pallet as far as they could from the drafts coming through the arrow slits, then carried Celophe over to it. The woman's pulse fluttered under Jaena's fingers, hummingbird-fast and faint.

"Let me see her." Othane said. He got to his knees and bent over the sick *taylenor*.

Still on his knees where the guards had tossed him, Faran retched and vomited onto one of the rush mats.

"All the hells," said Ishen, the *taylenor* who'd been Commander Sri's personal courier. His hand clutched his stomach. "That was all we needed to make this place more livable."

Jaena whirled to snap at the man for his insensitivity. Then she saw his face, pale as tallow, and remembered what these *taylenor* had already gone through. She rolled the mat with its contents and shoved it behind the privacy screen. Metten bent over Faran, a hand on the boy's arm, then winced as the motion aggravated his injured rib.

Ishen coughed and projected his voice towards the mage-healer. "How is she?"

"Not well." Othane sat back on his heels. "There's nothing I can do for her here."

"Please!" Ishen choked out the word, but Othane only shook his head.

"You helped me, and I was near death. Can't you save her?" Metten asked.

"There's nothing I can do. It's not the same."

Jaena looked at the mage-healer. His hair had been gray when she'd met him weeks ago, but his face had been youthful. Now, his forehead was furrowed. Deep lines bracketed his mouth. There was a weary slump to his shoulders. In the middle of her own troubles, she had almost forgotten Herrein had been stealing *taylen* from Othane, too.

"I'm all right," Faran said breathlessly. "I can stand." He wobbled to his feet, leaning on his brother for support.

Jaena settled down against the wall and watched the others. Ishen and his countryman Ewen leaned back and closed their eyes. Faran murmured to Metten, no doubt telling about what had happened to him in Herrein's presence. And Othane stared out the arrow slit as an early, frost-tinged darkness settled on the Pass. Winter was here after a long and beautiful autumn, and night fell early.

Celophe cried out from the pallet, and Othane went to her. A glow of light coated his hands as he comforted the Ull-fasten *taylenor*. It was the only light in the cell.

Yellow light reflected through the tiny observation window as someone set a lamp down on the floor in the hallway outside. The door scraped open. A husky guardsman handed in a tray of bread and a jug of water.

Jaena asked the man if he would have the mat taken away.

He gave a honking laugh. "Nah. Yer stuck with it. I ain't touching it."

But he threw in a pile of blankets, and left the lamp on the floor outside when he left, which provided a wavering dim light. Jaena sent him a silent thanks for that.

It was hard to think about eating, with the stink of Faran's vomit still sour and strong from the rush mat behind the privacy screen. But Jaena's hands were shaking, and she knew she had to eat.

After they choked down the food, Ishen spoke up. "I was born in Cassahn, you know."

Jaena really looked at the man for the first time. Until now, she'd tagged him as "Sri's courier", and refused to think about that too deeply because it brought back the memory of the Commander's terrible death at the hands of Herrein's guardsmen.

Now she looked past his pallor and the wariness in his dark eyes. Ishen might have been her own age, with medium-brown hair dark with sweat, and a square solid face that under other circumstances might have inspired trust.

"I didn't know," she said.

"I was just about to apprentice to my town's baker. I'd barely noticed the *taylen* – just an odd feel about things, no more – when my parents brought a stranger from Ull-fasten to me and told me I had to leave my town and go to a foreign land."

"And you went."

"I didn't want to go. I'd been chosen for the apprenticeship – it was an honor, my town was famed for its bakery. I had a future. The woman from Ull-fasten wore strange clothes and smelled of foreign spices. I was afraid. I said I wouldn't go."

Everyone in the cell listened to Ishen, faces turned toward him in the near-darkness. Except for Celophe, who was unaware of anything around her.

"What made you go?" Jaena remembered sitting on the single step of the donkey cart, talking to Wiel in the dusk in the clearing near his village.

"The woman convinced me. She showed me *taylen*, and told me about Herrein. My parents cried and hugged me, and I knew I'd never see them again."

"I'm sorry," Jaena said.

Ishen coughed. "I gave my *taylen* to the service of Ull-fasten, in return for saving my life. Not everyone did, but I was grateful. They trained me in magery and asked if I wanted to join the guard. Life was good. And then they kidnapped Celophe from the border, along with the other mages, and I swore I'd get her back."

"You knew her, before?" Metten asked.

"She was the one who came to get me, in my town in Cassahn. She rescued me before a Seeker -- someone like *you* -- could take me to be eaten up by Herrein." The hatred in the tone was palpable.

Jaena caught her breath. She'd almost forgotten her guilt, as she tried to tell Herrein his battle against Ark-amne was misplaced. Now it returned to wrap around her shoulders like lead.

"Jaena didn't know about any of this," Metten said.

His loyalty almost brought down her defenses. Tears leaped to her eyes.

"It isn't known here," Faran added. "I've never heard a whisper of it. I've never met another *taylenor*. It must be held as a great secret."

"Council knows," Metten said. His eyes met his brother's. *Our parents knew,* hung unspoken in the air between them.

"Yes, Council knows. And the mothers." Jaena drew up her knees, folded her arms on them, and bent her forehead into their shelter. Even after everything else that had happened, Thara's betrayal still hurt.

Silence fell. Ewen, the second Ull-fasten mage, had been silent through the day, watching them all from half-lidded eyes. Now he sat forward and grabbed a blanket from the pile the guard had dumped in the corner. He stood shakily and walked toward Jaena. "Here. It'll get cold."

She looked up. It seemed an act of great kindness in light of the conversation that had gone before. "Thank you."

"You're here, after all," Ewen said. He handed out a few more blankets and went back to lean against the wall near Ishen.

The glow dimmed from Othane's hands, and it was dark.

Gray dawn crept through the arrow slits. Jaena shivered on the rush mats, blanket clutched around her.

Othane hunched near the pallet. His long fingers pressed Celophe's wrist. He pressed an ear to the Ull-fasten mage's chest, then put his cheek very near her mouth. He shook his head, then pulled the blanket up to cover Celophe's face.

Jaena pulled her blanket about her and stood to do her duty to Celophe, as a priest.

"What's going on?" Faran asked. He was rolled close to his brother, who was still asleep. No doubt it was nice and warm under their shared blankets. Jaena envied them.

"Celophe is dead." Ishen turned away from them.

Her vocal cords were rusty with disuse and the effects of the chill, dry air. The first measures of the song were no more melodic than the croaking of a frog. Jaena tried again.

"Here." Ewen held out water from the jug.

"Thank you."

After a sip or two and a hummed prayer, Jaena was ready.

Celophe had been through a lot at Herrein's hands. No doubt she'd accepted – even wished for – death. Now her soul perched on the mage's shoulder, waiting. A few notes – off-key as usual, but fluid enough – filled the cell and rose to call Imn-ashu. In the cold, stone cell, the music seemed a breath of spring, a reminder of peace. In a moment, the goddess' familiar presence rested there, almost like a touch.

"Oh goddess, she's really here," Ishen wavered.

Celophe's soul left eagerly, fluttering up and into Imn-ashu's care. The goddess' presence remained for a moment, hovering. A flush of warmth filled the room, then Imn-ashu was gone.

Jaena let the last notes fall into emptiness, thanking Imn-ashu. Whatever bitterness she felt about being held in this prison, with no help from the goddess she served, she buried deep away. Imn-ashu would not intervene, since apparently intervention required using *taylen* that did not belong to her.

Jaena wished that wasn't so, and then she was glad after all that Imn-ashu had never succumbed to the temptations that had driven Herrein mad, that tainted even Ark-amne's existence.

"Thank you," Ishen said. "For Celophe, I thank you."

A blast of air blew the blanket off Jaena's shoulders.

Metten sat up. "What was that?"

The dim chill of dawn had strengthened into feeble daylight while Jaena sang Celophe's soul. Now it grew darker again. Gusts of wind drove through the arrow slits and grabbed at their hair and clothing.

Metten climbed into the wider area around the arrow slits. One hand on the stone, he leaned as far as he could and peered out.

"This looks familiar," he said.

He moved away and beckoned to Jaena. She looked out the narrow opening and saw a storm lowering across the otherwise clear Eastern sky, a black front as solid as the mountains beneath it.

It didn't look like a natural storm.

"I think that's a mage storm," she breathed. "Like Herrein raised, to kill the demons on our way back from Uthen."

"Yes, but who's doing it? Herrein or your friend the Eastern Mage?" Othane stood, stretching his shoulders.

The darkness came from the east. Jaena thought this might be Arkamne's next tactic. How much energy had she needed to make such a thing? How many *taylenor* had offered their strength? Jaena felt sick.

The cell door slammed open. Guards with shielded lamps jammed the hall. Erdo pointed at Othane and Faran. "You two! Herrein needs the strongest ones."

Jaena shook inside at what she was about to say, but knew she had to say it. "I'm strong. Take me, too."

Metten hissed at her.

Jaena ignored him. She must convince Herrein to work with Arkamne; together, they could destroy every demon and send them back to the pit they'd sprung from. How could she do that, locked in this miserable cell with Celophe's dead body and two depleted *taylenor* who hated her?

There was no need to convince anybody. A gust of mage-wind blasted through the narrow opening with enough strength to stagger Erdo. A bolt of lightning cast the room into wild chiaroscuro.

A screech echoed down the hallway. "Bring them! Bring all of them!"

Erdo shrugged. "You heard him."

Jaena joined Othane and Faran while guardsmen hauled the others to their feet. They bumped shoulders with each other and the guardsmen as they stumbled down the hall.

The room they entered was large, with windows looking out over the Pass and away to the Eastern skies. Perhaps it had once been a refuge for whatever warrior guarded this barren place. Iron grilles that had been meant to protect the open windows from projectiles now lay twisted off their hooks in a corner. The resulting view of the mage-born storm was expansive and terrifying.

A spear of lightning stabbed down into the mass of inky black that roiled into the Saarnen Pass. Its light illuminated the shapes of demons crowding into the gap. A shriek rose all the way to Herrein's windows as the bolt of electricity picked up several squirming shapes and flung them, jerking and seizing, to their deaths.

Jaena remembered Herrein's storm, the one that had killed the attacking demons on their return from Uthen. In spite of the grim conditions, a bit of hope lit inside her heart. Maybe Ark-amne, clearly full of renewed strength, could destroy the demons for good, by herself.

Then all that would be left to deal with would be the insane Mage Defender of Cassahn.

That same mage spit in anger as he watched another bolt spear the demons. His shield barrier was still active down in the Pass, keeping the demons from entering Cassahn; but the weird blue glow was even dimmer than it had been last night. Its glimmer was a ghostly after-image in Jaena's vision. It was almost gone, depleted of strength. No doubt that was why the last of Herrein's *taylenor* were crowded into this room.

Thunder rolled across the sky. With it came a sheet of lightning, a plane of *taylen*-made destruction that settled across the valley, full of heat and death.

"Goddess," Metten whispered.

The terrible lightning must have killed many demons. Some tried to run away. Even now a dark shape thrust at Herrein's failing shield, its forequarters vanishing as if into fog as it tried to push through the weakened shield into Cassahn.

"To me! To me!" shrieked Herrein.

Guards clustered into the room after the miserable *taylenor*. There was no way to physically attack Herrein with Erdo and his men ready to protect the mage. Jaena didn't know what drove their loyalty – maybe simply fear for themselves and their families, convinced that only Herrein lay between their loved ones in Cassahn and gory death by demon attack.

That was wrong, of course. But Jaena had no time to explain. *Goddess be with me,* she prayed, humming under the crash and slam of violent mage-attack in the Pass.

"Singing to the goddess," Herrein said contemptuously. "You think Imn-ashu will save you? Go ahead and sing. I'm going to repair the shield wall."

He stretched out clawlike fingers. Jaena's heart thumped against her ribs.

"Herrein, you're worn out," Metten said, fast and desperate. "Look at you! If you keep going on as you have, you'll eventually run out of *taylenor* to draw on. You'll use your magery one last time, and it'll be too much for you. Why in the gods' names don't you just run?"

Herrein sneered at him. "You have no idea what you're talking about. Just a little more effort and I'll win this accursed campaign. The attack is ready. We'll let the Easterners kill the demons, and then we'll be on them. They'll be worn out. We should be done with them by sundown. Then there's Ull-fasten – with hundreds of *taylenor*, a rich reserve. I'll never lack for *taylen*."

"Lord Metten is correct," Othane said. "You can't feed your magery like this forever. You look ill, Herrein. You don't have long remaining to you. Death awaits you as certain as those demons across the border."

"Death will never find me," Herrein said, grinning. Jaena looked into his reddened eyes for a moment and shuddered. Herrein was past sanity; whatever process he had begun during this long, last drain of energy after the hundreds of years he had spent carefully replenishing himself, something had gone out of balance.

"You're deluding yourself." Jaena tried to keep her voice calm, but it shook. "Mage Herrein, you know me; you trained me for years to be a Seeker. You can save yourself and us if you work with Ark-amne. You're both fighting the same battle! Why try to bring her down?"

"Listen to the priest," Othane said.

Herrein grinned. Apparently he had been chewing on the inside of his mouth; blood stained his teeth now, and crept into the folds of his lips. "A priest of whom? A goddess who won't step foot into the world, even to save her?" He spat pink-tinged saliva onto the floor.

A horn blew from somewhere below in the fortress, a sound of human battle far removed from the cataclysm of magery outside. Shouts and the metal clash of weapons echoed up the stairwell.

One of the guards slammed through the door, protocol forgotten. He signaled at his commander.

"My lord mage," Erdo said in a clipped rush, "We're being attacked from below."

"Go, go! It must be those Ull-fasten bastards. How did they get in? Take who you need. Leave enough guardsmen to protect me and go!"

Enough guards to protect me turned out to be three. With their swords drawn, their trained reactions between the sick *taylenor* and Herrein, they were an effective barrier.

"It must be Hashu," Metten whispered. "Great timing." He had edged closer to the front and was eyeing the three guardsmen analytically.

"Don't," Jaena whispered back. "You can't beat them alone and with a broken rib. I have another idea."

Metten looked at her disbelievingly.

A knot pulled tight in Jaena's gut. Something *pulled* – Herrein, beginning to leach *taylen* to reinforce his shield.

Ishen, the courier, fell to his hands and knees. He shut his eyes and clutched at his stomach with one arm.

The drag of energy grew stronger. Jaena hunched over to protect her core, bending with her arms crossed. Metten called her name, the familiar voice sounding very far away. She couldn't respond; the room tilted, and pain began to spike behind her eyelids.

There wasn't much time.

Jaena had lost sight of what was happening outside with Ark-amne's mage-attack on the demons. The crash and roll of thunder continued. A more human battle echoed upward from the lower level of Spar Fortress as the Ull-fasten attackers presumably hacked their way through Herrein's defenders.

None of it would matter if the last of Cassahn's *taylenor* died here in this room, and Herrein lived on and on to prey on another country's gifted, to grab them and feed off their energy to extend his mad, ancient life in a populace that had no idea what was going on.

A robed form slid into the room – Mother Thara, holding a dagger she'd gotten from somewhere. She stood in the door behind them, waiting. That made four defenders. Jaena had no idea what they would do when she tried her only remaining strategy.

Time was running out while Jaena had been trying to find her own *taylen*. She had never touched it before; it was masked inside her knowledge of her goddess, disguised as prayer. She had never before tried to use it without calling on Imn-ashu – but she knew, instinctively, that she must not call on her goddess now.

Herrein's hands were encased in magelight. *Taylen* flowed to him. The blue iridescence from outside, in the pass, grew brighter. The mage's eyes gleamed.

Metten, beside her, groped for his sword, which of course was no longer there. Cursing, he dropped to his knees. He fit right in with the two *taylenor* who had lost the ability to stand. He dragged himself through the crowd and threw himself at the guards at knee-level.

He hit the first guard at the knees. The woman went down hard. She was too close to her attacker for sword work, but twisted and kicked sideways with a booted foot.

Another guard turned on Metten, sword-arm raised to strike.

Herrein wobbled and flung out his hands; the fight had thrown him off balance. The *pull* that stole their energy eased, leaving the afflicted *taylenor* hunched over and gasping.

Jaena could spare no time to watch Metten. She had finally managed to reach her own *taylen*. Strong and pervasive, bright in spite of the cord that escaped her own being and wound across the room into Herrein's hands. There was no hint of Imn-ashu in its golden light. This was her own *taylen*, pure and simple, like the mist that had floated across the village on the morning she had found Wiel.

And Herrein stole it. Pain throbbed behind her eyes, and her mind refused to focus. She could barely remember the first thing all *taylenor* were able to do, their first ability, even untrained.

Then she remembered She called out to the others: "Pull!"

Ishen choked on his own vomit on the floor. Othane stared at her, glassy-eyed.

"*Pull,*" she ordered. "Even Faran, you can do it. Look at Herrein, feel his *taylen* – and pull."

"This is forbidden," whispered Othane.

"It's the only way." Ishen's square face was raised, his eyes held a spark of hope. "Pull, Othane."

Jaena grabbed at the brilliant cord stretching between herself and Herrein. She *pulled*.

She'd never done anything like this before. Her *taylen* had always been so subtle she'd thought it the gift of Imn-ashu – the gift of pulling concealment about her when enemies tried to find her, the gift of Seeking other *taylenor*. Not this time. This time the *taylen* came pure and physical, wrenching at her as she tried to pull back at her own strength, pull away from Herrein.

Surely she could do it. It was the first thing any *taylenor* could do. Even Wiel had done it, untrained and frightened in the Arahn forest when that first demon had barreled out of the night at them.

Herrein's face jerked up. He stared at her with the white showing all around his eyes.

Jaena drew her own *taylen* back away from him with a steady power.

Herrein shook his head wildly. He released his draw on her energy.

Jaena's strength rushed back in, adding power to her will. She knew Othane stood beside her, and she wondered if some of the flood of *taylen* was from him. Herrein staggered away from the window, whimpering, as all the mages in the room began to stir, regaining strength. The awful drain of energy was gone.

Herrein stood diminished in the middle of the room. "Give it back!" he spat. "Give it back! You don't know what will happen!"

Her *taylen* coiled inside her like a fire. The pain went away from behind her eyes, and the room stopped spinning. A glow ignited in her belly. Othane had been right: this felt good. The surge of someone else's *taylen* felt like wine, like a drug. She pulled harder.

"What are you doing?" Thara stood up from where she'd been thrown by Metten's attack on the guardsmen. Metten himself sat on the floor with a guard's short-sword at his throat. Blood seeped through his tunic, dripped on the floor; but there was no spurt of arterial blood, no fainting or other signs that the injury was immediately fatal.

"Get back!" Metten's guardsman ordered. "Against the wall!"

Metten put up a placating hand and began to scoot backwards.

Beside her, Faran stood up. There was a healthier glow about him. He was pulling too, she could tell. All of them were pulling – drawing back all their own *taylen* – and then more.

Lightning crashed outside. A stink of dead demons blew into Herrein's tower room. The stench below must be smothering.

The blue light from Herrein's shield wall stuttered. Herrein swayed on his feet.

"No, no!" Thara cried.

The guardsmen looked around, confused. No one was attacking Herrein. They all looked back at Thara, waiting for clarification.

Thara pointed at the recovering *taylenor* and ordered: "Kill them!"

"No! I need them," Herrein muttered. "Take them down, don't kill them."

Ishen, eyes glittering with new-found strength, rushed the guardsmen who had just been ordered not to kill him. Ewen followed, blasting new-won *taylen* in a half-visible disk at another of Herrein's defenders.

Metten twisted away from the wall, arm flung up to block his guard's thrust, crying out in pain as his ribs took a kick from the man's heavy boot.

Herrein stumbled back. Jaena's concentration wavered. The steady pull of *taylen* from the old mage faded.

Pale movement in the corner of Jaena's vision. She spun, but was too late. An iron-strong arm wrapped around her throat. Jaena choked out a cough. The sleeve had dropped back, showing the arm pale and sharp as a sword. *Thara*. Neglected in the doorway as the younger mages and Metten fought Herrein's guards, the woman had made her move.

Jaena reached up with both arms to grab Thara's wrist. She yanked hard. Thara's arm gave, just slightly, then stiffened against Jaena's throat. Jaena froze as she felt a blade digging through her tunic, sharp against the skin of her back.

"Stop," Thara ordered. Her voice was calm as Jaena remembered.

"She's got Jaena," Metten shouted from the melee across the room.

The guardsmen and *taylenor* untangled themselves from each other. One Cassahni guard lay motionless on the floor, dead or stunned. Metten clutched his ribs and did not get up.

Herrein giggled. He tried to straighten from his hunched-over stance.

"Get these *drathen* under control," Thara ordered.

Outside, an explosion of lightning cracked in the eastern sky. It vanished, leaving afterimages in Jaena's vision. The morning light now seemed dark as night.

She didn't know what was happening outside. But she could see their chance of success fading as Herrein's men regained control.

A door slammed open down the hallway. A man screamed. Boots echoed in the hall, along with the clash of arms. Herrein's guard was beleaguered here on the upper floor. Hashu avenged his fallen Commander by assaulting Spar Fortress from within.

Across the room, Ishen gave Jaena a long look, full of some meaning she could not understand. Thara's arm at her throat yanked back. Then Ishen moved, lightning fast. He turned into his guards-man's arm and slammed up on the man's elbow to disarm him. Evading the man's quick countermove, he grabbed the sword and with one brutal thrust, shoved the blade at an angle between the man's ribs to his heart.

"No no no!" screamed Herrein.

The guardsman jerked and spasmed on his own sword.

Jaena stepped back hard, throwing all her weight into Thara. She drove her heel into the arch of the woman's foot. Thara stumbled, off balance. Pain seared Jaena's side as the knife pierced her.

Jaena staggered, shocked; she'd never felt something like that before. Her side was on fire.

Thara scrambled behind her, pale robe twisted around her knees. Faran slammed Thara's wrist to the floor and hammered on her wrist until she dropped the knife.

Blood slipped along Jaena's side. Her nerves thrummed. She wavered on her feet.

Now, before she fainted. "*Pull*," she shouted.

Hampered by Herrein's command not to kill their attackers, the Cassahni guardsmen were at a disadvantage, but they recovered fast. One guard had fallen. Another, wounded, hauled a staggering Metten to his feet. One burly man stood in front of Herrein, sword drawn, knife in his left hand. None of the *taylenor* could get past him.

But they could pull.

Herrein's *taylen* fled him. There wasn't much of it left; the old man was weak and ancient. What there was, was tainted somehow, as if infused with Herrein's malevolence.

Herrein made a small, weak noise. He waved helplessly at his guard. "Useless!"

Herrein's burly guard stared at him, puzzled.

"What have you done?" Herrein croaked, standing in the middle of the room. His hands were outstretched as if he tried to grasp something.

"We took it away," Jaena said.

"Like you've done to dozens of us over the years," growled Ishen.

"I'm still here," Herrein said.

"Yes, not dead, surprisingly." Othane stood tall, with his shoulders back, some of his strength returned to him. His face was flushed. He put his hand on Jaena's shoulder. "That took a lot of energy. Are you all right?"

She felt weak, as if some of her life had bled away; her mouth was dry, and the knife wound burned. The room, cold with wind and full of people, seemed loud and painful.

"I think so. But it hurts."

"She was *stabbed*," Faran said. He held Thara down on the floor. "This woman stabbed a *priest*."

"I'll take a look." Othane helped her to a carved chair that had been shoved up against the wall. "Sit. You're breathing all right, so don't panic. You'll be all right. I have enough *taylen* now to help you."

"Stop!" Herrein shouted. "What about me?"

"My lord, what should I do?" the remaining guardsman asked. He turned from one of the *taylenor* to another, not sure where to strike or what to do.

"The Mage Defender's power is gone," Metten told the man. "You'd be wise to give up your weapons."

Ishen and Ewen began disarming the two other guards.

"You've killed me," Herrein mumbled.

"My lord, you're not dead."

"Imn-ashu doesn't kill, and I'm sworn to her peace," Jaena told the man. Then she laughed. There was blood on the stone floor, the scream of wounded warriors in the hallway outside the closed door, and wounded, bewildered guardsmen in here. Mother Thara who had supervised her childhood education had just stabbed her. Outside, the strikes and booms of Ark-amne's storm had ceased, but the stink of dead demons rose in a bitter wave.

All this around her bore no sign of peace. She laughed again, then clutched her side. Tears welled up in her eyes.

"Sit," Othane told her with unusual gentleness.

Jaena nodded and sat on the carved chair.

Othane put a hand on her shoulder and bent over her, trying to provide a modicum of privacy as he checked the wound in her side.

The world seemed pale and watery all of a sudden. Metten, who had his own injuries to slow him, brought her water. The mug had been knocked to the floor in the melee, but it was whole. The water cooled her burning throat.

Warmth suffused her side. She closed her eyes. Othane was glowing, the visible sign of his *taylen* limning his hands as he worked to heal her. She pulled away a little, grateful for the help but worried that the exhausted mage used too much of his gift. Soon, she thought, he wouldn't have any left.

Othane straightened, then leaned one hand on the wall for support. "That's just for now. Drink this, and I'll help you more later. You'll be fine."

"What about me?" Herrein shrieked. "Your Goddess has killed me!"

"Not the Goddess," Jaena said, exhausted. "It was just us. Working together." She didn't bother to protest that Herrein wasn't dead. She knew his death was near, probably just out in the hallway now at the edge of a sword, or maybe at the hands of the flame-haired Eastern Mage who no doubt hurried across the cleared Pass to him now that Herrein's barrier was down and the demons were dead.

Herrein slipped to his knees with a thump. There was a red dribble down his straggly beard; he was bleeding from the mouth again. The burly guardsman helped him to his feet.

"I'll call for help," Erdo said to the mage.

Herrein snarled at him. "There is no help, fool. This woman has just killed me while you stood and watched and did nothing."

Erdo frowned. "I don't understand."

The clash of arms in the hallway snapped Erdo's head around. "They're at the door. Stay put." He eased the door ajar and peered out.

The door slammed inward, knocking him backwards. Herrein's guards who had been defending the fortress had been backed upstairs until there was no room left. They almost fell into the room, their backs to the mages inside, still fighting. Jaena grabbed Faran's arm and struggled back toward the window, away from the clash of steel.

The Ull-fasten attackers raged into the room, rapidly overpowering the defenders.

Erdo fell and was trampled under booted feet. Another Cassahni guard dropped his sword from a nerveless hand as his throat was sliced open with a stroke of an attacker's short sword. Blood spattered the room. Jaena could no longer see past the clot of fighting men and women to where Metten lay on the far side of the room, or where the Ull-fasten mages were.

There was no way out. Jaena held tight to Faran's arm.

Mage Herrein sat with his knees pulled up to his chest, trying to push himself through the wall it seemed. He whimpered, flinching when the action drew near him.

Jaena drooped onto Faran's arm. The strength began to run out of her, like water poured from a jug.

"I'll help you," Faran said. "You can draw on me, can't you, like Herrein did?"

"No," she said. "No, I can't." Then there was a cry, and she felt a black curtain come up over her vision. The wall scraped against her back; she knew she was falling.

CHAPTER TWENTY-THREE

The red fog rolled in, alien in these dry and rocky heights, following the angles of boulder and cliff with ambiguous intention.

Jaena stood on the bridge that spanned the gorge between Spar Fortress and Cassahn, where the hostage exchange had taken place just days ago, watching the red fog that was not a fog.

Her wound felt swollen and tender. Othane had stopped the blood loss, but was too depleted of *taylen* to do more. The *cernen* bound the wound, gave her water and herbs for pain, and told her to rest. Instead here she was, looking down as the red fog slowly deepened, covering the remnants of the bloody battle in Saarnen Pass.

Metten had been carried away on a stretcher toward the *cernen's* tents in the Ull-fasten encampment. He'd complained the whole time in a gasping, hoarse voice. Othane thought that he'd received one too many kicks in an already-cracked rib for him to be roaming around untreated. He hoped that last impact hadn't done some internal damage.

Faran, who was basically unharmed, accompanied his brother.

Jaena reached out as if she were a Seeker again. *Taylen* threaded through the redness. The fog felt dry and hot, more like fire than like

222 • ANNE MARIE LUTZ

the drift of a mundane mist. It swirled around Jaena like hands, or maybe like red braids, twisting.

She nodded, and the Eastern Mage took her.

* * *

Ark-amne stood alone in the blasted ruin that was all that was left of the cavern where she'd slept away the last five hundred years. She swung to face Jaena, her demons-teeth necklace swinging, her fiery braids twisting almost of themselves.

Jaena steadied herself from the odd, jumbled passage and extended her senses. There was *taylen* in this room, clinging to Ark-amne, licking around her limbs – but nowhere else that Jaena could feel, no *taylenor* at all left in Ark-amne's realm.

"You've taken all of it," Jaena breathed. "Are they all dead, then?"

"Not all. But they knew what they offered. They were heroes, if you like." Ark-amne paced towards her. "Not like the *taylenor* in your country, kept ignorant, their gift and their lives stolen by that monster Herrein so he could live forever."

"Well, that's all over with," Jaena said calmly.

"The monster lives."

"I'm a priest of Imn-ashu. I may not kill someone who is no threat to me."

"Others can kill, and have done so liberally. Why does the monster Herrein still breathe?"

"He's powerless now, and insane as well. He's more than two hundred years old, and weak. I think nature will take care of Mage Herrein without our help."

"Do you expect me to go meekly away while my enemy still lives?" Ark-amne paced away, bright with anger and the *taylen* of others. Her mail glittered where it wasn't blackened and eroded with demons' blood.

"Do you plan to go away at all?"

Ark-amne swung around. Demons' teeth tangled together on her necklace. "I've honored you, priest of my sister. Don't bait me."

Jaena caught her breath. Ark-amne was terrifying and beautiful. Jaena thought only a whim kept the Eastern Mage from destroying her where she stood. "I thank you, for my own sake, and my goddess' sake."

"If you think I will meekly go down into the caverns and sleep for another five hundred years, until the demons spawn again, you're mistaken."

Jaena was appalled. "No! I don't think that."

What must it have been like, lying in a mage-enforced sleep in a stone tomb, waiting for the demons to be reborn from the pits? Had Ark-amne dreamed? Had she stirred in her sleep, or wakened sometimes to stare at the ceiling of the cavern that was her prison? And then, what would it have been like to awaken in a blast of fire and brilliance as the mountain blew apart above her head? *Imn-ashu, she is your sister. Imn-ashu, please guide me.*

"I brought you here to warn you, for my sister's sake. I will enter Cassahn through the Saarnen Pass today. Your mages are depleted, your common guard units are drained of strength, weary from fighting each other. They are all afraid – every one of them." Ark-amne's copper eyes looked down on her. "Your task is done, your mage neutralized. Take this gift and get away. I can't guarantee your safety in the madness of battle."

"You know I can't leave," Jaena said miserably.

"Spar Fortress will be mine by tomorrow, then Iryor by next week. I will not leave such a dearth of power in your land, where any *taylenor* might follow Herrein's example."

As if to underline her threat, booted feet echoed just outside the cavern. There were people out there, light flashing from their chain mail, weapons at their sides. There were no *taylenor* among those armed men and women, but strength of arms would be enough, now that the Ull-fasten mages were dead or drained.

Only Othane remained powerful, and his strength alone would not be enough against Ark-amne's forces.

"I swear there will be no more like Herrein." Jaena took a deep breath. "And that includes you, honored Ark-amne."

Copper eyes flashed like sunlight on bright metal. *Taylen* spat through the room. Jaena put both hands up in front of her face, shielding her eyes.

The Eastern Mage's voice boomed from every direction at once. "How dare you compare me to that monster?"

A shout of anger from the guards at the door. Jaena stood tall. Where was her goddess?

"You steal *taylen*," Jaena shouted above the din. There were black spots in her vision from the flashes of light, from fear of Ark-amne's anger. How far could she go without harm, just because Imn-ashu favored her? Surely the rope that had been played out for her wasn't endless, and Ark-amne could draw it taut at any time.

"I steal nothing! I take what is freely given, and use it for the ends ordained for me. Are you regretting my help against the demons now?"

"Of course not." Jaena tried to find the right note to reduce the anger in the room. "With Herrein too damaged to defend us, you're the one who saved us. Cassahn will always owe you for that. As I will, too. But we can't have anyone else ruling our land who takes and uses the *taylen* of others. It's wrong."

Ark-amne spat. "What is your authority to say so, you, a Seeker raised by the Mothers of Arifell to help Herrein farm the *taylenor* like sheep?"

"I don't have any authority. But I'll see to it that it happens." *Because I must. For Wiel.*

"You don't know what awaits you. You're going to be reviled, Seeker. Imn-ashu hasn't done you any favors by giving you this task. You'll be hated for the rest of your life for your part in Herrein's evil, while my sister refuses to intervene in your behalf because she is too good to take *taylen* from people who offer it." Ark-amne's braids snaked up around her head into a crown of living flame.

Fear shook Jaena's voice. "I know. It doesn't matter."

But it did. Imn-ashu was worthy of her reverence for the same reason Jaena was afraid. The goddess of peace and music, who showed her presence by comforting the desperate and taking the souls of the dead to rest, would never take *taylen* from a human being and use it to act in the human world. Not even when her priest called on her.

The weak side of Jaena wished that for once, Imn-ashu would. She shoved that side back and faced the unpredictable mage before her.

"The Ull-fasten people use *taylen*, but only their own. Their *taylenor* use their own gifts in service of their people, but it's a crime there to take the gift from someone else – even if it's given freely. Those are the people who have destroyed Herrein -- "

Ark-amne laughed. "*You* destroyed Herrein. By committing that same crime, priest of my sister. Don't think I don't know what you did."

"The Ull-fasten ride to Iryor tomorrow. They'll overthrow Council, with little difficulty I expect. They've been saving *taylenor* from Herrein for years. They have mages here – more back in their homeland. They are a worthy, dedicated people to rule Cassahn."

"It's *mine*."

"No," Jaena shouted back. "It's mine!"

Her own words shocked her. She stepped back to defuse the confrontation, frightened of Ark-amne but even more of the ridiculous claim she had just made. What was she doing, a priest with no power claiming an entire land against the will of a mage like Ark-amne?

She stood and shook. But she must. For Wiel, and for Marki and Tia, she had to make sure a monster like Herrein never happened again.

The *taylenor* needed a refuge, a place of learning where young *taylenor* could grow without being manipulated. She must make sure everyone knew, everywhere, that stealing *taylen* was evil.

And right here, standing exhausted in front of the Eastern Mage, was the time to start. She needed to claim the land as a priest of Imn-ashu, reminding Ark-amne of the love she held for her sister. If Ark-amne raged into Cassahn with her army behind her, there would never be a chance to save the *taylenor* again.

Something touched Jaena's shoulder, and warmth suffused the space between her and the Eastern Mage. The sweet aroma of *hibon* flooded the air. Jaena closed her eyes in gratitude. Perhaps she wouldn't die in this place after all.

"I see you, sister." Ark-amne's voice rang with anger, but the under-tone of respect was obvious.

Jaena opened her eyes fast, looked around her but saw nothing. If Ark-amne saw the goddess, it was with a sight denied to human beings.

Ark-amne sighed. She seemed to dim a little, as if the fire that burned in her hair and eyes was banked. "My sister supports you, Priest. Will you sit on a throne then, and decide the fates of others?"

"No!" Jaena was appalled.

"It might be a far better place than it is, now."

"I didn't mean that. I have no place on a throne, Imn-ashu knows."

"Then how is it *yours?*"

"That's not what I meant. I meant it's mine as a *taylenor*. I deserve a safe place in Cassahn – all *taylenor* do, a place where they can trust no one will misuse them for their gift. Even you, honored Ark-amne. I owe it to them, for what I've done."

"If you think you can overrule human nature, little priest, think again. This battle will barely be won before some *taylenor*, somewhere, will be trying to steal and use the gift of another, for what ends does not matter. Evil lives, even if your Herrein dies."

"The Ull-fasten care about these things. Commander Sri almost slew me when she found out I was a Seeker. In their country, each *taylenor*'s gift is theirs alone. I'll learn from them. They'll make good rulers, and your Eastern land will be safe from us."

"Will you kill the ones who fight you, then?"

Jaena deflated. "I don't know. The goddess doesn't permit it."

"And you think blessed Imn-ashu will stand behind you on this? My sister who won't lift a hand to save her own beloved priest, even from – this?" She raised a hand.

Taylen surged. A force like a massive hand slammed Jaena into the rock wall behind her. The breath exploded out of her. The uneven surface of the rock wall pressed into her, and the unhealed knife wound shot pain throughout her right side.

Jaena slid down, arm clutched to her side. She gasped for air.

Ark-amne looked around. "I don't see my sister coming to your aid."

"You know she won't." Jaena's fear had evaporated along with the pain, and now she was just angry. She dragged herself to her feet. "You've shown you can play with me, and I'm tired of it. I respect you for the good you've done for us, and for the love you hold for the goddess. But you aren't welcome in Cassahn – or even here, among your Eastern people -- as long as you continue to use the *taylen* of others. What's keeping you from growing to be like Herrein?"

Ark-amne shrieked at the insult.

"But you could!" Jaena said.

"I will not."

"How can we trust you?"

Ark-amne's glow dimmed all at once, as if part of her fire had been doused. She whirled and stared at the nothingness near Jaena's right side. "No! You can't send me to sleep again, sister. I won't do it!"

Imn-ashu was still present; there was a palpable presence, but no voice.

"What do you mean? Surely the ancient mages sent you to sleep?" Jaena clutched a hand to her side. Something warm trickled down her lower back. She was bleeding.

Ark-amne gave a desperate laugh. "You've seen my power. No human mage can defeat me. No, it was my own beloved sister, keeping me out of the way, keeping me away from her precious *taylenor* and her sheeplike priests but ready to act when the demons spawned again."

"Imn-ashu did it?" Jaena's jaw dropped.

"She has no compunction about taking action against *me*. I am not one of you. She'll keep me out of the way, again. Don't do it, I beg of you sister." Ark-amne's shoulders dropped in weariness. "Anything but that. It was cold and lonely, that half a millennium. Even asleep as I was I felt the weight of the mountain over my head."

Stunned and speechless, Jaena saw the Eastern Mage talking to empty air – only not empty, but full of a great presence, a being that swept Jaena with the warmth of approval while threatening her sister with a sleep not far from death. *She can't risk it. She can't risk letting Ark-amne free.*

A clatter at the open doorway: Ark-amne's people had perceived some change in the atmosphere in the great open space, and loyalty sent one of them inside. It was a bearded man with thick bare arms, his quilted coat slung from a strap at his side. "Honored Mage, do you need us?"

"No! Go, and wait." Ark-amne waved him away. "Stay ready, Captain Simar. If you don't hear otherwise from me within the hour, the order is given."

The man bowed and retreated, but the bustle of preparation beyond the door hushed to a waiting silence. Somehow, the decimated armies of Ark-amne knew their assault on Cassahn depended on the outcome of the conversation in this room.

Ark-amne turned back. Jaena didn't move; this was between the goddess and her sister, the ancient Eastern Mage.

"Don't send me back to sleep, sister. I will burn your country with fire and light if you so much as try, I swear it. If I can't escape your bonds, then my people will do it for me. They're loyal, you know – as loyal as this Seeker is to you."

Jaena edged back against the wall. She hurt all over, but she didn't dare to slump down while this odd pleading confrontation continued.

A wash of strength swept through the room. Not the pervading peace Jaena sensed when she sang souls to Imn-ashu; not the warmth and fragrance that accompanied the goddess' comfort. This was a wave of power that had nothing to do with *taylen*, as foreign to Jaena as this strange land. It felt old and serene yet massive, like a mountain that had watched the world around it forever.

With it, Ark-amne fell to her knees. The crown of light in her red braids dimmed. The demon's teeth necklace broke and slivers of venom-soaked teeth fell to the floor. The fire that had licked around Ark-amne's arms went out, leaving the space lit only by fluttering lamps in the sconces and the dimness of the approaching dusk in the wide sky over the broken cavern.

The wash of power receded. Ark-amne fell forward, supporting herself on her hands on the rocky floor. Her head drooped.

A hollow keening went up from the people peering in at the doorway.

The ruined cavern felt empty. Something that was there before was gone. Reaching out, Jaena searched for *taylen* and found none – none except her own raw ability, small and untrained next to the fire that had belonged to Ark-amne.

Ark-amne looked up from the floor. Her copper eyes seemed more brown now, and her wild braids hung like ordinary hair to her shoulders. She seemed smaller, and lighter – it almost seemed she wouldn't be able to lift the sword in its scabbard by her side.

She lifted an arm, lay her palm flat on her chest, as if testing her heartbeat – or something else. Then she looked around the blasted cavern and shivered like an ordinary human with the deep chill in the air.

The Eastern Mage gave a small, stunned laugh. "Thank you, my sister."

"What happened?" Jaena whispered, half to herself.

Ark-amne pushed herself up from her position on the floor. She was the same height, yet she no longer towered over Jaena. Her voice was soft and wondering. "She took it. All of it. I hadn't thought of such a thing."

"You can't simply ... draw more?"

Ark-amne shook her head. "It's gone. The *taylen*, the potential for *taylen*, the place in my body where it lived. A solution to our problem indeed, Imn-ashu. I thank you."

The something that took up such a huge space in the room began to drift away. Warmth suffused the air again, then chilled to the usual air temperature in this mountain hold.

Thank you, Imn-ashu. Jaena began the song as the goddess' presence left them. Soon all that was left was Jaena's solitary flawed voice, strong enough to make Ark-amne bow her head.

Imn-ashu was gone.

Jaena wondered what life would be like now, for someone who had been almost a goddess, and now an ordinary woman. "Will you miss it?"

The red-haired woman who was no longer the Eastern Mage shrugged. "Probably. It was like my blood. It ran through me always. Maybe my life will be counted in short years now, and I may have to earn the respect of my people again. It doesn't matter. It was a curse you know, sentenced to sleep while life above continued, emerging only to battle the demons. I will never go beneath the mountain again."

Ark-amne called out to the people milling around the entrance.

Simar strode in, hand on his sword hilt, his eyes spearing Jaena as if he expected to be ordered to slay her. "Honored Mage!"

"Stay sharp-eyed, Simar. Pass the orders. But we will not be invading Cassahn."

Simar frowned at the mage. Probably he couldn't sense *taylen*, but he must see the physical difference in his ruler. "Is all well, Ark-amne?"

"All is well indeed, Captain." Ark-amne smiled. "Though you'll have some things to get used to. My sister has spared me."

Simar bowed.

Ark-amne's chin went up. "I've been freed from my fate – at great cost, but it will be worth it. Make camp and tend those who need it, Simar. Keep a sharp watch on the Pass, peace is not made yet."

The Captain saluted and turned on his heel. Jaena wondered what was going through the man's mind. She wondered if these people would follow Ark-amne so willingly anymore, now that their ancient Mage was reduced to ... whatever she was. Still more than human, for sure, sister to Imn-ashu. But no longer a defense against the ancient evil.

"I don't have the *taylen* to send you back," Ark-amne said to Jaena.

"The Pass is open." Jaena limped away from the wall. "What will you do?"

"Your leaders will hear from me. If you're wise, you'll warn them I am still strong, and my people undaunted."

"I don't think anyone will take you lightly."

For a moment the old wildness seemed to swirl about Ark-amne.

"They would be wise not to." Then the wildness subsided, and Ark-amne was again a warrior with piercing brown eyes – but quite ordinary. She asked, "Do you need a *cernen*?"

"Probably. But I want to get back."

"Then you may go. You will hear from me, you and your Ull-fasten mages. I'll call your guide."

Jaena's heart lifted. "Mkot?"

"Yes, he made it through, hard-headed as he is. He'll take you through the Pass to your people. Tell them to expect emissaries from me by noon tomorrow."

"I will. That would be to Hashu, military Commander of the Ull-fasten forces, or maybe Othane, the chief Mage who is with them. And may I ask, honored Ark-amne – me as well?"

"Oh yes. I'm holding you bound to this endeavor, after what you stood and declared to me." Ark-amne gestured toward the door.

The military unit that had been clustered outside was breaking into small groups now, following Simar's orders. The activity was businesslike, with maybe a thread of dismay in the tone of the muted talk. One of the guards, a woman no older than Jaena herself, growled at her as she passed.

This place was no safer for her than it had been, but this time because of what the goddess had done to her sister. *I need to get out of here before someone decides to take revenge.*

She walked towards the outside. The boulder still blocked the way, the pikes bearing demons' heads. The muttering grew louder behind her.

Mkot waited for her outside in the gathering dusk, his quilted coat buttoned tight. A spot of dried blood showed through the bandage at his temple, but he smiled at her from behind his beard.

Jaena grinned. It felt good to have a reason to be joyful, amidst all the destruction and carnage. "You are well!"

"You look worse for wear yourself, Priest."

She laughed, then gasped as pain lanced through her side. "I am. But I'm starting to think there's a way through this. Will you take me back to the Ull-fasten camp?"

He nodded. "Those are my orders. If you can keep them from holding me hostage I'd be grateful."

He led the way around the mountainside, avoiding the steep path they'd taken last time to avoid the battle and walking directly toward the Saarnen Pass. The way was easier, beaten down by many footprints, the dangerous places flagged by Ark-amne's people. But the sun had sunk behind the Cliffs of Cassahn, and approaching night hid minor obstructions that were enough to trip her up.

Jaena's temporary good humor evaporated as they walked past the remnants of the Last Battle. Stretchers with bodies were still being brought in. Demons lay in terrifying numbers around the battlefield, jaws gaping in death. There was a pile of them marking the line where Herrein's mage shield had been. An acid stench still clung to the area. The physical remains of a hard-fought battle lay here and there – a crushed shield, half-eaten-away by demon's acid; a broken spear. Bodies of men and women who had fought on the first day, before Ark-amne had summoned the mage storm.

These people had given everything to fight beside their Eastern Mage. Jaena wondered if even now, Ark-amne was being forced to fight a new battle against her own people, winning a new right to rule them now that her *taylen* had been taken away.

CHAPTER TWENTY-FOUR

H alpen flung the tunic against the wall of the tent and glared at Rall.

"It's all they offered me, my lord," Rall said. He picked up the crumpled shirt and held it out to Halpen.

Halpen looked at the thing – rough as burlap, the kind of thing peasants wore. He reached out and took it, swallowing his pride. He knew he had no choice; it still rankled, that the Ull-fasten would scorn him like this, even though he was a de Morn of Cassahn.

"Assist me, then," he ordered Rall. He stripped off his grimy shirt and went over to the basin of warm water the man had brought. Rall made himself useful while Halpen washed, then took the soiled clothing away. Halpen hoped he would burn it; it was crusted with dirt and who knew what else from his failed escape attempt and his captivity. When Rall held it up, Halpen swore he smelled horse shit. It was unfit for him to wear. This peasant garb he had been given was not much better, but at least it was clean.

Commander Hashu and the other Ull-fasten invaders had been as surprised to see him in the underground passage to Spar Fortress as he'd been to see them. They'd taken Wiel off Rall's shoulders, laid him on a stretcher and carried him away. They'd detailed a young shieldsman – almost a child, no stubble even on his face – to get Halpen and Rall to the rear while the main force ascended to begin their assault on the fortress.

When they'd emerged from the ancient tunnel and begun to climb back to the Ull-fasten camp, two older guards had joined them. One was a brute, poking Halpen in the back with his knife just because Halpen demanded a rest. Then, the violence of the struggle at the Pass had become obvious. The dark skies punctuated by blinding flashes, the piercing crack of mage-lightning and the wails of demons rising like an opening to hell. Halpen moved faster then, without complaint.

That had been hours ago, and the wild crash of battle in the Pass had subsided. The dark clouds had retreated en masse in unnatural order. The initial unnerving silence had given way to the sounds of people returning from battle: the exhausted, the wounded, and those who aided them.

He drew on the peasant trousers he'd been given and belted the rough tunic. He ate the honeycakes and dried meat they'd left him. After that, he almost felt himself again.

Rall came back and Halpen asked him, "Is the *taylenor* boy still alive?"

"I don't know, my lord. I haven't been allowed to move around freely."

Halpen fumed. "I want you to get us some supplies. Whatever you can, so we can get out of here. We'll walk along the ridge trail to Rivasha, then parallel the -- "

Rall was shaking his head.

Halpen looked at his servant incredulously. "What!"

"I'd suggest there's no point in leaving here, my lord. When this battle is done, it will be safe for you to return home to Iryor. Or it won't be safe anywhere at all."

"Hmph." Halpen turned away. "Do it anyway. These people don't respect me, and I'd rather not wait around to be traded for a hostage again."

"My lord." Rall bobbed his head and ducked out of the tent while

Halpen fumed at the false show of obedience. Rall was indispensable, of course, and the man damn well knew it.

He stepped outside to find his young shieldsman sitting on a pile of fallen rocks within sight of the tent. Probably he was one of the few who could be spared from the post-battle cleanup or the garrisons Hashu must have left stationed at Spar Fortress and the Pass. It was clear these Ull-fasten didn't take him seriously, that his sole guard was a gangly boy.

"You," Halpen said.

"Yes, my lord. I'll be with you through the day," the boy said. "Orders."

"I want to talk to Hashu."

"Commander Hashu is still in the fortress. You'll have to wait."

Halpen sighed. It was just one more indignity, being forced to wait on a minor warlord like Hashu. He hoped the Ull-fasten wouldn't hold a grudge for Halpen's earlier escape. Perhaps bringing Wiel back would soften their vengeance.

He looked over the rock-strewn landscape. The eerie blue glow of the mage shield had long since faded, leaving the Pass wide open to any who might wish to enter Cassahn. Yet there was no sign of intrusion from any of the Eastern forces. All was bare and empty there, except for the tangled black piles of dead demons and the bodies of fallen men and women. A few shapes inched along in the distance, carrying stretchers, retrieving their dead. The Eastern Mage was conspicuously absent; the battle had fallen into a hushed suspension, both sides depleted, unable to muster strength for an attack.

Halpen jittered. He wasn't sure he wanted to know what had happened over there. The Eastern Mage or whoever fought from the far side of the pass was surely just as dangerous to *taylenor* and nobles as mad Herrein.

A clot of warriors emerged from Spar Fortress' open entrance and crossed the bridge. The sentries saluted the scarred man in front. Blood-spattered Commander Hashu stalked across the battleground with a febrile tension about his shoulders.

Halpen turned to walk shoulder-to-shoulder with the Commander. "What's happened over there?"

Hashu's second, a middle-aged woman whose blond tied-back hair was tipped in blood, cast Halpen a jaundiced eye but made no move to eject him.

Hashu said, "What in the hells are you doing running around out here?" He glared at Halpen's teenage shieldsman, who hunched his shoulders. "Shieldsman, get this *prisoner* back to his tent and set a watch."

"Sir!" The boy set a hand on Halpen's arm to draw him away.

"Commander, I'd appreciate an update!" Halpen said.

Hashu's second came around like a bear disturbed in winter. Her hand was on her sword hilt.

Hashu moved away towards his tent.

The shieldsman yanked at Halpen's sleeve. "Come on."

Halpen decided the best thing would be to go, as soon as possible. He turned and began walking towards the rear. "I want to see my friend Lord Metten. Where is he?"

"I've got orders."

Back in his tent, his guard intensified, Halpen fumed. He'd saved the *taylenor* boy. What more did they expect? When Rall came in some time later with tea, Halpen pounced on him for news.

"The battle against Herrein is won, my lord. The old mage is under heavy guard in one of the tower cells, but they say he's very sick. Mage Othane stayed to tend him."

"Did he really? Thought he hated the old bastard."

"I wouldn't be surprised if he does."

"Huh. What happens next?"

Rall shrugged. "You would have to ask Commander Hashu, sir."

"I tried that." Halpen fumed for a moment, then brightened. "When will we be able to leave this place?"

"My lord." The tone was exasperated.

Halpen turned around and stared at his manservant in surprise. He'd never heard that tone of voice from Rall before. "What?"

"My lord. This is an army dealing with the aftermath of a great battle. There are wounded everywhere, and still a threat from the Eastern Mage across the border. Things are in disarray, and tempers are on edge. There is no way I'll be able to coax a couple of horses and a week's road supplies out of the supplymaster. You must resolve yourself to stay here for now. Herrein is defeated, and I think you are in little danger."

Halpen turned back around so Rall wouldn't see his face. "When I return, the Council will have these Ull-fasten people before them on charges."

"I believe the days of the Cassahni Council are over, my lord. I don't know who will rule Cassahn after the defeat of the Mage Defender, but I assume it will be either Ull-fasten or some representative of the Eastern Mage."

"All the more reason I should get out of this place."

Rall did not reply. The man busied himself about the tent for a few moments, lighting a shielded lantern against the deepening darkness, and then ducked under the tent flap and out into the cold.

Halpen sipped the tea Rall had delivered, and thought. The letters of safe passage and financial support his father had given him were lost, destroyed by Greencloak and his confederates. Without money in Ull-fasten he would be a landless nobleman, probably forced to work for his keep. Unless one of his father's old friends was willing to recognize him – but the Ull-fasten people here seemed to universally disdain him.

Without money he could not even afford to pay Rall. Halpen was already deep in arrears in paying the man, who worked more from habit than for recompense, he thought. He didn't know what he would do without Rall.

Ull-fasten had been his only haven while the Mage Defender chased him across Cassahn to capture him and steal his *taylen*. Now that Herrein was dead, Ull-fasten began to seem vaguely unpleasant.

At least in Cassahn, Halpen's parents would be there. Cast out of the Council no doubt, shorn of their office and influence; but the family home was a town house in the city, with plenty of servants, horses and carriages, and money.

Halpen smiled. Yes, that's where he wanted to go. He would no doubt be vilified by his peers for his role in this fiasco, but he would endure that. A man of his stature deserved the comforts of life. His parents would provide a substantial allowance, as they had always done, and his friends would no doubt get over their awkwardness over his defection and invite him back into their circles.

A tall form ducked under his tent flap with no warning. It was the blond woman who had been walking with Hashu. She was still in battle-dress. Her mouth drew down at the corners with exhaustion.

"You don't know me," she said. "I'm Naar, Commander Hashu's new second. I've come to tell you to get out."

"What?"

"You're a nuisance more than anything else." She crossed her arms over her chain-mailed chest. Streaks of blood had dried on her forearm. "The Commander agrees. We'll be better off without you, and we can see no more need for you. So, we release you. Take your man and go."

Halpen stood up. "Well, then. I'll need an escort to get me down the ridge trail at least to Rivasha, then --"

Naar shook her head. "Just go. Take your man, and you can have a week's trail rations from the supplymaster. You have until dawn, and then go."

"But -- "

She took a sudden stride toward him. She was less than an arms-length in front of him, hand on her sword hilt, controlled violence in her face. Halpen stepped back, appalled.

"Just. Go." She stared at him a moment longer, then spun on her heel and ducked out of the tent.

After a stunned minute, Halpen went to the tent flap and looked outside. "Hello?"

There was no reply. Halpen stepped outside. In the near-distance, yellow light illuminated the upper-level arrow slits of Spar Fortress, and a glow as of firelight flickered at the top level windows – the floor where Halpen had been kept, where he'd rescued Wiel. Here, in the Ull-fasten encampment, it was deep dusk, dark but for the occasional pinprick light of a shielded lantern. The air was crisp and cool, without a hint of woodsmoke since no campfires were permitted. A low hum of conversation came from a nearby tent, and there was a cry of pain from the *cernen*'s tents in the rear.

His teenaged shieldsman was nowhere to be seen. In fact, the area immediately around his tent was clear of any guards at all.

He was alone, free to go.

He went back inside his tent and lay on the cot. He pulled up the scratchy blanket that had been provided. He thought a long time before sleep took him.

CHAPTER TWENTY-FIVE

The Saarnen Pass, technically open now that Herrein's shield had fallen, was nevertheless closed as if a portcullis had dropped over it.

Armed men and women, wearing mail over their quilted coats, were stationed behind boulders and outcroppings but were visible to the Ull-fasten sentries. Even from the cliffs they had an air of grim watchfulness.

Jaena knew the Ull-fasten had no intention of invading the East. Nevertheless, Hashu cursed low under his breath when he saw the defensive arrangements.

"I suppose this tells us your Ark-amne is in trouble," Hashu said.

"I have no idea what it means," Jaena replied. "But I *think* they're in confusion, and shutting down the only point of entry until they resolve it."

The commander glanced at her. "If Ark-amne isn't the leader over there, who will be?"

Jaena shook her head.

Hashu growled. "That's what I feared. Will they attack us through the Pass?"

"Well, they were going to, at Ark-amne's command. But that was before. Now – I have no idea, Commander. You'd better ask Mkot. But Ark-amne did say to expect emissaries from her by noon tomorrow."

"And darkness falls now, and no moon tonight. Soon we won't be able to see our hands in front of our faces without a torch."

With fire discipline in place in camp, the only light allowed would be shielded lamps used far in the rear. But there was no risk of someone falling over the cliff in the dark. With the battle over, Spar Fortress was lit; a reassuring yellow glow from fireplaces and candles within, a beacon that reassured them of success.

"Get the Easterner up here," Hashu ordered. "I'll see what he's willing to tell us. Go, get some rest and food, visit this young lord of yours. For now, we'll assume we must be ready for anything. At least they have no more mages. I'm sick to death of mages."

Jaena agreed with that. She edged through the group of Hashu's lieutenants. Mkot awaited her there, flanked by a couple of wary guardsmen, shifting from foot to foot with nervousness.

"Tell him what you know about what could be happening over there," she asked him. "Please."

"I won't betray Ark-amne."

"Nobody's asking you to. I think Hashu only wants to know the East won't invade as soon as his back is turned. I think he wants to know who might be in charge now that Ark-amne is no longer a mage."

"No one will betray Ark-amne," Mkot declared.

Jaena hoped he was right. Mkot was loyal, but very young. Maybe he was too naïve to understand what might happen with an altered power structure in the East. Or, maybe he would be able to tell Hashu who the leaders might be in any coup against Ark-amne.

On her way back to the darkening encampment, she wondered what was happening to the Eastern Mage now. With no *taylen* to give her more than ordinary ability, would her people still follow her? What was the power of centuries of worship and Ark-amne's personality worth?

The *cernen*'s tents were to the rear. Jaena went there immediately, hungry and so thirsty her lips wanted to stick together, but desperate for news about Wiel and Metten.

The *cernen*'s tents were a scene of controlled chaos.

Attendants carried water and blankets, and removed wads of blood-stained fabric. Shielded lamps provided a wan glow that turned the scene inside nightmarish. Canvas screens hung from wooden frames between cots in an attempt to provide privacy, but the number of wounded overwhelmed the preparations. Some lay on spread-out bedrolls on the dry ground, while others propped up against piles of feedbags or other supplies.

The smell of blood was everywhere, along with a whiff of other unpleasant excretions. The sound of sobbing came from behind one screen. Two mage-healers, wan and shaking from the use of their *taylen*, hovered over the most sorely-wounded. The *cernen* moved between the cots with bandages, water and cups from which emanated the grassy smell of herbal painkillers.

A woman lay near Jaena, moaning in pain while a *cernen* worked to straighten a dislocated shoulder. This woman was among the luckiest of the wounded; her injury would heal quickly. The canvas screen beside her was splashed with red, indicating that whoever lay behind it was not so fortunate.

"Hai, out of the way!" ordered a rough voice. Jaena jumped aside as two attendants carried a laden stretcher out of the *cernen's* tent. The stretcher swayed and bumped against her arm. The body on it was covered with what appeared to be a saddle blanket.

The attendants veered left as they exited the tent. Jaena looked after them and saw an intimidating line of bodies, each covered with something – a blanket, a cloak, whatever fabric had come to hand to give them dignity. There would be work for her tonight, as all these souls must be sung to Imn-ashu. There was a priest among the Ull-fasten, but Jaena felt that as priest and *taylenor*, she should do this task herself. She must not be too tired to do it; these people had given their lives to rid the world of Herrein's evil, and to save the *taylenor* in the fortress. She wondered if Commander Sri lay among them.

As cautiously as she could, trying to respect the wounded and their caregivers in the cramped tent, she moved between the partitions, looking for one face. A face that wasn't there.

"There's another tent," said a harried *cernen*.

Thank the goddess. There was another tent, and that meant there was still a chance Wiel lived.

Jaena made her way to the second *cernen*'s tent. The atmosphere in this one was calmer. A single lantern hung from a pole in the center of the tent. The wounded lay on makeshift cots or blankets padded with straw underneath to protect them from the chill seeping through the ground. Most of the wounded in this tent were sleeping, blanketed bumps with their faces turned away from her. Jaena began to move from one cot to another, still looking.

Wiel wasn't there.

Surely he couldn't be dead. Othane had said he'd been rescued from the fortress. But Herrein had kept him so long, feeding from the boy's *taylen*. Maybe he'd been too weak to live.

She remembered the dead boy in the village they'd passed on the way up the ridge trail, empty of *taylen* and life like a hollowed-out gourd. And the Ull-fasten mage Celophe, who'd died in Spar Fortress. And how many others – all the *taylenor* lost in this latest battle, and all the ones Herrein had used throughout the years, to keep his position and extend his life far beyond his time. Little Tia, and poor Marki. *Marki*, she thought with a pang. So many years ago, but she would always remember him.

She stood under the single lantern, feeling lost.

A voice hailed her in a loud whisper from the rear of the tent. Metten lay propped-up at an odd angle on a pile of blanket-covered straw, smiling. She hurried over to him and sat on the ground next to him.

"Are you all right? What did the mage-healers say?" She kept her voice soft to avoid waking the sleepers around her.

"No mage-healers, they're busy with the serious injuries. A *cernen* was here to see me though. That's why I can't sit up straight." He lifted his tunic to show Jaena the fabric wrapping his chest. Deep bruises purpled his skin around the wrap.

She touched the wrap gently, feeling how taut it pulled around Metten's broken rib. "Can you breathe?" she asked, only half in jest.

"A little." Metten shrugged, then paled. "The worst is, I keep moving."

Jaena drew his tunic back down over the wrap. A scream of pain sounded from the other tent, and she winced. Tears welled up in her eyes.

"Jaena, dearest? What is it?"

She shook her head, unable to speak.

"I'm all right, you know." Metten pushed back a strand that had come loose from Jaena's hair tie. "Faran's all right, I saw him. He's doing what he can to help the *cernen*."

Jaena felt herself coming apart. She looked away from the sympathy in Metten's dark eyes, looked over the bundled figures of the sleepers into the black corners of the tent. She was afraid to speak.

"You look exhausted," Metten continued. "Have you eaten? Here, they left me some water. Drink some of this."

Jaena drank from the leather sack he held out to her. It helped; the water slipped down her throat like nectar. She took a deep breath and pushed back the tears. Later, when she found a place to be alone for a little while, she could let go. Now she had to find Wiel.

Metten looked grave when she asked. "I don't know, Jaena. There's another tent, have you checked there?"

"He's not there. If he's dead --"

"You knew all along he could be dead." He took her hand. "You've done more than anyone could have expected."

"But I have to know for sure." *Imn-ashu, I must know.*

"I know Hal brought him out. Rall told me. He still lived then."

"I'll look." She let go his hand and stood.

"Come back when you're finished?"

She nodded and made her way out of the tent, threading her way between the rows of sleepers.

Outside, she looked around helplessly for a moment, wondering where to go next. Most of the camp lay silent under the stars, sleeping. The *cernen*'s tents behind her were the only hubs of activity.

An attendant emerged from the *cernen's* tent where the most seriously injured were being treated. The man supported a mage-healer, a slender man who sagged with weariness.

The attendant began to lead the healer away towards another tent. "Come," he said with great gentleness. "Food and water, and rest. You can't help them if you're half dead yourself."

"Wait." The mage-healer held up a hand that trembled with exhaustion, and turned to Jaena. "I know who you're looking for – I tended him earlier. The Cassahni boy is in his own tent. Will you show her, Tave?"

The attendant nodded. "Wait here," he commanded Jaena before leading the mage-healer away.

A few minutes later, Tave reappeared. "Crazy mages, won't stop until we make them. We need them too much to let them spend themselves like that."

"Do you know where Wiel is?" Jaena heard her voice break. She clenched her hands, trying to shore up her control.

"Come with me."

Tave led her across a dusty clearing to a small tent. It was dark and looked empty. "Here." Tave handed her the shielded lantern he carried. "Go in. I know who you are, Priest, and that you mean no harm."

"Wait. Has Othane seen him yet?"

"Othane is with Mage Herrein in the fortress. But we've had another mage-healer here to see the boy. He said he's done all he can."

That didn't sound good. Jaena pulled back the tent flap and entered.

The lantern threw shadows around the tent, enough to see the blanketed form on the cot and the jumble of healing supplies set aside on a cloth.

"Wiel," she whispered. "Are you awake?"

The boy turned over. Jaena's lantern showed his pale face, cheekbones sharp under the skin. Wiel's dark eyes opened and looked into hers. They held no recognition.

"It's me, Jaena." She couched down next to him. "I've come to see if you're all right."

Wiel did not respond. In the flickering light of the lantern his eyes looked endlessly dark, as dark as the Eastern pit the demons had sprung from. Jaena shivered and held back tears.

She took his hand. "Wiel, I am so sorry. I've been thinking about you every day, every hour. I don't deserve to ask your forgiveness."

The cold hand tightened on hers. "Not your fault." The voice was a mere whisper.

"Goddess help me, it was." Jaena bowed her head. Then she thrust back her guilt; she could deal with it later. Wiel deserved more from her now. "I am so glad to hear your voice. Do you need anything?"

The boy shook his head.

"Water?"

"No." Wiel wheezed like an old man who'd smoked a pipe for many years.

Jaena cringed, hearing the gurgling in his lungs. She closed her eyes and sang the beginning of the goddess' song, warm and low. *Imn-ashu aid him*. She knew, none better now, that the goddess did not intervene in the lives of humans. But comfort was worth a lot, and strength to endure what the mad old mage had done to Wiel.

"She's here," Wiel whispered, and closed his eyes.

Jaena felt nothing.

"I can feel her hands on my shoulders." Wiel's cracked lips bled as he smiled.

Thank you, Imn-ashu. But – is he ready to go, so soon?

Jaena's fingers had slipped from Wiel's hand to his wrist. The boy's pulse fluttered under her thumb. She reached out to feel his soul, daring and frightened, because she'd never sensed the soul of a living being before. She felt nothing; the soul still firmly held in Wiel's body, thank the goddess.

Wiel sighed. "She's gone. Blessed Imn-ashu." He coughed, hard and long, until his face was red. Jaena helped him sit up and lean forward to ease his breathing.

"All right now?"

He nodded. "They told me what you did, Priest Jaena."

"What I did?"

"How you brought the Ull-fasten army to rescue me and the other *taylenor*, and --"

"Well, they were on their way when we met them."

"And you agreed to be traded as a hostage for me."

Jaena hung her head. "I'm so sorry that didn't work out as we planned."

"And you and the other *taylenor* stole all the *taylen* from Mage Herrein, so he was next to dead."

"Well, yes, we did that."

"And your friend and his man rescued me from the tower when I was almost dead myself, even though I don't remember any of it."

"I owe them a great debt for that," Jaena said seriously. Though she could barely imagine spoiled Lord Halpen doing such a thing.

"And then ..." Wiel paused to cough until he almost choked.

"Please don't talk so much. You'll make yourself sicker."

When he could draw a breath, Wiel continued. "And the *cernen* said you went to Mount Nimn to talk to the Eastern Mage, and convinced her not to attack us, and now she's powerless just like I am."

Powerless?

Closing her eyes, Jaena sought *taylen* in the little tent. Wiel had been so full of the gift, *taylen* overflowing so it lay throughout his little village like mist, calling to her as she rode in on the donkey cart. But Wiel was right; there was so little left, just a dusting, a memory of power more than anything else, sifting through his being. To all purposes there was none at all.

Yet, the boy still lived.

Weak, skeletal, gasping for breath, but alive.

"I hope the *cernen* is helping you."

"Yes, and the mage-healers. I'm much stronger now." His eyes went out of focus again, just for a moment. "But they said I'm unlikely to walk by myself again. I can't get the breath to do it, you see."

"I'm sorry, Wiel."

"You didn't know."

"What can I do to -- " She almost said, *make it up to you*. Then she stopped. Wiel, a boy of fifteen, would live his days in a bed or a chair, struggling to breathe. Maybe he'd live until he was sixteen. How could she make up to him a life stolen away?

"I want to go home," Wiel whispered.

"I'll take you there." She squeezed his hand, then let go. "Back to Bless-us-goddess?"

"Yes. But – oh, Goddess, I can't. What will they say when they see me? What will they do? My friends, they'll be afraid to come near me." A tear leaked down his cheek.

"Stop, before you make yourself worse. I'll take you anywhere you want, Wiel. You're a martyr for Cassahn. Back to Bless-us-goddess if you want. Or to the hospital, in Iryor." She raised a hand as if to stop a nonexistent protest. "Mage Herrein will be dead soon, I think. Mother Thara will be in prison, if she's lucky. It will be safe. Or, maybe the Temple would be better for you. There's music there always, and the goddess is there."

"I'll think."

"I'll let you rest. I'm so glad you're here, Wiel." Jaena stood. Perhaps it wasn't right with Wiel so sick, but a terrible weight had dropped from her shoulders now that she knew he was still alive.

He lay down. Jaena pulled blankets back up over him. He was so small on the cot, so unlike the vibrant laughing boy she'd taken from his parents, promising she would watch over him.

When Wiel was asleep, she left the tent. She must get food, and water, and a few minutes rest in her tent. The long rows of dead waited for a priest to sing their souls to their rest with the Goddess.

CHAPTER TWENTY-SIX

J aena heard the Ull-fasten army moving around long before dawn illuminated the eastern side of her tent. The guards would be grabbing bread and cold meat for breakfast before heading out to relieve the sentries at the edge of the cliffs. The grooms would be feeding and watering the horses. And the mage-healers and *cernen*, most likely weary beyond words, would still be caring for the wounded.

She hoped Wiel still lived.

Her throat felt sore and dry. She reached for the bit of honeycomb she'd asked for last night, and began to chew it. The sweetness of the honey burst in her mouth and coated her throat.

She had sung the souls of the dead for a long time last night, her voice creaking with strain. Commander Sri's soul had been among them, and Guardsman Ael's who'd stayed with them on the long walk to Spar Fortress, and others Jaena had met. Imn-ashu had swept the souls away as if in a cloak, wrapping them all in peace as they left behind the concerns of the mortal world.

Commander Hashu had stood next to her, his scarred face unmoving, weeping silently.

Jaena had sung until she could barely speak, then picked up her flute and played the goddess' song, the one that was played daily in her Temple in Iryor. The simple music sounded lonely and mournful, its only accompaniment the wind at this rocky place at the top of the world.

When she was done her voice was gone. One of the *cernen*, a round motherly-looking woman who reminded her disconcertingly of Mother Rhody, had given her warm tea and the bit of honeycomb for use in the morning.

Later today, people would be detailed to bury the dead.

The rising sun turned the inside of Jaena's tent golden, and a familiar voice called her name.

She emerged into the frigid air to see Mage Othane, wrapped in a frayed blanket over his coat. He looked haggard but at peace, the lines of worry gone from about his eyes.

"The old mage is dead," he told her. "Are you willing to sing his soul to Imn-ashu?"

She felt as if the breath had been knocked out of her. "What?"

"There's no other priest better suited to the task." The rising sun gave a chestnut glow to the side of his face and reflected off one eye, turning its color almost silver.

Jaena closed her eyes for a moment, adjusting to what was going to be required of her. "I'll do it." The air stirred and struck cold. "I'll need a few minutes, though. Where is he?"

* * *

It turned out that Herrein's remains were still in the fortress. Jaena walked with Othane across the bridge where they'd tried to exchange hostages, back before Sri was killed, before the terrible battle against the demons in the Pass, before Jaena had met Ark-amne. So much had happened since then. It felt as if weeks had passed rather than only days.

The inside of Spar Fortress was bitter cold, in spite of the thickness of the stone walls. Herrein had been moved to a space on the second level, and someone had tried to stuff wads of cloth into the arrow slit there to block the wind. That was more kindness than the mad mage had shown to his captive *taylenor*, Jaena thought, then shoved the bitterness back. The old man was dead now, and the time for anger was past.

Othane showed her where the body was, then gave an odd little bow and retreated to give her privacy.

At first, Jaena's eyes refused to identify the tiny heap on the cot as a body at all. It was a mere bump under the blankets. Jaena stared at it for a moment and then, because she couldn't stop herself, lifted the concealing cover over Herrein's body.

It wasn't Herrein at all anymore: not the mage who'd held such power over her, from when she was made a Seeker to when he'd finally tried to steal her *taylen* to fight the Eastern Mage. The body looked more like a jumble of bones than anything else, the flesh fallen away, bones collapsed into themselves as if they belonged to someone long dead.

The man had been more than two hundred years old when he died, his madness eating away at his body as well as his mind, the last of his *taylen* fleeing his body as all the *taylenor* in the room pulled it away. This was what was left.

Jaena had expected to feel disgust, or maybe hatred. Instead she felt a terrible pity. She covered the body. She would sing Herrein's soul to Imn-ashu with as much honesty as she did anyone else's.

She cleared her throat, ignoring the soreness, and began. Her voice croaked now and then, but the goddess was forgiving.

Imn-ashu came to her quickly, warmth filling the little space. The goddess as willing to take this man's soul as any other. Jaena bent her head and closed her eyes, feeling the goddess' presence in the little space, and looked for Herrein's soul.

And did not find it.

The souls of the dead were fragile things. Usually they longed to go home, and went with Imn-ashu quickly, enveloped in her embrace. Sometimes they seemed confused, and fluttered around looking here and there as if not sure where to go.

Babies' souls and old people's souls seemed most ready to go. The warriors in the Ull-fasten camp had all waited to go to the reward of their dedication. Jaena had sung a murderer's soul once, and it had leaped into the goddess' arms like a drowning person reaching for a rescuer.

Herrein's soul was not to be found.

Jaena's voice began to fade into a scratchy hoarseness.

The goddess reached out. The sense of presence filled Jaena's heart. Imn-ashu drifted over the pitiful pile of bones, waiting, holding in the room longer than Jaena had ever known her to.

Tears rose up inside Jaena, and a great wonder as she knew she was experiencing something extraordinary.

A few seconds, or hours, or days passed, caught in time as Imn-ashu waited for the dead mage's soul. Then sorrow filled the room, an almost physical weight that pressed down on Jaena's shoulders until she had to bend. A moment's fear at the intensity of it – Imn-ashu wouldn't hurt her priest, surely – and then the weight was gone, the warmth vanished to be replaced by stinging cold, and Imn-ashu was gone.

Jaena blinked at the sudden gray dimness, which seemed like bright light after the fog she'd been in.

Herrein's soul was long gone, it seemed.

She bent her head and left the little dark room.

Outside, an attendant asked her if it was all right to take away the mage's body now.

"Yes," she replied. "I'm done."

She walked down the hollowed stone steps that curved around the inside of the fortress, back into the world of people.

CHAPTER TWENTY-SEVEN

Metten came to get her just when the sun was at its zenith, at its highest point in the low arc of early winter.

He moved slowly, taking care for his broken ribs and bruises. She ran her hand up his arm in lieu of a hug. "You're doing better."

"Well enough to be a messenger." Metten smiled at her. Even pale from his injuries, his face seemed full of light.

Jaena caught her breath. With the shadow gone from their lives, she noticed again how beautiful he was. "What's your errand, then?"

"The Eastern emissaries have come and gone. Naar – that's Hashu's second, do you know her? She sent me to get you."

She followed him all the way to the edge of the cliff, to the bridge that spanned the drop that separated the Cliffs of Cassahn from the plateau where Spar Fortress stood. Guardsmen stood looking out toward the East, but none stopped her; they didn't seem to be on alert, just staring eastward with their hands shading their eyes against the brilliant sun.

Commander Hashu and his second, a tall blond woman, turned to greet her.

"They're pulling back," Hashu said. "Look."

The Eastern sentries, quilted against the cold, still stood keeping watch at their stations, watching the open Saarnen Pass. But the rest of the forces were melting away, a stream of people winding through the paths and crevices back towards the little village, and deeper into the East.

Jaena thought she saw a bright red head amongst them. Maybe it was Ark-amne riding that big horse in the middle of the group. She wished she could see farther, but the brilliant light almost blinded her. Then the figure turned the horse, stopping the column, while it stood in the stirrups and held a hand palm out towards the watching Ull-fasten army on the cliff. Sunlight turned the figure's hair to fire.

A gesture of acknowledgement. A wave of farewell. Ark-amne lived, at least, and seemed unhurt. She had stopped the whole army in its path to tell Jaena so. It was just like her.

She smiled at Metten.

"The emissaries told me the army would withdraw, but leave sentries to guard the Pass. Your Eastern Mage is a woman of her word." Hashu nodded as if confirming something to himself.

"Did you think she would lie?" Mkot walked up, ignoring the big guardsman who escorted him.

Hashu cast a narrow glance at the Easterner. "Merely that she might have been kept from honoring her word."

Mkot snorted, clearly deeming that a diplomatic evasion.

"She no longer has the *taylen* that earned her the service of that army," Jaena said. "I wondered, too – if she'd be challenged by one of her commanders."

"Well, now you see in what reverence we hold Ark-amne." In spite of his words, there was a hint of uncertainty in his voice.

"Once we've confirmed they've left the Pass to us, you may return. Thank you for guiding Priest Jaena back to us. We won't forget it."

"I did it for Imn-ashu. We honor the goddess as Ark-amne does, you know."

"I know." Jaena stood on her toes and reached up to give Mkot a hug around his shoulders, bristly beard scratching at her arms and face.

"Thank you. I hope to see you again. Goddess' peace go with you, my friend."

Mkot turned red.

"How will you find them?" Metten asked.

"I'll meet Ko, he's one of the sentries there – you can see him from here, he bears the flare on his shield so I can find him. He'll give me orders. It's all arranged." Mkot looked around him, at the exhausted Ull-fasten army and its encampment. "You know we won't abandon the Pass. You know this, right?"

"I assumed," Hashu said.

"Legend says the demons won't return for hundreds of years. That's why Ark-amne – well, anyway, we don't trust in legend. A watch is always kept. Someday one of us will have the courage to go down and destroy them in their own pit, but until then -- "

Naar snorted. "Not courage. Foolishness, you mean."

"Don't even think about it, Mkot," Jaena said.

Hashu turned from the cliff and spoke, his tone formal. "We'll rebuild the barrier in the pass as soon as we have the resources. We swear an oath to maintain a watch here at Spar Fortress, in time of peace or war, and signal to your country and our own if any sign of demons is seen. Even hundreds of years won't dull our watchfulness. I told your emissaries this, and I'll say it to you as well. Tell your Eastern Mage."

Mkot nodded. "I will."

Jaena said her goodbyes and left the Commander to watch the Eastern withdrawal.

She wanted to visit Wiel again, but an attendant sitting outside his little tent warned her away. "He's sleeping, Priest."

At least he was still alive. She nodded and went to find Othane.

Othane was resting on a cot in the quieter *cernen*'s tent. When she greeted him, he looked around at the other wounded and put a finger to his lips. "Outside."

Metten joined them and they walked through camp towards the horse picket line, gradually leaving behind the clutter of the encampment. Paying attention to her footing on the rough ground, Jaena didn't look up at Othane until they had arrived at a fairly-private spot near the horse lines.

When she did, her words froze in her throat.

When had Othane become *old*? His hair had been gray as long as she'd known him, but his face had been unlined and fresh, a young man's face. His shoulders had been broad that first time he'd stooped to enter their tent in the Ull-fasten camp to heal Metten. Now his body seemed frail. His angular face had sunk in upon itself, and lines creased his lips and eyelids. He stooped as he walked, the sign of fragile bones.

"Oh Othane, I'm so sorry," she said.

He grimaced. "I suppose I know what you're referring to."

"Do you feel all right?"

"I'm not my old self. I was very sick in that cell. Even the crime I committed didn't replace it all. The use of *taylen* is a terrible thing, Priest, but I knew what I was in for."

"You knew you'd need to use it to defeat Herrein."

"I knew." He shrugged. "Some others didn't want to come. That's their right, to use or not use *taylen* as they see fit. My own sister stayed at home."

"Everyone here owes you immense thanks. And you committed no crime."

He shook his head, his hair brushing the tops of his shoulders. "You won't convince me, Seeker. It was a crime, no matter how necessary it was."

"I for one am glad you committed it, then," Jaena said tartly. "If you and the others hadn't joined me in the fight, we wouldn't be here now. And you know it."

"I know it. Nevertheless, I'm doing penance." He gave her a shrewd look. "And you plan to do so as well, I think. I heard from Commander Hashu what you promised the Eastern Mage."

"Yes, well, it was more a promise to myself. I owe every *taylenor* in Cassahn the safety of a peaceful life in their own homes – or in another place I'll make for them. I owe it, personally, because I helped Herrein. Don't try to talk me out of it as Hashu did."

"If you lead the *taylenor*, you'll be in a position of power in Cassahn."

Jaena spun to stare at him. "Is that what you think? That I want to lead them? Do I seem like that to you?"

Othane held up a hand. "No, no. Seeker, you strike me as a quiet woman who wishes to worship her goddess in peace. If anything you seem to have an overdeveloped sense of responsibility – a common disease of priests, I believe. But you must be aware of the position this will put you in."

"I won't lead the *taylenor*, just provide a haven for them. That's all. To try to pay my debt." Jaena looked back at camp, at the little tent beside the *cernen*'s tents, where Wiel slept.

"I honor you for that." Othane gave a little bow. "I wanted to tell you I'll be going with Commander Hashu and the main army towards Iryor. We'll expect a fight, of course, but I believe Herrein stripped the place of defenses in his rush to get here. So you can expect Ull-fasten will prevail, and you'll have to deal with military rule when you set up your place for the *taylenor*."

"You've been reasonable so far," Metten said.

"And plan to continue."

Metten nodded. "What are your plans for Council?"

"You'll have to ask Commander Hashu. It will also depend upon how fiercely they resist us."

"I have family on Council," Metten said.

"All of them part of Herrein's duplicity. Is it not so?"

He sighed. "I suppose so."

When Othane made his way back to the *cernen*'s tents, Metten stayed behind. They walked into the horse picket lines together. The tents and sentries of camp vanished behind big warm bodies and snuffling noses.

Jaena ran a hand along a bay's withers, noting the deep scratches bordered with puffy flesh along the mare's flanks. "This one's hurt."

"They weren't in battle here, but some of the horses were injured at the battle of Rivasha, when we came across the bridge. Didn't you know?"

"I never thought about it. It's too bad they had to bear this. Poor thing." The mare nickered at Jaena. The spotted gelding along the picket line next to her shook its head as it chomped from its feed bag.

The presence of the big horses warmed them as they shouldered through the line. Jaena relaxed.

They found a groom checking one of the pack-horses' hooves. The girl grinned at them and waved them on. "I know who yer lookin' for, Priest. Yer donkey's over there."

Metten grinned. "I see her."

Two donkeys were picketed near each other on the line. The white splash on Ears' forehead gleamed at them. Jaena went to her at a half-run, leaving Metten to limp along behind. By the time he caught up she was cradling Ears' face while the donkey nuzzled her.

The donkey's bray of greeting blared into Jaena's ears. All the horses nearby turned their heads, and two grooms grinned at them.

"All the gods, what's that racket?" Metten said, covering his ears.

"She missed me. She's saying welcome back, where were you?" Jaena laughed harder and tried to hold Ears' face away from hers. "I'm back, Ears! I'm glad to see you! Oh goddess, she's loud."

"You don't say." Metten gave a helpless wave as Ears' greeting continued to resound through the horse lines.

"What?"

"I'll wait for you back here!" he yelled, trying to be heard over the racket. He laughed, but as he walked a little distance away he clutched one hand close to his side.

Jaena calmed Ears and said a polite hello to Ears' donkey companion as well. She pulled out the stubby carrots she'd saved from going into the stew and fed them to Ears and her friend. The donkeys shouldered around her, being affectionate.

"I missed you, donkey. More carrots once we resupply, or even an apple if I can find one. Good Ears!" She pulled the donkey's head down to her shoulder and gave the jennet a big warm hug. "I missed you."

Ears finished the bit of carrot and lipped Jaena's hair.

After a few more minutes Jaena stepped away. She rejoined Metten where he stood at the edge of the picket lines, still guarding his injured side.

Halfway back to the *cernen*'s tent, they heard a familiar voice. "Hai, Met! Priest!"

Halpen jogged up to them, looking very different in a servant's homespun tunic and leather coat. His face was the same though: set in discontented lines, a flush of anger on his cheeks.

"Hal! Good to see you, man!" Metten greeted his friend joyfully, clasping the other man about the shoulders and pulling him in for an embrace.

Halpen frowned and held back, arms held out stiffly. "They said you broke a rib."

"He did, so he should avoid wrestling with people," Jaena said tartly.

"I'm fine, all wrapped up like wool on a spindle."

Jaena forced down her dislike of Metten's friend. She owed the man a great debt. "Lord Halpen, I want to thank you for saving Wiel. They said you and Rall brought him out of the tower – I think you saved his life, because he wouldn't have lasted much longer."

"You're a hero, Hal!" Metten added. "You and Rall."

"That's the thing! If I'm really a hero, you'd think they'd let me stay!"

Jaena forced back a laugh.

"I thought you'd want out of here," Metten said.

"Well, I did. But Rall refused to find supplies and horses, and then that rude woman who's Hashu's second pretty much ordered me to go. A week's trail rations, she said, no escort or horses. Anything could happen to me alone out there – I'm almost sure there's more bandits, waiting to prey on people like me."

Metten's eyes shone with suppressed laughter. "Why don't you stay, then?"

"She said I had until dawn. It's past that now. She's a brutal-looking woman, Met. What if she comes to kill me?"

"For staying in the camp?" Jaena shook her head. "She probably just wants you to stay out of her way."

"Rall will protect you, Hal. Where is he?"

"I'm here, Lord Metten." The slim manservant nodded to Jaena and Metten as he approached. "I was looking for Lord Halpen. I'm very glad to see you both well."

"And you. I owe you and Lord Halpen thanks, Rall. You carried Wiel out of that terrible place. If there is ever anything I can do for you, please ask. I'll never be able to repay you, but I can try." Jaena put every bit of sincerity she had into the words. She wanted them to ask. Without them, she would even now be mourning the boy she'd stolen from his parents in Bless-us-goddess.

Rall gave a little bow.

"Well, I remembered you wanted to save him." Halpen cast Jaena a speculative glance. "If you mean it, about helping, you could chase that blond bitch away. Tell her who my family is, or something. I don't think she'll listen to me."

"I've spoken to Second Naar, my lord." Rall went so far as to put a hand on Halpen's sleeve. "If you remain out of the way, I think you may remain with the Ull-fasten army for protection on the way to Iryor."

"Well. Good!" Halpen looked at a loss. "She was unreasonable when she spoke to me. I'm glad you were able to convince her."

"I believe she has other things to worry about."

Metten's face was red. Jaena hoped Halpen would go away before Metten started laughing at him.

Halpen turned to go with Rall. He looked back at his friend. "Well, then. Call for me when you feel better, and we'll have a drink. I'm out of *aum,* but Hashu might have something."

Rall and Halpen had barely walked out of earshot when Metten broke into laughter.

"All the gods, did you see his face? Poor Hal." Metten clutched at his side, trying to stifle the huge gasps of laughter that strained his bound ribs.

"Easy." Jaena wrapped an arm about him. "You'll hurt yourself."

"Too late, too late!" Metten puffed through his lips, trying to ease the pain. "No one wants him. Poor Hal!"

"Come over here." Jaena led him to a slab of rock that jutted out from the escarpment. "Sit down."

Metten almost crumpled as he sat. Once there, he wheezed until his breathing slowed and the redness faded from his face.

"There," Jaena said. "Are you all right, or should I call a *cernen?*"

"Goddess, no. The *cernen* have enough to do. I'll be fine."

They sat for a moment, watching the activity as the Ull-fasten prepared to break camp. The most seriously wounded would remain for now, along with a mage-healer and *cernen*, and some attendants. Sentries would be posted at the rubble of the Saarnen Pass. Everyone else would pack up and head out on the next stage of their journey, traveling back to Rivasha on the ridge road and after a resupply, into Cassahn. There, Janea had no idea what would await them. It all depended upon what news had reached the Council from the battles at Rivasha Bridge and at the Pass.

With Herrein gone and Mother Thara in shackles, the Cassahni army decimated at Rivasha and the Council frightened to death for their lives, she thought the Ull-fasten would have little trouble establishing rule over Cassahn.

And then Jaena would become a Seeker again, this time to offer training and refuge to any *taylenor* who wanted it. Where she would be sure to teach them how to protect themselves against those who wanted to steal their *taylen* for themselves.

Herrein's story would be told down the ages if Jaena had anything to say about it. It would be a cautionary tale, a warning: the story of Herrein the Monster.

Someone laughed in a tent nearby. A line formed near the central fire, the first open fire that had been permitted in days. The cooks were handing out roast meat and dried fruit. The aroma and sizzle of the meat reached them where they sat. Things in the camp were returning to normal.

"I'm going to help you, you know," Metten said.

"You are?"

His expression grew solemn. "You have noble intentions, my dear-

est. But you're going to have to put up with a lot. You helped Herrein –
not your fault, but there it is."

"That's what Ark-amne said. She said I would be hated for the rest
of my life." She swallowed sudden tears. Where had they come from?
Maybe she needed food, or sleep.

"No tears, now." Metten wiped one away from her cheek. "You're
strong, my love. And I intend to be with you every step of the way, so
you can lean on me. Once my ribs are better, that is." He smirked, then
grew serious. "And if you allow it."

"If I allow it?"

"Let me take care of you, Jaena. It looks to me like you're going to
be taking care of everyone else. I want to be there for you."

Jaena looked around her at the dusty rocks, the tattered camp with
its wounded, its battered soldiers. All at once it seemed the best place
in the world. A glow lit inside her. If Metten were to stay with her,
then she could do anything.

"I love you, Jaena. You know that?"

"I know. I love you, too. Thank the goddess you didn't die in that
evil tower. I don't know what I'd -- "

"It's over. I'll be your protector, forever, if you let me." He leaned
into her, then cursed under his breath as his ribs pained him.

"Once you can sit up straight," Jaena said. "Yes, my love. I'll be
happy to work with you beside me for the rest of my life."

They heard a familiar complaining voice approaching them a few
seconds before Lord Halpen stepped out from between tents and
walked toward them. He carried a piece of hard bread with a slab of
meat on it. He broke off a piece as he walked toward the rock that
Jaena and Metten sat on.

Licking his lips, he closed his eyes for a brief moment of enjoy-
ment. When he reopened them, he stared at Metten and Jaena sitting
close together on the rock.

"What!" he exclaimed, eyes widening.

"Hal, you can be the first to wish us happy," Metten said.

Jaena blushed.

"Gods and demons!" Halpen cried. "Does this mean I'll have to put up with the Seeker for the rest of my life?"

Jaena stood up. "Just as I'm going to have to put up with you! If you're Metten's true friend anyway."

"Well, I am." He licked the meat juices from his fingers. "I suppose I wish you very happy. There. Now Metten, I've reconsidered. Do you think you can convince that Naar to order me a horse for the return journey?"

THE END

ABOUT THE AUTHOR

Anne Marie Lutz is the author of the two Color Mage novels, *Black Tide* and *Sword of Jashan*. Her short stories have appeared in several publications including the "For the Road" anthology, Strange Fictions Zine, and Bards and Sages Quarterly.

She was raised in the Youngstown, Ohio area, and currently lives in central Ohio with her family. She is a graduate of the Ohio State University (Journalism and MBA). She enjoys reading and traveling when she can. She is currently working on another novel.

You can follow her on her blog at annemariesblog.wordpress.com, or on Twitter or Facebook.